ALPHA
AND OMEGA

Also by Lou Paduano

The Greystone Saga

Signs of Portents

Tales from Portents

The Medusa Coin

Pathways in the Dark

A Circle of Shadows

Greystone-in-Training

Hammer and Anvil

The Gifts of Kali

The Final Gauntlet

Greystone Lost Tales

Army in the Obelisk

The Last King

The DSA

Season One

The Clearing

Promethean

The Bridge

Spectral Advocate

Dark Impulses

Broken Loyalties

Season Two

The Wellspring

Foundations

The Missing

Cracked Chrysalis

Secret Histories

Terminal Point

ALPHA AND OMEGA

Greystone Book Six

Lou Paduano

Eleven Ten Publishing LLC

GRAND ISLAND, NEW YORK

Eleven Ten Publishing LLC
282 Fareway Lane
Grand Island, NY 14072

Publisher's note: This is a work of fiction. Names, characters, places, and incidents either are the product of the author's imagination or are used fictitiously. Any resemblance to actual events, locales, or persons, living or dead, is entirely coincidental.

Printed in the United States of America
Edited by JP Services
Cover art design by GetCovers

First edition published 2025

Library of Congress Cataloguing in Publication Data
Paduano, Lou
Alpha and Omega / Lou Paduano

LCCN: 2025907110
ISBN-13: 978-1-944965-61-7 (hardcover)
ISBN-13: 978-1-944965-60-0 (paperback)
ISBN-13: 978-1-944965-59-4 (eBook)

For Missy

CHAPTER ONE

Portents was in her blood. From the docks of Riverside, down the RDJ, and out to the Grove, every inch of the city influenced her being. They were the stories that created a wealth of imagination in a child. As an adult, however, Melanie Gates knew the city to be more than just the place where she grew up. To her, Portents was home.

The patrol car settled along King's Lane in the Knoll, another night on the job. Gates kept her hands tight to the wheel. Her keen eyes locked on the alleys and the mounting shadows that filled every crack and crevice in the sun's absence. Three months on the job had granted her comfort with the route, but a nervousness fluttered in her stomach; like something waited to snatch her away from her perfect little life.

That was the fear of a child, not the grown woman she purported to be, though few saw the difference in her youthful gaze. Twenty-five meant little in the eyes of the world these days.

Still, her fear made her wary of the night in Portents. Gates understood the dangers of the brooding metropolis, and the unspoken rule passed down from her parents.

Gates sought to change that edict. She hoped by her presence, her unyielding diligence, she might pierce the darkness of Portents and bring back some light to her city. She wanted to hear the laughter of children in the streets, to see her elders happily walking down the block without fear of violence from every shadow.

Those were the ideals of that self-same child, and she kept them close to her heart every day.

Those ideals were not held by her partner, Richard "Dickie" Delmar. Dickie, for all his experience over his decade-long career with the department, viewed the patrol as nothing more than a casual drive through town rather than a means of serving and protecting the innocent citizens of Portents.

Gates tried not to take his callousness personally. For all her drive, it pained her to see colleagues and friends merely muddle through work for the paycheck waiting at the end of the day. Her recruitment to the Central Precinct had been the proudest day of her life. She shined her badge daily and carried its weight on her shoulders. She never viewed the responsibility as a burden but a privilege.

Carrying Dickie's weight, though, was becoming troublesome.

"You're quiet tonight."

His words caused Gates' hand to slip from the wheel of the car. She blinked hard to tear her eyes away from the darkness permeating the shopping district of the Knoll.

"I'm sorry?"

Dickie offered her a wide grin that pushed his cheeks up and caused his glasses to lift from his beady brown eyes. "Don't get me wrong, it's not a bad thing. I'm actually enjoying the silence. Usually, though, you're asking ten questions a minute. About the route. About the problem children in each neighborhood. Where the illegal card games are being played. Where the dealers have been gathering of late." He took a deep breath, and she waited, sensing more on the horizon. Dickie was nothing if not verbose when the mood struck him. "Then there are the questions I really enjoy. Like what uniform you should wear for what formal occasion, as if the brass would ever include us in anything of importance. Or my favorite, where to eat at break time."

"Okay," Gates said with a laugh. She pointed at Dickie's bulging gut. "That last one is you. Or rather, that stomach of yours."

Dickie patted his belly. "Give it another decade, Mel. Meals are the only priority in this life. Speaking of which…"

He tapped the window. Through the falling rain, Gates noticed the neon lights of the convenience store at the corner of Gentry and Forest. She tapped the blinker of the car, though no traffic was around, and sidled along the curb in front of the shop. Shifting the car to park, Gates unlocked the doors.

"Have at it, Dickie," she said.

"Now what have I told you about that?" he said as his seatbelt retracted. "Call me Del."

"Everyone else calls you Dickie."

"Yeah, but then we could be Del and Mel: team supreme. Completely interchangeable."

"Which means I get stuck with any tasks you don't feel like doing," Gates said with a grimace.

"Now you're catching on." His hand settled on the handle of the door, then he stopped. "Okay, kid. What's your deal?"

Gates held her tongue for a second. She peered around the area, through the rain and through her growing wariness. "I've been thinking, is all. I keep reading up on those random acts of destruction throughout the area over the last few months. Not for money. Not for anything other than to cause chaos, from all appearances. And then there's… Well, I don't know, Dickie. There's something going on in this city, isn't there?"

"There always is," Dickie replied. "If it wasn't those clowns or this killer thing, it would be something else. What are you—"

Gates turned toward him, hands in front of her. "I mean, it's darker. Portents feels darker somehow. You can feel it, can't you?"

Dickie opened the door. He stepped outside, the rain patting his hat and sliding down to his shoulders. Holding the frame, he peered back at her. "That's Portents, Mel. You could have gone anywhere to be a cop. What kind of person picks this place?"

"You did."

He laughed. "I'm an idiot. What's your excuse?"

Gates sighed. Everywhere she turned brought with it another memory. "This is home."

Dickie shook his head. "Home is a bed and a sixty-five-inch flat screen. You can find that anywhere. But Portents?"

"I've lived here all my life. I can't imagine being anywhere else." Gates slipped from the car and rounded the front for the sidewalk. Her gaze shifted from the convenience store to the closed storefronts along the opposite side of the street. She drifted up to the apartments above each shop. All held darkened windows. The patter of the rain trailed her steps, like the beating of her heart. It grew faster and heavier with every passing second. "Something just feels… off."

Dickie scoffed, tossing his hands in the air. "The weather. The phase of the freaking moon. Or the fact that you're nothing but skin and bones."

"And you're hungry. Got it," Gates finished with a smile. She shrugged her shoulders, then held out her hand for the waiting door. "Go."

He passed her for the entrance. "Ham on rye?"

"With the spicy mustard this time."

"Living dangerous, kid," Dickie joked. "Don't let that come back to haunt you."

Dickie entered the shop. The chime carried along the block until the door slipped back into the frame. He left Gates with the falling rain and the growing shadows of her home surrounding her.

Heavy footfalls carried her from the shop down Gentry. The Knoll, while mostly residential, held small nooks of businesses throughout. They were the butchers and the bake shops, the small storefronts that lived and died along with their neighborhoods.

Gates recalled each one from her childhood. There was Vilente's, where she used to buy ice cream with her friends on hot summer days, or Halley's, who always carried the best comic books during the cold, blustery winter months. Both no longer existed, passing to new owners with new dreams. Change was inevitable, but she didn't care for the one that gnawed at her thoughts tonight.

Portents remained her home, but it carried something else on the wind, more than the clouds perpetually stuck over the spires of downtown. What it was, Gates failed to recognize, and that worried her almost as much as what she found at the back of the convenience store during her short stroll.

Lying outside the mouth of an alley rested a woman's handbag. The contents fell from the shallow opening, lipstick, compact, wallet, and a dozen receipts lying on the sidewalk, all soaked from the storm.

Gates moved for the bag. Next to the purse, tucked into the alley's shadows, was a larger bag with the CostSmart logo emblazoned on its side. She carefully peered inside to see three shirts and a pair of jeans. They still bore their tags from a recent shopping excursion.

"Hey, Mel," Dickie's voice called over the rain. She could hear him chomping on the chips that came with his sandwich. "You think we have time to swing by Cusimano's for some pastries when they open? I've been dying for… What are you doing?"

Gates stood from the bags. She drew her sidearm, eyes locked on the deep black of the alley. "Found these." She kicked lightly around the items at her feet. "I think there's something behind the dumpster."

One step into the alley and the shadows swallowed her. Dickie called to her from the sidewalk, his nerves up. "Mel?"

"Shine your light this way," she said. "I see… I see…"

All words left her when she rounded a dumpster tucked along the back wall of the deli. All sense of her world vanished, and her so-called home became a much different place.

"Oh, Lord," she muttered. The prayer offered little comfort. Neither did Dickie's light when it finally penetrated the darkness. The light reached a pair of legs jutting out from behind the dumpster.

"Is that…"

Gates nodded, her hand over her mouth and nose to block the smell. Even with the rain, a rank stench caught in her throat. Crouching at the side of the body, Gates stared into the eyes of a young woman. A single stab wound through the neck told her the circumstances of the woman's demise.

The smile on the victim's face told the rest of the story.

"It's him again, isn't it?" she asked to Dickie, who loomed over her. The terror in his eyes gave his answer. His light lowered, and he reached for his radio to call it in.

The Kindly Killer had struck again.

CHAPTER TWO

Greg Loren desired nothing more than the mother of all storms. Blistering winds coupled with raging torrents of rain and a cascade of thunderclaps that could wake the dead. He prepared for such an event, his worn-out trench coat snug on his shoulders. He dreamed of the rain washing over him, cleansing him of every malicious thought and terrible dread he carried with each breath.

So, of course, the rain immediately stopped once the call came in. All weather halted, like the city had simply taken a breath of its own to calm itself from the news of another strike.

Another murder.

Loren waited to be notified. He sat in anticipation as he watched dozens of officers pulled from their duties to attend the fresh scene. The news spread like wildfire. Whispers, innuendos, and quite a few glances passed in Loren's direction. None, however, brought his invitation to the party.

Patience at an end, Loren left the confines of the precinct. The storm was upon him within, if not without. It churned with each footfall that carried him from the Rath Building for the Knoll—the same walk he took with the start of each shift. The thought of another murder sent waves of burning agony through his veins. Another murder meant another failure in his eyes, the same failure that had trailed him ever since the death of his wife.

The case was all he knew anymore. Each victim had become ingrained in his mind. Every scene had been memorized and cataloged for future study. For all his knowledge, Loren remained ignorant in far too many ways. Now his ignorance had left him out of the case completely.

He couldn't let that stand.

By the time he arrived at Gentry, cordons barred the street

from foot traffic. Officers littered the block, pushing back the first reporters to catch wind of the latest news. Leaks continued, even under the tightest of orders. Promises were handed out like bribes for a newsworthy headline or ten, all to be cashed in at a later date for fortune and fame when the killer finally met his end.

Loren looked forward to that day very much.

This one, though? Not at all.

Head down, Loren cut through the cordon with the raising of his badge. He didn't have to make eye contact to be recognized. All knew who he was and his reason for being at the scene. Called or not, the case was all he had left, and Loren refused to take any dismissal sitting down.

He slipped by forensic technicians in a frenzy to gather what they could before the next wave of showers hit the area. From there, he circled the plainclothes detectives, Jefferson Quinn and Alan Messick. To so much as glance in their direction gave the impression of asking for permission, something Loren never cared to do. Instead, he pressed on for the open alley behind the convenience store.

A hand stopped him from entering—one Loren had been waiting for since his arrival.

"What are you doing here, Greg?" The slim, middle-aged Hispanic man with salt and pepper hair asked. Captain Alejo Ruiz's eyes thinned at Loren's presence, evident disapproval at the detective's presence.

"You know why I'm here, Ruiz," Loren said. He shuffled off the hand. Ruiz quickly cut him off from the alley.

"Then you know why I didn't call you in," the captain said. Friends for as long as they had known each other, times like these made things easier to think of Ruiz as Loren's captain and little else. The more professional things turned, the uglier they became as well.

"It's my case."

"It was." Ruiz took a deep, calming breath. He lowered his voice and pulled Loren close. "You look like crap, Greg. Have you slept?"

Loren sidestepped Ruiz. He didn't bother to rise to the man's bait. "Where's the victim?"

"Dammit, Greg…" Ruiz sighed. "You can't just barge in on an open investigation and expect—"

"Don't," Loren snapped. "Don't you dare cut me out. I've spent months on this case. I've… I need to see this through."

Ruiz stared him in the eyes, bloodshot and weary to match his own. A slow nod caused droplets of rain to fall from his hair. Before they had touched the ground, Loren stood in the alley.

He stopped at the sight of the young woman's body behind the dumpster. She sat with her back against the brick wall of the cafe next to the convenience store. Fully clothed, there was no sign of physical harm anywhere on her extremities. Nothing screamed out to Loren about a struggle between the woman and her assailant.

The only injury had surely caused her death—a sharp stab through the throat. Blood spatter ran across the side of the dumpster. She lay where she'd died, pulled into the alley's darkness and out of view of anyone who might have saved her from such a grim fate.

"Her name was Lydia Giles," Ruiz said, the initial report in his hands. "Twenty-six years old. She worked at a salon a few blocks over."

"Which one?"

Ruiz squinted to read his sloppy handwriting. "Uh, Ophelia's on—"

"Breckenridge," Loren interrupted. "I know where it is." He crouched beside the victim. His gaze never left her, trailing up her body for evidence, though he found nothing but frustration in the effort. "She leave work with anyone?"

"No," a voice said from the front of the dumpster. The sound of a woman behind it caused both Loren and Ruiz to turn at the arrival of the officer. She held her hat tight in her hands, timid in approach but with a fierce look in her wide, green eyes. "She didn't leave with anyone last night, sir."

Ruiz beamed at the officer and held out his hand for her to join them. "Greg, this is Melanie Gates. She's one of our latest recruits from—"

Loren shifted away from them with a loud grumble. He tossed a wave as he returned his focus to the body. "Great. Congratulations. What time?"

"I'm sorry?" Gates asked, confused.

Loren sucked air between his clenched teeth. "What time did the salon close?"

"Nine."

"And the body was found at?"

Ruiz stepped ahead of Gates. "Delmar called it in at 11:30."

A large window of time. The late hour didn't help matters. It limited the number of potential witnesses who might have seen the victim walking the Knoll on her way home, if that had been her destination. Too many questions vied for Loren's attention, not the least of which centered on the change to the dead woman's lips.

They twisted in a curling grin, the calling card of their killer. Those grins haunted Loren's every waking moment. He stood from the body, unable to take the sight any longer.

"Ronne been here yet?" He shook his head at his own question. "No, don't answer that. I can't smell the aroma of death that seems to trail her."

Ruiz's arms crossed over his chest. "She's not your biggest fan, either."

Loren peered past Ruiz for the departing Gates. She offered an angry glare back before joining the cordon with the other officers. "Who is these days?"

Ruiz slapped at the detective's shoulder. "Gee, with your winning personality, Greg, how can you be surprised?"

"You want to know what surprises me, Ruiz?" Loren pointed to the deceased and the sneering grin. "This."

"Don't start—"

"Seven victims in as many months. That we know about." Loren paced the width of the alley, his hands strangling the air before him. "I'm no closer to finding this bastard."

"We will," Ruiz said. "We have every available patrol on the streets looking for this guy."

"When they aren't distracted by the nutcases breaking into local businesses for the fun of it," Loren shot back. "Any idea who they are?"

"None," Ruiz answered. His own frustration came through clearly. "We never arrive in time to catch them in the act. Surveillance footage is never clear, not enough to make any kind of identification."

"Of course."

"Hey," Ruiz called, ending Loren's pacing. "We're doing our best. All of us."

"Yeah," Loren commented, a nod towards Gates. "The wealth of experience."

Ruiz's gaze thinned. He closed the gap between them, then dropped his voice to a whisper. "Gates found the body. This poor woman could have stayed hidden for another day or two before—"

"I know." Loren threw his hands in the air. "I know!"

He slammed his hands against the brick, then settled beside the body once more. "Seven months, Ruiz. Seven months and he still doesn't make sense to me. A different method used with each kill, like he just picks something at random seconds before the act. Yet when he strikes? Precision. One blow, maybe two. Never unrestrained when all signs point to that." He leaned close to the open wound that caused the woman to bleed out. "What was it this time?"

"A pen," Ruiz said. "From the victim's purse."

If it wasn't that, what would he have used? Loren agonized over the methodology of his opponent. The not knowing caused the storm to churn in his guts faster. He needed the damn rain.

Attempting to stand once more, Loren found himself next to the upturned lips of Lydia Giles. "That damn smile."

Ruiz held out a hand to help him up. Loren hesitated for a brief second. "Come on, Greg. Let Hady's team handle the scene."

Loren took the hand and found his footing. "Don't handle *me*, Ruiz."

"Then don't force me to, Detective." Ruiz tracked his lowered gaze and caught Loren's eyes once more. His own were filled with nothing but concern, the very thing Loren hated to see. "When was the last time—"

"I slept, Ruiz," Loren snapped. "Dammit, I slept."

"A full eight hours?" Ruiz pressed. "In a bed?"

"The couch is—"

"All the answer I needed." Ruiz shook his head, concern replaced by judgment. "Now you see why I didn't call you for this? You're pushing too hard."

"If that's what it takes to catch this guy, I'll—"

"Make a mistake."

Loren scoffed at the accusation.

"You have, Greg, and you will again," the captain continued. "And people will get hurt because of it. You especially."

"Me?" Loren asked. "Or my career?"

"Both, if you have it your way." The clearing of a throat from the sidewalk interrupted their less-than-private discussion. Ruiz nodded to his subordinates and waved them over. "Quinn and Messick can handle the scene. They're up to speed on the case and—"

"I can—"

Ruiz shuffled Loren for the street. "Let the department—let *me*—finish this one."

Loren ripped away from Ruiz's grip. He took a step back for the body, then stopped. At the far end of the alley, a shadow shifted in the dark. A figure slipped in and out of view in the blink of an eye.

Ruiz reached for him. "Greg?"

"Did you see that?" Loren pointed toward the shadows. "A woman. She was…"

He trailed off, unsure of what he saw—if he saw anything at all, the way he felt.

"Greg?"

Loren shook his head. "Forget it."

The last thing he needed was a psych evaluation on top of everything else. He had already been through enough questioning from everyone since losing his wife. Their stares spoke to their doubts in him. He never included Ruiz in that group, though, until now.

Ruiz ushered him from the scene, the hand a guide as much as a forceful shove away from the murder and mayhem that followed Loren's life. The captain wanted him out, away from the case and away from the answers he needed.

"Go home, Greg," Ruiz said. "Get some sleep. Promise me."

He wanted to fight for access. He needed the case more than Ruiz or anyone could understand. Surrounded by a dozen officers and even more analysts, Loren swallowed the argument.

"Yeah," he muttered. "I will."

Ruiz left him with a nod. He joined Quinn and Messick at the body. Forensics gathered evidence. Hady's team arrived and set to their tasks. Everyone worked to solve the case, except Loren.

They left him alone in the street, feeling nothing but the storm inside his veins as the rain began to fall again.

CHAPTER THREE

Quick steps took her away from the alley, while quiet curses followed each stride. Loren had almost seen her. Soriya Greystone wasn't ready for their first meeting. Not while the Kindly Killer remained at large.

The enigmatic murderer sat at the heart of all her troubles of late. She had been hunting for her elusive prey since Loren lost his wife. In her failure to save Beth, Soriya had promised to look after Loren. She could think of no better way than to catch the killer he had sought mercilessly for so long, especially if the killer had been behind Beth's sudden fall.

Soriya's guilt over the loss of her friend carried her out of the alley and across the street. The bright lights of squad cars faded to the background. The deep dark of Portents stood before her, and she welcomed the thick shadows like a warm blanket on a chilly night.

Rain dampened her mood further. The killer had struck again, and left no clue to his identity. She had studied the previous victims endlessly for some insight. All appeared to be randomly selected, almost by chance rather than sought after by the murderer. The only clear thought carried throughout the investigation was that the killer was male. The force behind the strikes used against his victims and the height required in each circumstance made the determination clear.

That was it: Kindly was a man. No other evidence presented itself, not after months of searching.

It was no wonder Loren looked so exhausted. His face had been haggard and desolate, like the man had not found a peaceful rest in ages.

Soriya's anguish accompanied her as she left King's Lane, heading to the bottom of the hill that linked the district to the rest of the city. Riverside sat to the east, with Grant Square to the west.

Her promise to the memory of Beth remained unfulfilled. Her own diligence to see a killer caught came up short with each passing night, and each new victim added to Kindly's tally. Yet, Soriya discovered no new insight into the case. Her mind crashed against nothing but dead ends, despite the months spent on the hunt.

She needed a distraction.

The city was typically full of them. Myths and legends hid within Portents. Most were benign, wanting nothing more than to live their lives among humanity. Despite their extraordinary origins, they worked, played and loved as anyone else and none were the wiser. There were always others though that wanted more, and took what they desired, until Soriya put a stop to them.

That was the job, and had been her task—one she had trained for since the age of five. During her training, Soriya learned to battle the worst of the worst, from this world and every other out there. Minotaurs. Witches. Gods and goddesses alike. All brought their own delusions of power and glory, always at the expense of the innocent and Portents.

But for all her training, for all the threats Soriya had tackled since assuming the mantle of the Greystone, the Kindly Killer remained active in her backyard. He took lives without worry of being caught, and his pattern of attack made him more brazen. The gaps between deaths narrowed with each subsequent victim. Where weeks would slip by, now only days passed before another body dropped.

So lost in thought, with the pounding rain offering nothing but a soundtrack for her anger, Soriya barely heard the horn of the sedan down the block on Lascombe. Only the twin beams from the car's headlights alerted her to its presence, and to her own position right in its path.

Soriya leaped toward the far side of the street. She felt the heat of the car's engine against the bottom of her feet. The driver's side mirror skimmed across her legs in her flight from certain death.

Knees and elbows slammed into the sidewalk. Soriya's body flipped end over end until she hit the solid brick edifice of the nearest building. Slowly, she rolled to her back and stared into the rain pelting her face.

"Idiot."

A car almost ended her life. Not some demon from the netherworld, not a mythical beast loose in her city, but her own distraction while crossing the damn street. Soriya slapped the ground, then fought her way to her feet. Her knees screamed when they touched the ground. Layers of skin had definitely been lost on her elbows as well.

"I can't believe I almost…" She stopped at the sight of the sedan.

At the end of the block, it turned back in her direction. Gray paint chipped in several places with streaks of other colors dotting the chassis as if it had collided with a rainbow or a plethora of brightly colored objects—hard. The car was old, an antique compared to most vehicles on the road. Its hood jutted out far from the windshield and the rear on both sides shot up like horns. The engine boomed as the driver stepped on the accelerator while the car stayed in park.

"What is—"

The sedan shot forward like a bullet from a gun. There was no mistaking the intent this time. The car hopped the curb on a straight path for her position.

The occupants hadn't been warning her with their flagrant use of their horn: they had been announcing their arrival. They did the same this time, and she saw them through the front windshield.

There were two of them. They hooted and hollered at her, demanding her full attention. Both wore masks, hiding their identities. None of that fazed Soriya in the slightest.

No, what kept Soriya frozen in the path of the murderous sedan was the fact that the driver's mask bore a massive smile across the face.

CHAPTER FOUR

"What the hell is this now?"

Even through their masks, Soriya heard the cries from the occupants of the sedan as it barreled once more toward her. She ignored them as much as she did the wounds already inflicted during her previous evasion. Bending at the knees, Soriya waited for the lights of the car to bear down on her.

Caught between their twin beams, the roar of the engine like thunder in the storm that surrounded them, Soriya leaped into the air. She flipped forward, hands to the roof of the assaulting vehicle, which then propelled her beyond the bumper and back to the curb at the end of the block.

The sedan continued on in its haste. It sheered along the side of the brick edifice, slicing off the passenger-side mirror with ease. From there, its victim out of reach, the car bounded off the sidewalk and back to the street.

Soriya caught her breath, chest heaving from the sudden threat. All frustration dissipated, replaced by intense anger. She turned to face her attacker, who skirted down another block before skidding to a halt under the screeching of brakes. A wide turn through the empty intersection brought the car back around in a standoff.

Instinctively, Soriya's hand fell to her hip. Through the thin fabric of the pouch tied tight to her belt, she felt the power of the Greystone within. The ancient weapon waited to be unleashed on the two masked hooligans looking for trouble—something Soriya had no problem obliging.

She ran at the car with a scream on her lips. Two blocks out, she barreled toward her enemy like it was only two steps away. The distance wasn't the issue for her. The anger pulsing through her body gave her the strength to run fifty blocks, much less two, without pause and without remorse.

Soriya's issue was in the arrival of an additional complication. Pedestrians rounded the corner equidistant from both parties of the standoff. They caught the attention of the driver the instant they came into view.

There were three of them—two boys and a young woman. Her immediate impression was of kids, which Soriya found funny considering their destination was clearly the bar scrunched in the middle of the block and she was not yet of age. Oblivious to the roaring engine, or the rising squeal of the tires over the wind, the trio laughed and joked with reckless abandon on their way to the double doors, complete with blacked-out glass windows.

"Oh, no," Soriya muttered, stumbling in her effort to reach the sedan. She had been so intent on a showdown, she had failed to compensate for the newcomers to the field, or the danger they faced with their presence. There wasn't time to stop the car.

"Run!" she yelled. The rain and the roar of the racing sedan muffled her entreaties. Warnings went unheeded and flat-out ignored. Soriya ran faster, pushing through the wind. A hundred feet out, then fifty, then twenty, and still the car raged ahead.

The trio's laughter cut out the moment the car hopped over the curb for their position. Curious looks passed between them, questions muttered between close friends. One grinned widely, sensing a joke on the horizon where none was warranted. The other two shared a skeptical glance and nothing more. They made no motion to flee, no panic to hide from the impending crash.

Soriya launched for them. Arms outstretched like a shield, she soared across the sidewalk to encompass the trio as they reached the doors to the bar. Hands slammed into their shoulders. Two fell against the door and into the bar. Soriya's head clipped the third in the ear. The weight of her body, the force behind the tackle, sent the young man crashing after his friends and out of the path of the sedan. The car sparked with fury against the door frame on its way down the rest of the block.

"What the hell, lady?" the young man exclaimed. He held tight to his ear as he struggled for his feet. The other two pulled him up, one by the elbow and the other from the armpit.

The girl to his right rubbed at her neck. Realization sat in her gaze, but she said nothing. Their companion followed suit.

Soriya, however, had plenty to say in their place. "What the hell are you doing out at this hour?"

The young man chuckled at the question and at her indignant anger, complete with hands tight to her hips. "You're kidding, right?" He showcased the bar at his back. "It's ladies' night."

All looked around the establishment, the only one on the block still open despite the unwritten warnings of the city at night. A lone bartender occupied the counter, his bald head reflecting the overhead lights. Five others sat at the bar, needling their drinks. None bothered to engage with their neighbor, and none were women.

The young man's companion shook his head. "She don't look like she's kidding, Mikey."

Soriya gritted her teeth. "Go home. It's not safe in Portents at night. Especially tonight."

She started for the street. The sedan idled at the intersection. Before she could step out to face it, a hand grabbed her by the arm.

Mikey seethed, "You don't get to tell me…"

"Mikey," the woman of the trio called. Soft steps brought her to his side. She offered Soriya an apologetic nod, then turned back to her friend. "Listen…"

"Nell, you can't be serious. We just got here."

"And now we're leaving," Nell replied. "Before some other maniac tries to kill us." She continued through the still open door, pausing only to mutter, "Thanks for the save and all that."

Mikey stood incredulously in the bar. His friend joined Nell in the door frame, barely able to lift his nervous gaze from the ground. "Not you too, Jim. Nell, she—"

"Will kick your ass, moron," Nell shouted over his tantrum. She held out a hand, an irritated wave ushering him from the establishment. "Come on."

"This is so stupid," Mikey grumbled under his breath. He pushed through Soriya, shoving her at the shoulder only to have her move at the last instant. He stumbled and caught the edge of the door with his chin. "Dammit."

"Serves you right," Nell said.

"There's no reason to just leave, Nell," Mikey said. He rubbed at his chin as he made his way to the sidewalk. "One drink and we can forget—"

The car's engine roared. Tires squealed, and the sedan launched for their position with fresh zeal.

"Or we can get the hell out of here!" Mikey screeched. "That works too!"

They barreled down the sidewalk and cut through the closest alley for the connecting street. Soriya watched them depart, knuckles tight to her sides and waiting for something else to go wrong.

"At least one of them had common sense," she said to herself. Spinning on her heels, Soriya faced the assaulting vehicle once more. It gave no pause at her presence. One victim was as good as the next, it seemed. "Seems to be a rarity, though."

The masked driver honked the horn wildly. The wheel swerved to match, causing the sedan to skid against the brick in a wave of sparks just as it shattered through the canopy over the bus stop.

Soriya didn't flinch. She made no move to save herself, nor to launch at the fast-approaching death heading her way. The dance had become tiresome to her. It was time to change the pace.

With only a second to spare before becoming a squashed bug along the front grill of the six-cylinder nightmare, Soriya jumped into the air. She brought her legs up to her chest, knees almost to her cheeks. In the next breath, the lithe figure slammed her legs back down and landed squarely on the hood of the car.

Her balance was precarious. Every shift threatened to throw her clear and back to where she'd started. The pink ribbons adorning her left arm sensed the weakness in her position and sprang to life. Snatching for the thin seam of the hood, the Ribbons of Kali slipped inside and held tight to prop Soriya up.

Soriya smirked. "Pull over."

For the first time, her attackers came into full view. The driver was female, pale skin and slight in stature, with dirty blonde hair in thick curls. The male passenger had a medium build with scars decorating his tanned arms.

Both bore the same mark along their necks, what appeared to be the tattoo of the masks they wore. The driver's grin stretched from ear to ear. Her passenger's frown was her polar opposite. She could see neither of their eyes through the mask, only two black holes offering no clue to the mania in their actions.

"It appears we've picked up a passenger, my sweet," the frowning figure said. No alarm filled his voice, no concern at Soriya's presence in the least. It was like she had interrupted their weekly trip to the grocery store.

"We should greet her accordingly, dear." The woman's smile reflected the joy in her words, and she immediately cut the steering wheel sharply to the right.

Soriya fell to her left knee, but stayed upright. The ribbons saw to that much, at least. She tightened her grip and leaned toward the windshield.

"I said, pull over."

Her fist shot out at the glass, though it held firm against her attack. A second strike caused a shallow crack to form. The third splintered it further, and the crack spread from the initial blow.

The driver let go of the wheel, foot still hard on the accelerator, and reached into her pocket. She pulled out a banana, bruised and mushy. "What do you say, dear? Comedy?"

Her companion shook his head. "I'm afraid not, my sweet." He ducked his hand behind his seat. When it returned, he carried a large automatic machine gun. "This looks to be a tragedy."

"So true, so true," the smiling woman said. She tossed the banana out the open window and gripped the wheel.

Soriya's eyes widened. The frowning passenger didn't hesitate. He didn't even maneuver the weapon out of the moving vehicle for a clear shot. He simply opened fire, through the windshield and all.

With less than a second to consider her next move, Soriya willed the Ribbons of Kali to retract. They rebounded from their position throughout the hood and snapped along her left arm. Soriya was already diving from the car when they fell back into place. Her body skidded against the pavement.

Momentum sent her rolling clear of the street to the curb. She felt the concrete jab her in the side. Her vision blurred, but she could see a hand waving from the driver's-side of the departing sedan. Her frowning companion continued to fire bullets randomly in the air, though the sound was lost under their shared hollering.

"Bon voyage!"

"Ta-ta for now!"

Soriya grimaced with pain. Her entire body screamed, bruised and bloodied from the affair. Still, she fought her way to her knees and let out a long, labored breath.

"I had to ask for a distraction."

CHAPTER FIVE

It was too soon. The shadow knew it the second he took off into the night. Every instinct begged him to turn around and head home. There was television and reading and a million other mundane activities to distract his attention. Yet, he continued to walk in the opposite direction.

The itch was too strong to ignore.

His compulsion typically dimmed in the aftermath of a kill. The shadow went about his everyday life, feeling nothing but free following the sudden release of his pent-up rage. His first kills had brought entire weeks of peace. For a time, he wondered if he had dreamed up the early incidents. They remained surreal in his eyes, impossibilities in the light of day.

Weeks, however, ended just the same. The urge returned, and with each subsequent act it came back fiercer than ever. Now he barely made it hours before sensing that nail-biting fury struggling to burst through his skin.

Work failed to comfort him. His job was the source of his pain. Though he fought it as best as he could throughout the day, the urge won out. It always won out.

Because of people like *her.*

Her car sat in the back corner of the lot outside the midtown plaza. The lights overhead offered her little in the way of comfort, as noticed by her swift gait from the locked door of the shop. They were few and far between, some blinking and others out altogether.

Whatever name she held mattered little to him. The woman, bold and brazen in her every act, treated him the same as everyone else. Rudeness dominated her behavior—an intolerable arrogance that placed her higher than everyone else in the world. She had treated him with the same disregard she did all those around her.

Her disrespect gave her power, and she had wielded it against him. Trailing her steps, the shadow continued to hear her hateful words from earlier that day. They fed into the growing itch, burrowing deeper and deeper through his flesh.

"Are you deaf?" She bellowed in his ears. Her fury was all-encompassing. The laughter of everyone else in range helped prop up her poor behavior as if it had been nothing more than a joke. "Or are you just dumb? Move!"

The shadow stood his ground, out of principle more than anything. His good intentions did little to soften her demeanor.

"Are you questioning me?" she cried. Stolen garments were clearly tucked under her shirt, though she did everything possible to distract from her crime. "Are you calling me a liar?"

He wanted to, but weakness kept his lips sealed. When he made eye contact with the woman, his sudden strength only set her off further.

"Where's your boss?" She poked him in the chest and pushed him against the wall. "Get me your boss so I can tell him what a waste you really are."

The woman departed with her stolen goods, laughing her way to the door in the wake of her threat.

The shadow struggled to shake away the memory. Rudeness was an infection. It seeped through society like a plague. Instead of wiping people out, though, it provoked them to spread more ill will to those around them. People fell to rudeness to get their way. Others merely ignored the poor behavior rather than struggle against it for fear of recrimination.

The shadow couldn't ignore it any longer. The compulsion refused to allow it and gave him the will to follow through on his feelings.

Pulled from the past and back to the present, the shadow halted in the darkness of the empty parking lot. The woman continued toward the lone car. She cursed the late hour or the clear night she'd wasted stuck at her terrible job. Whatever the words, they were lost under the pounding of the shadow's heartbeat.

At the side of her car, the woman's keys fell from her grasp.

They clattered against the pavement like the ringing of a bell.

"Couldn't spring for keyless entry, could you?"

Her wide girth prevented an easy retrieval. She crouched, a hand along the car for support. Before her free hand snatched the keys from the pooling puddle at her feet, the shadow grabbed them.

"Hey!" The woman jumped, shocked at the sudden arrival of company. The shadow, however, remained calm. The keys dangled from his finger between them, taunting her to act. Recognition came quickly to her eyes. The insolence of their previous encounter shifting her shock to anger. "What the hell do you think you're do-ing?"

"Helping," the shadow answered.

Her laughter echoed in the night. No word of thanks entered her thoughts. "Yeah, right. I don't need your help."

She reached for the keys. The shadow pulled them away at the last second.

"I wasn't helping *you*," he said.

"What?" Fear filled her eyes. The car key settled between his fingers. With a blistering cry, she shouted, "Wait!"

The key jabbed through her left eye in a swift blow. Her stout body crashed against the side of the car. Blood streamed from the wound, which he held firm as her body convulsed under his assault. When it stopped, when her body finally surrendered to fate, the shadow removed the key from the woman's eye. She slid against the cold frame of the car and settled against the pavement.

The shadow dropped the key into the puddle at her feet. He stared at the crimson seeping down her face in a long trail of bloody tears. It stained her cheek and dotted her still open mouth. He reached out for her lips, fraught with terror at her sudden death, and twisted them into a smile.

She looked happier than he had ever seen her. He preferred her that way.

Satisfied, he stood. "You see?" the Kindly Killer said in the cold shadow of the night. "I was helping myself."

CHAPTER SIX

Gates stepped out of the locker room with her uniform tucked tight to her side. Her badge continued to glint under the dim overhead lights. She caught her own reflection on its shining surface.

Staring deep along the department's emblem, her own eyes faded from view, only to be replaced by another pair. They were youthful like her own, but no longer carried the spark of life in them. Two days after discovering her body, Lydia Giles stuck with her. The suddenness of the poor woman's demise, the cruelty behind the act, followed Gates everywhere, like a ghost.

Delicate fingers ran against the badge, wiping away the image without success. Lydia continued to stare into her, a crooked and hellish smile forced upon her face for all eternity.

Gates needed rest and was thankful for the quiet shift. Her patrol with Dickie "I suddenly prefer Del" Delmar had turned up nothing of interest. There were the usual bad boys skulking the corners, and other hot spots to visit. Mostly, however, they simply wandered through Portents like tourists seeing the sites.

There was a nervous energy to their work, though. She felt it in everyone's movements at the precinct. The entire department was hungry to catch the Kindly Killer. They worked with nothing else in their mind but the capture of the elusive killer. Every disparate personality came together for a common goal. She always thought it possible of all who resided in the city of her birth: if they stood together, nothing could knock them down. She hoped the feeling stuck around.

Her own feelings, though, circled back to the Kindly Killer. He was still somewhere in the city—free to plan another death, to take another innocent from the streets at a moment's notice.

Gates closed her eyes and drew in a deep breath. She tried to push work aside and focus on the rest to come. Unfortunately, there were also several chores for her mother Gates had been avoiding all week.

"Great," she muttered, not quite ready for the fight to come. Gates squeezed her uniform between her palms. Her fingers hid the badge from view, a reprieve from the weight it carried.

"They'll give anyone a badge these days," a voice called from down the hall.

Gates recognized the voice immediately. She tucked the shirt into her open gym bag, a smirk on her face. "They gave you one, didn't they?"

Gates rushed for the waiting figure of a man. He greeted her hug with wide arms. John Pratchett was a sight for Gates' very weary eyes.

"It's so good to see you, John," she said into his chest. She squeezed him harder than her uniform, double-checking his existence before letting go. "Sorry. They call you Pratchett, don't they?"

"Last names are big around here, yeah." Pratchett laughed and rubbed his neck. They had spoken several times on the phone since her recruitment, but Gates hadn't seen Pratchett in months. "You look good, Mel. Dickie treating you all right?"

"He tell you he prefers Del now?" Gates said with a groan. "He's trying to get people to call us the Del-Mel team. John, he's trying to make that a thing people will say. To our faces."

"I can start if you like."

"Don't you dare."

"So not the best?" Pratchett asked.

Gates sighed. "Besides that and adding an entire hour of cardio to my daily workout thanks to his love of carbs? Things have been good, John. Really, I…" She trailed off, a glimpse back to the bag at her side and the badge tucked within. "They're…"

Pratchett's hand fell to her shoulder. "What is it?"

She patted his hand thankfully, a false grin on her face. "Nothing. Sorry." Gates shifted away from him. A few steps away, she spun on her heels. "It's just this case."

"The Kindly Killer?" Pratchett shook his head. "Terrible name."

Gates couldn't help but laugh. Her hand covered her lips quickly. "It really is."

Sullen eyes trailed her movements through the corridor. "I

heard you found one of his."

"Yeah." Gates pulled the uniform loose once more. She un-clipped the badge and held it before her. Lydia Giles remained, cold and lifeless. "She…" Gates slipped the badge into her pocket and zipped up her bag. "She was my age, John. And then gone… poof. Just like that."

"Mel."

"I'm fine. I am." Gates waved off the discussion, shaking away all thought of the deceased woman and the monster who took her from the world. "But listen to me. You didn't come to talk about work. Unless you're back." The notion caused her eyes to widen. "Are you back? Because that would be amazing, and—"

"Not yet, Mel," Pratchett answered in a muted tone. His hand returned to his neck, and he slowly backed away down the corridor. "I'm getting there. I need a little more time to figure some things out."

"What kind of things?"

His reticence surprised her. Gates grew up with little Johnny Pratchett. They went through grade school together, shared the bus together. Even then, Pratchett had been so easygoing, so light-hearted. The look on his face was anything but, and it saddened her, but not as much as his silence on the subject every time she pressed.

Not that it stopped her from trying again. "I've asked around, but no one seems to understand why you're on leave, John." His gaze fell to the floor, unable to meet hers. "Hey. We go back. You can always tell me anything. Usually it comes with a bad joke or two, but…" She reached out and took his hand. "I'm here if you need me. You know that, right?"

He squeezed her hand. "Yeah. Of course."

Still unable to meet her eyes, Pratchett scanned the second-floor corridor. At the sight of a fast-moving detective, he stopped.

"This, though?" he whispered. "Some things are complicated."

Gates leaned around Pratchett to trail his wayward attention. She huffed when she saw Loren. "Like him? Pfft. Nothing compli-cated about Loren at all."

Pratchett's eyes widened in surprise. "No?"

"Nope. Guy's just an ass."

"Mel," Pratchett intoned.

She shook her head to stop the lecture. "I get it. It's the old boys' club around here, and I'm the outsider looking in."

Pratchett blinked hard. "I don't even know what that means."

"You've both been at Central a lot longer than me, is what I'm saying."

"Next time, just say that," he said, a chuckle on his lips.

"Stop," Gates shot back. "He was a jerk, John. Straight-up, arrogant, know-it-all jerk."

Pratchett considered his reply, then snapped his fingers loudly. "That explains it."

"What?"

"You haven't met Loren yet," Pratchett said. "Not really."

Gates threw him a thin glare. "John."

Pratchett stopped her with a raised hand. "What happened to him… What he's had to endure? He's one of the good guys, Mel. One of the absolute best you'll meet."

Loren pushed through the milling crowd at the end of the hall for the door to the parking garage. He offered no apology for his brusque behavior, and no one gave him a second glance, except Pratchett, whose eyes filled with sadness.

"I don't see it," Gates admitted, confused at her friend's adoration of Loren.

"You will," Pratchett replied. "Trust me."

"I do," Gates said with a pat of his arm. She tightened her grip on her bag and puffed out her chest. "Now step aside, Gigantor. Some of us have lives to attend to."

Pratchett cocked an eyebrow at her. "Really?"

She grinned. "We can't all be living off the system, lazing around all day and night, or whatever it is you do."

"I keep busy," Pratchett said in a whiny tone. "I do stuff."

"Sure." She hugged him close. "Come back to work, John."

"Soon."

She nodded. "See you later. Say hello to your uncle for me when you're doing your 'stuff.'"

"Only if you say hello to your mom for me."

Gates laughed. Pratchett knew exactly what her plans entailed, as she did his. So much for lives of their own.

She tossed him a wave and headed for the exit. The pounding of feet through the precinct, the collected energy of the law, fell behind her. So did images of Lydia Giles, though Gates knew they would return soon enough.

CHAPTER SEVEN

Ruiz hesitated at the door. Words ran through his thoughts; mock conversations played out the upcoming encounter. None went well in his mind. Still, the talk remained a requirement in the captain's eyes.

He had tried dozens of times to have the conversation over the last six months. The attempts had come from a place of friendship, which Ruiz counted Loren as one of only a few. Even in the shadow of his wife's death, with the changes in behavior and the lack of sleep and the terrible work ethic, Ruiz clung to that friendship tightly. His attempts to help Loren, though, had been rebuffed or blatantly ignored.

The Kindly Killer sat at the heart of the problem. No matter his motivation, no matter his obvious need, Loren could not look past the murderer among them. In his mind, the serial killer had taken Beth from him. His only way back to the world was to solve the case and bring down the man who had haunted his days and nights.

Ruiz supported that quest. Hell, everyone at the precinct had in the beginning. But with each failure, as each body turned up, Loren had pushed everyone else away. He had snapped at them because of his own inability to find the man responsible for the worst day of his life. Their sympathy fell away because of Loren's behavior.

Now Ruiz stood alone, cursing his need for the talk. He missed his friend, though, and this was the only way left to win him back—no matter the fallout.

"At least he'll get a good meal out of the deal," Ruiz muttered under his breath. He could smell the homemade barbecue sauce on the braised short ribs tucked within the bag at his feet. He lifted the peace offering, then knocked on the door.

A response came immediately, though not from the right

apartment. Behind him, the door to the neighbor's residence slipped from the frame. An elderly woman with thick glasses stared at him through the crack. Her thin glare caused Ruiz's cheeks to flush, and he waved.

"Answer the door, Greg." Ruiz knocked harder, three sharp raps against the slab. It wasn't until his third succession of knocks that steps approached.

"Coming," Loren called through the door. "I'm coming already."

The chain fell from the door loudly, clattering against the molding. The deadbolt twisted loose, and the knob turned sharply to the right before the door opened. Loren stood in the frame, confused.

"What do you…" He stopped at the sight of the bag before his face. "Ruiz?"

Ruiz looked him over with a glance. Unshaven cheeks and deep wells under his eyes spoke to the man's sleeping habits. He wore a ratty shirt with holes along the cuffs. The S-symbol adorning his chest was dull from age.

"I…" Ruiz caught himself when he heard the creaking of the door behind them. Both he and Loren slowly turned their attention to their unwanted guest.

Loren forced a smile and a wave. "Evening, Mrs. Abernathy."

She said nothing, continuing to eye Ruiz cautiously.

Ruiz shifted for the door. "Any chance I could come in?"

Loren hesitated. "Depends."

"On?"

"Who did the cooking?" he asked, pointing to the bag. "You or Michelle?"

Ruiz handed him the meal and stepped inside. "Don't insult the man who brings you dinner."

Loren waved once more to the woman before shutting the door and her view of their conversation. "I won't," Loren said. "As long as he didn't *cook* the dinner."

Ruiz sighed with mounting frustration. "Michelle says to enjoy it."

Loren smiled and clutched tighter to the feast in his hands. "Thank you." He moved to the kitchen with zeal. "Am I sharing this delicious meal?"

"It would be nice," Ruiz said. "I'm missing an art show at Zoe's school for this."

Loren ducked back into the living room with a raised eyebrow. "You're using me to get out of school functions now? For shame."

"Yeah, well, you haven't seen the artwork."

Cupboards opened and plates rattled against the counter. Loren tore into the bag to seize the meal within. Ruiz caught the scent of the ribs once more, this time joined by rice pilaf and steamed vegetables. He had suffered through the wonderful aroma the entire trip from the coves, and was eager to dig in.

As he waited, Ruiz scanned the living room of the apartment. A lone image of Loren's wife rested on the mantelpiece in front of a dusty mirror. The small television was positioned on a rolling cart next to a coffee table covered with paperwork. Ruiz recognized the files from the precinct and reached for those on top.

All pertained to the Kindly Killer. Images of crime scenes, forensic reports, Hady's personal notes on each case, and more littered the table. Ruiz followed the trail and realized even more were piled at the end of the couch.

When he turned for the far wall, Ruiz found the mother lode. His jaw slipped open. Dozens of images had been taped to the wall. Some were victims of the Kindly Killer. Others, the locations of their deaths. Index cards were pinned between them with scribbles, circles, and shorthand Ruiz failed to decipher at a quick glance.

He approached the wall as Loren's voice cut through from the adjacent room. "What can I get you to drink?" He entered the living space with two plates in hand. "I have water, more water, or flat ginger ale."

Ruiz simply stared at him, a finger to the covered wall. "Are we going to talk about this?"

Loren sighed. He shuffled a pile of casefiles to the floor with his elbow and placed the rapidly cooling plates down.

"There's nothing to discuss."

"You've turned your apartment into a murder room," Ruiz said with stark astonishment. "There's nothing to talk about?"

"No."

"This isn't healthy, Greg," Ruiz continued. All hope of sticking to the script he'd practiced during his drive faded at the sight of Loren's obsession. "It's—"

"All I have, Ruiz!" Loren shouted. He cut the captain off from the images, a hand slapping at them in frustration. "You want to kick me off the case, fine, but I'll be damned if I stop looking. After what this monster has done?"

"You don't know that he—"

"Don't say it!" Loren snapped. "Don't you dare say it."

Ruiz closed his eyes. He forced a deep breath. "What happened to Beth was tragic, but there is no evidence to suggest the Kindly Killer had anything to do with her death."

Loren's fists clenched tight at his sides. He paced the length of the living room for the front window overlooking King's Lane below. "You weren't there. You didn't see her. She died with a smile on her face, just like the rest."

"She had you by her side," Ruiz shot back. "Did you ever think it was because of you?"

The grieving detective slammed his hands against the sill, then rested his head on the cool pane. Rain fell in streaks along the glass.

"They still call it a suicide," Loren said. "The others at the precinct? They've all made their judgments."

"So have you," Ruiz replied. In the middle of the notes and locations and deaths adorning the apartment wall, an image had been tacked on top and circled. It was of a man in a gray suit with a receding hairline and a square jaw. "Who's Kenneth Winthrop?"

Loren retreated from the window, his eyes suddenly ablaze. He shifted next to Ruiz, tapping the image fervently. "It's him."

Ruiz stared at him in confusion. It did little to deter Loren.

"It is, Ruiz!" Loren ripped the image down and held it before him. "Winthrop owns three of the buildings where we found victims."

"Three?"

"That's right."

"And the rest?" The question was quiet, but hovered in the air between them.

"What?" Loren said. He shook his head, unable to understand or unwilling. "That's not..."

Ruiz pressed. "How does he connect to the rest?"

Loren spun the image around. Tired eyes begged Ruiz to listen. "This is him. He's involved. I know it."

"Like you knew it with Baxter," Ruiz answered, recalling Loren's other obsessions about the killer's identity. "And with Cross."

"Those were solid leads that didn't pan out."

"Those were lawsuits the precinct barely avoided, Greg!"

Baxter had held their interest for days, a viable suspect with deep ties to the mob. Nothing concrete ever surfaced, and an alibi had come forward during their investigation. The man might have been close to the mark, but Cross had been a wild shot in the dark from Loren.

The business magnate owned a construction company where victims five and six—Beckett North and Wyatt Andrews—had been found. Loren had gone after Cross like a rabid dog, despite the man's sterling reputation and complete forwardness with the case.

Loren had pushed him too far, however. He'd assaulted Cross, demanding to know his whereabouts the day of Beth's fall. Booze had been the culprit for Loren's surprise visit, and Cross had thankfully recognized the grieving widower at the heart of the conflict. No charges had been pressed, but the warning had been clear from that moment on.

Ruiz had no choice but to cement that warning now, rather than see it happen again. "You're seeing suspects everywhere, Greg."

"Better that than closing my eyes to the potential killer," Loren said. He tacked the image back on the wall, unable to take his eyes off his key suspect.

Ruiz saw nothing more than another mistake. "This isn't the guy, Greg. You know that."

Loren refused to look at him. He turned back to the lukewarm meal on the table. "I appreciate the support, Captain."

"Greg…"

"And the meal," Loren finished. He offered a stiff nod, then headed for the door. He reached for the floor next to the coat rack where his jacket lay and picked it up. "Be sure to thank Michelle for me."

"What are you doing?"

He opened the door. "I have some errands to run before work. I don't want to be late for my shift. The boss hates that kind of slip up."

"Greg, listen…"

Loren's hand offered Ruiz the waiting hall. "I'll see you at the station."

Ruiz ran his fingers over his lips. There was more to say. There always was with Loren. The damage, however, had been done. Ruiz ducked out into the hall. He spun on his heels, another argument on the tip of his tongue.

The door slammed in his face. He heard the snap of the dead-bolt and the chain slip back into place.

Ruiz wanted to knock again, his hand hovering before him. Then he let it fall away. He knew the futility of such an act when it came to Loren's reaction. Another fight was the last thing either of them needed.

The rumbling of his stomach reminded him what he truly need-ed. He clutched tight to his empty gut, the aroma of the ribs still in the air.

"Couldn't have waited until after the meal. Nope. Not me," he grumbled as he moved for the stairs and the cold rain outside. "Stupid, Ruiz. Real stupid."

CHAPTER EIGHT

Soriya slowly woke from a troubled sleep. In her dreams she'd been cut repeatedly, beaten and shamed while her attackers had laughed behind ever-widening maniacal grins. The sound echoed in her mind, even in her return to the waking world.

Shifting for the edge of her cot, Soriya rubbed the weariness from her swollen eyes. The simple act caused her to wince in pain. Her hands were raw, the cuts and scrapes along her knuckles, wrists, and forearms more prominent under the dim light of the bedroom.

Grumbles accompanied stiff movements from the bed through her room. Soriya grabbed at clothes hanging in disarray from every piece of furniture. Discarding the blood-stained attire worn the previous night, she quickly changed. With each move, she stretched sore muscles and aching bones, listening to the creaks and snaps of her body.

A trip to the sink in the adjacent room allowed her to splash water on her dirt-caked skin. She rubbed the fresh water deep against her cheeks and forehead, then let it drip upon her hands. The coolness burned against the raw patches on her fingers and palms, and she squeezed her hands closed tight.

Returning to her room, Soriya snatched her phone from beneath her pillow. The time flashed on the screen and she realized the late hour. She had wasted a whole day in nightmarish dreams.

"Time to go to work."

The notion rejuvenated her. All thought to the previous night, to the troubles that carried her through sleep, vanished. She cared only about the night ahead and another chance to end the threats that plagued her city.

Grabbing a quick breakfast-turned-dinner, which amounted to

nothing more than a granola bar and a bottle of water, Soriya headed out of the makeshift domicile into the Bypass Chamber.

Four stone pillars rose from the corners of a square platform. They soared to a ceiling forty-feet high, with glyphs and markings cut into the stone throughout. In the center of the platform, floating a few feet from the ground, was a glowing green orb of light.

The Bypass served as an extension to other worlds and times. Deep within its spinning surface was the means to see and learn the secrets of the universe. All questions could be answered, but at a cost.

It was a wonder to behold. However, it was not why Soriya turned toward the glowing sphere. She looked around for something else entirely—or *someone* else, at any rate. Relieved to find the platform empty, Soriya rushed for the metal staircase leading to the subway tunnels and the city beyond.

"Who were they?"

Soriya nearly jumped out of her skin at the voice. A cloaked figure with deep gray eyes stared at her from the bottom step, his arms crossed tight over his chest.

"Mentor!" she exclaimed. "You scared the hell out of me."

He departed the shadows of the stairs for the chamber with a huff. Soriya backed away at his approach, though not fast enough to escape his reach. He grabbed her by the wrist and lifted the sleeve. His eyes widened at the bruises coloring her skin.

"The two who did this to you," Mentor said. "The two in masks. Who were they?"

Soriya shoved her shirt back into position. The pain was excruciating, but she refused to cry out. "How did you hear about that?"

"I am not a hermit, though you might mistake me for one. I stay informed."

Soriya cocked an eyebrow. "You can just say the Bypass told you."

"It didn't." Mentor removed the newspaper from the deep pocket of his cloak and handed it to her. "They made the morning edition."

She scanned the article. For months, multiple districts had complained of random acts of violence. The perpetrators plagued various businesses, terrorizing and then fleeing into the night without a single clue as to their identities.

Soriya had met them the previous night. Coincidence or not,

the rest of the city woke to their first meeting of the pair as well. A traffic camera had caught the masked marauders during their joyride up the Knoll. The deed, however, was not a surprise to the miscreants. They waved wildly for the camera, as if they'd planned it that way, even in the midst of smashing into a mailbox and news-stand.

Soriya crumpled up the paper in her hands and tossed it back at Mentor. He caught it deftly, smoothed out the new wrinkles, and slipped the paper into his pocket once more.

A curious thought occurred to Soriya. "I didn't hear you leave. Usually, I can hear the groan of the door or the subway when you do, but—"

"I have my ways," Mentor interjected. His eyes fell on the far wall of the chamber, out of the natural light given by the Bypass at the center. Just as fast, his eyes returned to Soriya. "You also snore quite loudly after taking a beating."

"They didn't beat me," she snapped, unsure what annoyed her more: the snoring accusation or his summation of the previous night's endeavor. "They merely surprised me."

"A far too frequent occurrence of late."

Soriya grimaced at Mentor's smug words. Concern fell away and the haughty teacher took over. She grew tired of being the eternal student.

"Comedy and Tragedy," Mentor continued. "Your attackers."

"Yeah," she said, recalling the masks. "I picked up on that."

"What do you know about them?" he asked. At her silence, Mentor shook his head. "Nothing? Not one insight? Then where are you rushing off to?"

His hand stretched out to showcase the domicile and the library tucked within. Study had always been the priority to uncover the secrets of Portents. His approach had been her own for many years—if only to quiet the constant lectures from her aging teacher.

The role of Greystone now fell to her, and she had methods of her own. "I have to—"

"You're injured."

"I'm fine," she said. Mentor grabbed at her arm and squeezed. She cried out, then ripped free from him. Her hand grazed the bruises, and she tucked the arm in close. "I will be fine."

Mentor sighed. "Your mistakes of late have been costly, little one."

Soriya's fists clenched. "Oh, you're trying to push all my buttons now, is that it?"

"You can't keep doing this, Soriya."

"Doing what?" she shouted in frustration. There was more to his derision, and she tired of circling the matter. "Tell me, Mentor. What am I doing that has you so out of sorts?"

His gaze thinned. "Forget the detective."

Her eyes sparked at the admission. She should have known what his problem was from the start. "This is about Loren? You don't—"

"Your guilt clouds your judgment," he pressed, not caring for her excuses. "Bethany's death was not your fault."

"Yes, it was!" Soriya yelled. She could still see the missed call on her phone in the aftermath of her battle with the Daughters of Salem. While she'd protected the city, Soriya could not save the life of one she called friend and confidant. Portents had taken the priority, and the cost continued to haunt her.

"I wasn't there," she said in a low, sad voice. "She called, and I didn't... I should have been there. I should have saved her."

"Little one."

Soriya cringed at the name, eyes shut tight. "Please stop with that."

"Your guilt serves no one."

"I made a promise, Mentor," she said. "Loren needs me. There is a killer on the streets. I can—"

"I'm aware of your rationalization." The paper was back in his hands. "And of the situation. There was another victim."

He turned the page to show the profile of the deceased. Soriya snatched it from him and looked her over. "I'm going."

Soriya moved for the steps.

"Leave the detective to his grief," Mentor called after her. "There is only more pain down that road. Our work is too important."

She heard every word, but said nothing in return. Quick steps carried her to the door. The city awaited.

So did Loren. Despite Mentor's warning, Loren remained important to Soriya. After failing Beth, no one was more deserving of being saved in her eyes.

CHAPTER NINE

Gates put off visiting her mother all day. She felt too tired for anything but sleep by the time she reached home after her shift. The gloom of the day kept her in bed; the patter of rain against the windows of her apartment accompanied her through a series of nightmares. Images of the dying, including Lydia Giles, faded when she woke.

The afternoon waned in a series of distractions that amounted to little in the end. A bit of cleanup, dishes to the sink from the counter, a sweep of the floor where she had spilled some coffee grounds, and a consolidation of her laundry for her trip later in the week, stole away hours she didn't have.

The delays cost her. By the time she reached the grocery store, shoppers swarmed the place. Stock ran low on several items and Gates struggled to complete the list she'd put together with little to no input from her mother—mostly for Gates' own sanity.

Juggling three bags from the store down the Knoll in the rain rounded out the trip. Her grumbling complaints carried her to the apartment building on Cambridge, where Gates fought to find her keys without success. Picturing them on the kitchen counter next to her piling mail, Gates groaned in frustration and punched the call button for Kelly Gates in Apartment 3-B.

The buzzer rang twice without a response. "Come on, Mom. Answer the door."

Instead of the buzz of the door opening, static rose from the intercom. "Any cigarettes in there?"

Gates nearly dropped the bags on the stoop. Rain seeped into everything and her grip tightened on the contents of her excursion. "Are we really going to do this right now, Mom?"

A slight pause, then the voice returned to the intercom. "Are there any cigarettes in those grocery bags?"

"No, but—"

"Goodbye, Melanie," her mother said through the line.

"Don't you—" The static vanished. Gates pressed the bags between her and the brick edifice and slammed her thumb against the call button. Three times, then four, Gates hit the buzzer without success. She stared up, hoping to catch a glimpse of her mother in the window. "Open the door, Mom. I need you to—"

The door opened, not with the sound of a buzz of acceptance from the third-floor occupant, but by the withered hand of a sixty-four-year-old woman. Helen Janke, the neighbor from 2-E, had lived downstairs from Gates' mother for the last three decades.

"Key not working, Melanie?"

Gates offered the woman wearing a raincoat and boots an awkward grin as she moved for the open door. "Mrs. Janke. You're looking lovely today." Gates cocked her head to the call button. "Something must be wrong with Mom's buzzer."

Helen pursed her lips. "You should let Leroy know. I swear he gets lazier every year."

The neighbor let go of the door to open her umbrella. She made no move for the bobbled grocery bags in Gates' hands.

"I will." Gates turned back, her hand in a wave. "Thank you, Mrs. Janke. Have a great—"

The door shut without a word. Helen headed down the steps with no consideration for the visitor she had known since Gates was in diapers. She left without a word of concern or care, as if her own world was all that mattered and Gates had been an inconvenient interruption.

"—day," Gates finished. "Have a great day. Yeah, I will too. Thanks."

The trek up the stairs brought no more interactions. The building's occupants either settled in for the evening or had yet to return from their days. No looks passed through peepholes or greetings offered through cracked doors. The community Gates had grown to love failed to reciprocate those feelings, too buried in their own priorities.

At the door to Apartment 3-B, Gates lowered the soggy and tearing bags of groceries to the carpet. Her hand twisted the knob on the door to find it unlocked.

"Okay, Mom, I'm—" The door stopped opening at a crack.

While the deadbolt had been disengaged, the chain remained in place. Gates pushed against the door to no avail, then slammed her head against the wooden frame. "Please tell me this is a nightmare, and I'm about to wake up."

Bloodshot eyes peered through the crack in the door. "This is my nightmare, Melanie. Ruined by my own daughter!"

Gates sighed. "Not dramatic at all." She pushed at the door once more. "Now open up, please!"

Her mother huffed. "Fine."

The chain slipped and bony fingers pulled the door open. Gates let out a relieved breath. She bent down to retrieve the three full bags of groceries. Heaving them into her arms, Gates crossed the threshold of her childhood home for the kitchen off to the right.

Lamps were lit in the living area beyond, yet the room continued to be dim. Dust covered the tables, the smell of stale smoke in the air. Gates carted the groceries to the counter and plopped them on top, careful to keep them from spilling over.

"Don't worry, Mom," she called. "I've got it all."

"Good," her mother grumbled. She wore a heavy sweater despite the temperature. Brown hair lay in tangles, as if neglected for days. Her pants were faded from age, like her very presence. Still, there was the old fire in her words that Gates knew very well. "There's nothing for *me* in those bags."

"No?" Gates asked in surprise. "I didn't lug all this food four blocks in the rain for someone else."

Her mother shoved Gates to the side. Reaching into the first bag, she removed the top items. Each one brought more disgust to her face. "Lean turkey. Green vegetables. Where's the ground beef? Where's the sauce?"

"The doctor said—"

"Like he knows," she scoffed. "My mother ate—"

"Grandma ate crap all her life."

"And lived to be ninety," her mother exclaimed. "Ninety, Melanie! A glass of wine with a pound of pasta every Sunday until the day she died."

"Of a heart attack."

"In her sleep!" her mother bellowed, her finger raised high over her head. "At ninety!"

Gates didn't reply. The argument merely provided a distraction for the ebullient matriarch. Gates, however, saw through the ploy.

She noted the stains under her mother's fingernails, the fresh mint in her mouth, and the lingering stream of smoke that ran from the ashtray out the open window.

"Where are they, Mom?"

"What?" She played at confusion, though the effort failed to convince her daughter. "Where are what?"

"Who smuggled the pack to you this time? Was it Leroy again?"

"I don't know what you're—"

Gates stopped listening. She pushed past her mother for the living room. Quick glances brought back memories of brighter days and childhood dreams. Every hiding place came into view. Most were her own, though, tucked away in the corner with her toys or her books.

A snap of her fingers brought with it a return trip to the kitchen. Gates moved for the microwave cart and opened the false drawer beneath the unit where her mother had hidden small gifts for many years. Inside the shallow space sat an open pack of smokes. Gates grabbed the pack and held it in the air.

"Try again."

Her mother attempted to snatch it, but Gates held tight. "I paid the kid down the hall," she admitted. "Too much, if you ask me."

Gates shifted for the open window and her mother blocked her path. Surrendering in frustration, Gates settled on the small kitchen table chair and stared into the gloom outside. "Can't you just try for me?"

Her mother joined her across the table. "Can't you just visit your poor mother without a lecture?"

"I would love that."

"Good." Her mother opened her hand for the pack. "Then—"

Gates squeezed hard. "But her stubborn addiction keeps getting in the way." She tossed the pack through the open window.

"Melanie!" Her mother watched in horror as the pack faded from view, lost to the debris along the side of the apartment building. She continued to stare for a long moment, almost willing the cigarettes to return, then collapsed back against the chair. "You can't change destructive behavior, Melanie."

"*You* could." Gates took her mother's hand. "You could do it for me, Mom."

Her mother grimaced and rubbed at her bloodshot eyes. She looked tired. The weather always affected her.

Gates tried to pull her away from the rain outside, a soft smile on her lips. "I told Aunt Leslie—"

The mere mention of the woman's name snapped her mother back to the table. Anger flashed in her sharp eyes. "Why do you still talk to that woman?"

"She's my aunt," Gates said. "She's your sister."

"Who's too busy gallivanting around the country to be here with her family."

"She's coming back," Gates remarked. "She even talked about running for City Council again."

"Yeah, bossing people around was always her style. Like you, it seems."

"I'm trying to take care of you."

"And the city," her mother said. "Two losing battles, if you ask me."

Gates rolled her eyes. "Let's not start that again."

Her mother continued to look outside. From their vantage, they could see the downward slope of the Knoll and Riverside in the distance. "This neighborhood used to be so different. Parties in the streets. Kids riding bikes and shooting off firecrackers."

"Which you always hated."

Her mother ignored the comment. "Now, people lock their doors at all hours. Keep the shades drawn and windows latched. Scared."

Gates nodded. "The city can get through this, Mom. If more people stood up, we could make a real difference. I know we could."

Her mother chuckled and shook her head. "Always the dreamer." She reached out to pat Gates on the hand. "Someday, you'll have to wake up."

"Not a chance," Gates said. "I have too much hope. Even in someone as stubborn as you."

Their shared laughter filled the air, and for a moment, the rain seemed to lessen. Gates realized it was only a temporary reprieve from what waited for her once night fell and work took over. At the moment, however, she was content to bring a glimpse of light to her mother's life.

One she hoped to share with the rest of the city.

CHAPTER TEN

325 Hammond Way stood just north of the Knoll. No less than six local businesses that ranged from construction to real estate occupied office space within the building. An accounting firm shared the upper floor with a budding tech startup. The first floor split between three different tenants, each with their own lobby that opened up into a larger office.

Traffic patterns throughout the building faded in the evening hours. The tech firm used the stairs off the front entrance to get to their workstations, while most of the accounting firm called it quits with the dinner bell. Of the three offices operating on the first floor, only one had lights on within.

Winthrop Holdings was an intimate operation dealing with commercial real estate. A few partners helped handle the day-to-day operations, but most of the work ran through the man at the head of the business. A hands-on boss, Kenneth Winthrop worked longer hours than he required of the rest.

Loren had expected his visit to be quick. With the coming night, there was little time to delay before his shift at the precinct. He had snuck in with members of the tech firm, his face obscured behind the collar of his coat. When they turned for the upper level, Loren continued through the shared lobby and corridor of the first. Noticing the light in the Winthrop office, Loren tucked behind the entry door. He hid between the random couch and chair which decorated the space.

Waiting was never his strong suit, but he made the best of his situation. He kept his head close to the door; the soft voices of an administrative assistant and her boss barely heard through the obstruction.

"I'm heading out," the woman's voice called. "Unless you need anything further, Mr. Winthrop?"

"No, no," Loren's target replied. His voice was soft and fatherly, not the menace Loren imagined in his head on his way over. "I'm beat as well. Have a good night, Janice."

"You too, sir," she said. "Thank you."

Loren tucked tighter to the wall as Janice exited the office suite. Her heels clicked softly against the thin carpet runner, and she kept her eyes ever forward for the exit and the night ahead.

The moment she stepped away, Loren shifted from his position against the wall. He grabbed the door. With a quick scan of the suite, Loren noted the absence of Winthrop.

He ducked inside and crept deeper into the brightly lit space. A ski mask hugged tight to his face. It limited his peripheral vision, but he found his way to the assistant's desk along the left side of the room. At the approach of steps from the inner office, he ducked behind the desk for cover.

"Sir?" Winthrop's voice echoed in the suite.

Loren tightened at the call of the man's voice. He held a long breath, wondering if he'd been found out and how he might explain his presence. A deep chuckle filled the space as Winthrop laughed.

"When did I become a sir?" he said to himself. From the corner of the desk, Loren noted the man's stone-gray suit and bright red tie. Winthrop presented a look of prestige. His neatly trimmed snow-white beard clued Loren in to the man's age. "Better question is, when did you start talking to yourself? That's a slippery slope, Kenneth. Which means… I am done for the night."

Winthrop grabbed his coat from the rack outside the inner office. He tucked it over his arm before heading back inside. Less than a second later, he returned with his briefcase in hand. The door closed behind him, and Winthrop slowly crossed the length of the room. He flicked the lights out with a deep sigh at another day gone, then he departed the suite.

Loren heard the lock click and the knob rattle to ensure it held. Soft-soled shoes padded away until all sound left the space completely.

Standing, the masked detective headed for the inner office. There was no lock on the door. It surprised Loren, though he continued without pause to view Winthrop's workspace. The desk sat in the middle of the room. A mini-bar occupied the corner. A sofa with twin chairs made up a meeting space, which ran in front of the wide window overlooking the fence to the rear of the building.

The desk was cleared of work and of a computer, which must have been in the briefcase Winthrop departed with for the night. Still, the lack of files confused Loren, who paced the length of the office for some clue as to the man himself.

"You can't tell me this guy isn't suspicious," Loren muttered under his breath. "He talks to himself for crying out loud. Who does that?"

At the question, Loren turned to see a large mirror reflecting his masked image. Tired eyes stared back at him.

"Right," he grumbled to the man in the mirror. "Well, you don't have to be so smug about it."

Leaving the office behind, Loren shifted to the only other closed door in the suite. This one was locked. With no tools to handle the lock, Loren took a step back and kicked out at the knob. It bent under the force of his blow and gave way with the follow-up.

Loren knocked the broken knob aside and pulled the lock free. The door swung open, hitting against a filing cabinet. As he stepped inside, Loren noted several cabinets occupying the cramped room.

"Here we go."

He didn't know what he expected to find, yet set to work with urgency. His time was limited, the ticking clock always set in the back of his mind. Drawers swung open, files pulled, scanned, then returned out of order or upside down.

Reports mentioned dozens of real estate dealings. There were images of his holdings in Portents and major cities in six other states. Emails with clients and investors were sorted and cataloged. Winthrop diligently kept a paper trail for everything.

Yet, for all his searching, Loren found nothing to indicate his other proclivities in life. There were no victim profiles, no smoking gun of any kind to denote Winthrop's late-night activities.

"Come on," Loren murmured in his frantic search. "There's something here. There has to be. I can't be wrong. I—"

So focused on his search, Loren was oblivious to the sound of the outside door opening and of footsteps through the suite. He didn't realize company had joined him until light fell on his full hands and a sharp command filled the air.

"Don't move!" A pair of patrolmen stood in the doorway, flashlights in one hand and guns in the other. "Hands in the air!"

CHAPTER ELEVEN

A silent alarm for the file room must have been tripped. Winthrop might also have been aware of Loren's presence in the suite before his departure. Either way, Loren had been a fool. His actions had brought him to the brink of arrest, or worse, if he pushed his luck further. Which, of course, was the only move left to him.

Loren blocked the light from his eyes with his left hand. His right remained above his head. Before him, the two patrolmen, their identities still unknown thanks to the bright beams from their flashlights, approached with caution. Both carried pistols aimed for his position.

"I'm sure we can talk about this, guys," Loren said through his mask.

They leaned closer in confusion.

Loren sighed, then lifted the mask from his mouth. "I said we can talk about this, can't we, guys?"

The officer on the left raised his gun higher. "Don't move again!"

The second tucked his weapon away to remove the cuffs from his belt. He took a step toward Loren, who could only shake his head. "Or not…"

"You made a big mistake, pal," the second said. The cuffs opened as he reached for Loren's arm.

"Yeah, well, I was never very good at learning my lesson," Loren replied. He snatched the man's arm.

"What are you—"

Loren swung the officer hard at the row of filing cabinets. The cop bounced from the steel paneling of the cabinets, and Loren drove his head into the man's chest. He barreled him into his colleague, who tried to dive out of the way. The cramped space of the filing room made it impossible to avoid the collision.

Out in the main suite, Loren let go of the officer in his grasp. The shared momentum of the pair kept them on the back of their feet. They staggered, tripping over each other in a heap on the floor. A flashlight rolled, and limbs struggled to break free from the pileup.

Loren didn't hesitate. He rushed for the outer door, still open from the officers' arrival.

"Stop!" they called after him.

"Sorry, guys," Loren answered with a wave. "Can't help you there."

He ducked around the corner and bolted for the exit. The corridor remained darkened, though the dim light of the rising moon outside gave Loren a clear path for the door. What failed to help him was the mask he'd hampered himself with. He nearly tripped on a chair not quite flush with the wall.

The two officers renewed their pursuit, continuing to shout unheeded warnings. Loren wondered how many more were allowed before they would simply open fire. They answered him the second he cleared the building, when a snap of air boomed around him and the brick of the adjacent complex shattered just shy of his shoulder.

"Shit," he muttered. Frantic, Loren jumped from the side of the stoop to bypass the six-step walk-up. Worn-out sneakers slapped against puddles on the pavement as Loren circled Winthrop's office building.

More shots followed him, as did the cry of one officer. This was not directed at Loren, though. The officer had called in to the nearest precinct house about the robbery.

Loren didn't need another complication. He needed to escape before backup arrived. A fence divided the property from the adjacent street. Loren latched onto the chain-link and scurried up. When he reached the peak, he took a second to glance back. His mistake cost him.

The officers were almost to the fence. "Stop!" they shouted in unison.

Loren slipped from the peak of the ten-foot-tall fence. He managed to get his feet under him, but his left ankle rolled with the impact and he fell over into a pile of trash.

The resultant fall saved his life as the shot intended to wound him skimmed by a second too late.

His ankle screamed for relief, but Loren could do little more than continue to flee his pursuers. They clambered for the top of the fence while he fought through the trash bags.

Once free, Loren skipped along on his twisted ankle. His pace quickened the more he ignored the pulsing pain, and he soon found himself five blocks over from Winthrop's. All signs of pursuit faded to nothing.

Loren almost collapsed from exhaustion. He found a wall to lean upon and slid to the ground. His ankle had already swollen to twice its normal size. Not that he could tell until after he ripped the mask from his face. A thick layer of sweat coated the inside.

Tossing the ski mask into a nearby bush, Loren ran his hands through his hair. The rain felt like a godsend, and washed him clean in seconds. Still, his mistake stuck with him.

He couldn't believe what an idiot he had been. Ruiz was absolutely right to treat him the way he had. Loren had been nothing but sloppy... and lost.

Time slipped away in his struggle to his feet. Dejected and sore, Loren retrieved the mask from the bushes. He found a nearby trash can and dumped it inside, not needing forensics to find a trace of his stupidity.

Loren took his time in his travels by cutting across another block for Evans and the downtown district. He wanted the night behind him, and thankfully, work provided an adequate distraction. Now he just needed to reach his destination without collapsing from the pain.

CHAPTER TWELVE

Upon arriving at the Central Precinct, Loren made a beeline for the supply closet on the first floor. Emergency medical supplies were stationed throughout the building, but by and large, they were a patchwork of missing equipment and emptied boxes.

Loren didn't want to take the chance and went straight to the source of the resupply that never made it to the rest of the building. Even the smallest amount of pressure added to his ankle caused him to limp slightly. Pain, a constant companion on the best of days, increased by the second.

Ripping through the boxes of goods tucked to the rear of the closet, Loren removed a pack of gauze and tape. He slipped his sneaker off carefully, rainwater coating his hand with the act. He wiped his palm along his pants, then once futility set in, opened his jacket and ran his hand along the liner.

With careful precision, Loren set to work on wrapping his swollen ankle. It pulsed with each circuit, but the pain lessened with the pressure added at just the right spot. The gauze ripped at the end of the last loop, and Loren placed a piece of tape to secure it.

He stared at his sneaker. There was no getting around putting the damn thing back on his foot, despite his body screaming for mercy. With one swift motion, Loren dipped his foot inside and gently tucked in the laces rather than tie it tightly around the swollen mass. The measure brought little comfort.

No one appeared to notice when he left the supply closet. Walking through processing and down the interrogation wing, Loren cut around the corner for the elevator. He preferred the stairs normally thanks to the ability to escape to the parking garage at the rear of the Rath. The very notion of steps, though, drove daggers up his leg.

By the time he reached the second floor, Loren's breathing was labored. He needed a reprieve and heard his desk calling him all the way from the other side of the floor. He passed briefly by the breakroom and coffee machines. At the edge of the bullpen of desks and half-walls, Loren noticed the whiteboard filled with names, dates, and officers. A fresh line of red appeared at the top, with the names Quinn and Messick attached.

The Kindly Killer had struck again.

Just the thought of the killer reminded Loren of his failed outing. His lead hadn't panned out anything other than his own stupidity over the entire case. Reflection came with the only sense of honesty Loren allowed himself these days: he needed to refocus. A figure at his desk, however, refused to give him the chance.

Ruiz stood there, hands on his hips. He paced up and down the corridor until Loren rounded the corner and all pretense was dropped.

"Detective," Ruiz said through clenched teeth. "I'd like a word."

Loren looked at the clock. He was on time—okay, almost on time—so his punctuality wasn't the issue. There was no question of Ruiz's anger; his stance alone gave away that much. Rather than assume the reason, Loren attempted to play off the exchange innocently.

"What's up, Ruiz?"

Ruiz eyed him closely, settling on the wounded ankle for a second. He shook his head and pointed down the wide corridor. Without a word, he started walking away.

"I thought you wanted—"

"Not here." Ruiz waved him further down the hall.

Loren gave a muted groan. His chair beckoned him, so soft and inviting. Instead, he left the desk behind and trailed the captain, who stopped in mid-stride to give Loren a chance to catch up. Loren did all he could to keep from limping during their rapid travels.

The captain continued to glare in his direction with each step, but Loren kept his eyes forward during their travels. Soft-soled shoes stopped halfway down the hall at an open door to the right.

"In here."

Ruiz stood aside at the frame of the door. Loren peered in, curious about the boxes lining the walls and surrounding a lone desk at the center. The precinct had always used the room for storage, yet now there seemed to be a purpose behind it.

"What's this about?"

"Inside," Ruiz replied. He closed the door behind him to cut off the sounds that boomed throughout the rest of the floor.

Loren padded deeper into the room. He opened boxes at random to paw through the belongings. Files upon files were stacked in each. Some dated back weeks, others months, but all were cases handled by the department at one time or other.

"Something wrong with your office?" Loren said as he circled the desk. His left foot caught the leg of the chair and he nearly screamed. Ruiz noted the reaction, but said nothing. Loren recovered quickly, a false grin on his face as he used the stacks on the far side of the desk for balance. "I keep telling you leftovers spoil when you leave them on your desk."

Ruiz said nothing, a stern look across his face.

"What?"

"Are you insane?"

Loren chuckled. "I don't follow. What's—"

Ruiz rushed at him. "Are. You. Insane?" He grabbed Loren by the collar and pushed him against the window ledge. "You come here and act like everything is fine and normal?"

"It is."

Ruiz stomped down and caught Loren on his left ankle.

"Ow!" the detective exclaimed. "What the hell?"

"Say it again."

"I don't know what—"

Ruiz kicked the ankle again. He let go of Loren at the same time. The wounded detective cursed loudly. He fell to the ground, clutching his ankle close.

"Dammit, Ruiz!"

"You broke into a man's office not one hour ago!" Ruiz yelled.

"I didn't—" Ruiz raised his foot once more. Loren shot a hand up. "All right. All right!"

Ruiz stepped back. He ran his hand through his hair to calm down. "How dare you, Greg? How dare you look me in the eye and try to pass this off? Winthrop tops your suspect list and, suddenly, two uniforms find a guy in a ski mask at the man's office?"

Loren struggled to stand. He leaned hard on the window ledge, then sat against the vent attached. A hand remained plastered over his ankle to smooth out the pain pulsing through the swollen mass.

"What the hell were you thinking? What the literal hell was going on in that thick skull of yours?"

Loren considered lying. It was easier than admitting the truth, but both knew the score right from the start. He lowered his head in shame. "I screwed up."

"You're damn right you screwed up."

Hardened eyes rose. "I know, Ruiz. All right? I know how bad I messed up."

Ruiz circled the desk once more. "Find any evidence?"

"No."

Ruiz nodded. "Because there wasn't any to find. Want to know how I know that?"

"How?"

"I did the work, Greg." He pointed to a report on the desk. Loren limped for the file. He opened the sleeve and scanned the contents as Ruiz shifted behind him. "Background checks. Statements from those close to him, including—*including*—no less than four verified alibis for the dates of the murders. Do you know how long it took me? Go on, guess."

Loren sighed. "A couple hours?"

Ruiz slammed his hand on the boxes. "A couple fucking hours! Over the phone! I didn't break any laws doing it either!"

"Ruiz, I…"

"Oh, you screwed up all right!" Ruiz shouted. "After I warned you. After I begged you to take some time off. I'm taking the choice from you, Greg. You're off active duty."

"What?" Loren's entire world blurred. Without active duty, Loren lost access to the Kindly Killer case completely. It had been the only thing holding him together since his wife's death. "Ruiz, you can't!"

"I can do plenty, Greg," Ruiz said without sympathy for the man's plight. "I am three seconds from cuffing you myself for that stunt you pulled. Of all the idiotic moves you could have made."

Loren clenched his fists tight against the desk. Ruiz was right. That was the absolute worst part of the whole thing. Ruiz was right about everything.

"What is it?" he asked. "The punishment?"

"You're looking at it." Ruiz tapped the box to his right. "These are cases solved outside the department. By who, we don't know. But I want a formal review of each one. I want to know what hap-

pened and how we missed it. These cases need to be closed properly."

"By filing paperwork," Loren said with a scoff. "Come on,
Ruiz. I'm not some damn clerk."

"No," Ruiz snapped. "You're an officer of the law. Maybe it's
time you remembered what that means." From the door, he peered
back at the forlorn detective. "Now get to work. I can't stand being
in the same room with you anymore."

Ruiz slammed the door shut, leaving Loren to his work and his
guilt. He had earned the captain's wrath. His entire endeavor had
been the epitome of stupidity. It was no wonder Ruiz had lost all
faith in him.

Loren wasn't sure if he had any in himself anymore.

CHAPTER THIRTEEN

Glen Tripp walked the empty halls of Portents Commerce Bank the same way he always had over the course of his forty-two-year career. He started from his station near the lobby with a clear view of the monitors positioned throughout the building and the street outside. No other businesses held entryways on the block, so all traffic typically headed toward the century-old establishment. Few others ever passed by, not in the commercial district of the Knoll, and especially not at such a late hour.

For Glen, who marked the days until his seventieth birthday, the job held an obvious benefit: it kept him moving. He knew the score otherwise. Everyone in his social circle had already felt the aches and pains of retirement. Without the constant need to move, there came the desire to stop altogether. Once the body realized that was the case, well, it was only a matter of time before any movement at all was no longer an option.

That thought alone kept Glen from turning in his keys and his standard issue Glock. The other one that kept him circling the bank's empty corridors was the question of what the hell he would do with all his free time? Television held no interest for him. Books were the same, though he read through a fair amount of magazines during his morning and afternoon constitutional. (He really needed to cut back on the fiber.) Socializing, to Glen, was a beer before work with the other regulars at Josie's Grill and a Sunday visit from his nephew to watch the hockey game if he had the time.

Work was steady, with no stigma attached. Glen wasn't afraid of leaving. He was afraid of what would happen *after* he left.

Another circuit passed under his musings. Glen tried to force away the same dismal thoughts that collected in the bank's silence at night. Barely dusk, and already he found himself a stone's throw away from a snooze with another six hours to go on the clock. He should have skipped the beer at Josie's. His eyes were already tired and his feet shuffled along the tile floor. He needed to be prepared for anything.

To prove the point, the alarms went off.

Glen grabbed at his chest. He jumped half a foot into the air as well, but he preferred to recall the general alertness that came with the rise of the alarms.

Racing for the monitor station in the lobby, Glen checked every section of his domain for signs of life. They all appeared clear.

"What in the world?"

He double-checked himself, then repeated the process twice more for good measure. He cycled through the screens slowly and methodically, from the offices to the rear of the branch and those on the upper levels, to the vault below. No one appeared on them, yet the alarms continued.

"Dammit," he muttered. He pulled the phone from the cradle, hesitating to dial. Procedure dictated the call, yet he hated to do it for only a glitch with the electrical system.

The phone rang twice before clicking over. "Hello?"

"Yeah, this is Glen at Portents Commerce. We have an alarm."

The young woman on the other end sighed audibly. He heard the pages being flipped on her desk, the protocol clear the second he dialed. Still, he remained on the line while she retrieved the instructions, then relayed them in firm tones over the line.

"I understand," Glen said. "But I don't—"

He pushed his glasses to the bridge of his nose. The camera to the vault level flickered, but for a moment Glen glimpsed a hole in the floor.

"It's the vault," he said to the woman on the phone. "The monitors show..." The flicker sped up right before the monitor died completely. Glen switched to a different camera—there were eight pointed at the vault at all times—yet found all had been deactivated somehow.

"The monitors are down," he breathed through the phone. He peered at the receiver when no reply came. "Hello? Did you hear me? I said the monitors are down. They..."

The line went dead. Glen tapped the phone several times to regain the dial tone without success. Setting the phone back into the cradle, Glen fumbled for his weapon. Suddenly, the corridors that he had called home for decades appeared bleak, isolated, and oh so strange.

"Retirement is looking pretty good now, isn't it?" His slow steps carried him to the stairs off the right side of the lobby. Careful footfalls continued to echo as he made his way downstairs. "But no, I had to stay active. Had to keep moving so the reaper didn't catch me. Always repeating the same damn mantra. That it's going to be a celebration when he finally comes on the day I'm ready. A regular…"

His voice trailed off. A gaping crater in the floor spread before him, with a clear view of the subway tunnels that ran beneath the bank. How such a hole was managed without alerting Glen immediately shocked him into silence.

As did the balloons and streamers decorating the entire vault door and the surrounding pillars. Hundreds of rainbow-colored balloons floated around Glen. Streamers ran in loops down the pillars and tied more balloons in place. Additional streamers crossed vast expanses of the room to connect to its neighbor.

"… party," Glen finished, his mouth still agape. "How?"

A woman stepped out from behind the open vault door. She wore a mask with a wide grin on the face and carried a cake topped with two sparklers. Atop her head sat a triangular party hat with the word CELEBRATE adorning the side in an endless loop.

"Too much?" she asked at the sight of the stupefied guard. "Probably too much. I was just so excited and couldn't pick between the streamers and the balloons. And the hats? Well, everyone likes a nice hat, don't they?"

Glen's gun shook in his hand. He made no move to raise it against the approaching woman in the mask. His stunned look continued until she stopped right before him and held out the cake.

"Aren't you going to make a wish?"

"What?" Glen shook his head. "I… I don't…"

"Here," a voice called from behind Glen. "Let me."

Before Glen could turn, a sharp blade dug into his back. Heat rose from the entry and coursed throughout his body. Intense pain followed, and Glen staggered forward. His gun fell to the ground.

"You…" Glen pawed at his back for the wound, but it was out of reach. His attacker wasn't, however, and turned Glen around. He wore a mask similar to the woman's, only his face carried a frown. "You…"

The knife drove into his gut, opposite the first strike. Glen gasped, struggling for breath. The second the blade retracted from his flesh, Glen fell to the ground. His back slammed against a pillar and balloons popped upon impact.

The smiling woman placed the cake on a stand, then pulled the sparklers free to wave them in the air. She danced excitedly around her companion.

"What was the wish?"

"I can't tell you, my sweet," the man replied. "It would spoil the surprise."

The woman jumped at his words. "I almost forgot!"

She passed him the sparklers and returned to the stand. From the side pocket, the grinning fiend removed a small device. The second she activated the button on top, there was a loud click. She quickly passed the device to Glen, careful to make sure his finger remained locked on the button.

"Here you go."

"W—W…What?" Glen stammered. Blood filled his throat. It ran in a thick stream down his side. A puddle formed next to him. He glanced over at the cake on the stand. Beneath the top rack rested a stack of explosives piled up like cordwood.

Glen stared at his hand as a terrifying realization kicked in. He was holding a dead man's switch.

"Ready?" the frowning figure asked his companion. She snatched the sparklers from him, then danced toward the stairs.

"But…" Glen called after them. His voice weakened with each word. "You didn't even steal anything."

"Didn't we?" the man answered. The smiling woman giggled at the reply, though the man did what he could to rein in her enthusiasm. "My sweet?"

"Coming, dear." She curled up next to him. Together, they started up the stairs for the lobby. "Now, tell me. The wish. It was about us, wasn't it?"

"You know me too well."

With that, they were gone, and Glen was alone. Sweat pooled along his brow. He felt cold and clammy. Shock set in from the gaping wounds to his gut and back. He fought to maintain his grip on the trigger, but with each frantic breath, more and more of his vision faded.

"I… I can't…"

The switch slipped from his hands. Glen's eyes widened in pure terror. "Oh, my."

The entire world went white. Retirement was no longer an option for Glen Tripp.

CHAPTER FOURTEEN

Another patrol car drove down the block. It was the third in the last half hour. Soriya ducked deeper into the shadows to avoid being seen. She stood out from the crowd and questions were the last thing she needed from those unwilling to understand the truth about Portents.

Sticking to alleyways and back roads, Soriya surveyed the Knoll to the best of her ability. She started in the former Haymarket District just south of Allure. Her weaving took her east, brushing along Riverside and then back west to Grant Square, where the RDJ cut through to divide Lowtown from the rest of the city. The outskirts of the downtown area stood as the border for the Knoll and the bottom of the hill at King's Lane. She stopped there for a respite.

Her body begged for rest. Her wounds continued to ache, her bruises adding new layers with every passing hour. They were nothing compared to the mental beating Soriya gave herself during her travels. The Kindly Killer had claimed another victim while she'd slept. That made eight in the last seven months.

That had been eight too many in her eyes.

Her searching had brought no end to the misery. She sought some sign of the killer, some clue where he might strike next or against whom, and still she came up empty. Soriya wondered if Loren felt the same way. Her endless searching was for him. Her obsession with the case of a human murderer over the dozen other threats she should have been focused on was for Loren's benefit above all.

Loren needed closure, especially if the killer had been involved in Beth's death. Soriya did as well, though she failed to believe anything would wipe the guilt from her soul over failing to be there for her friend in the end.

Frustrated at the lack of progress, Soriya turned back up the Knoll for another round. The second she crossed King's Lane for Hammond, an explosion ripped through the air. Fire shot into the sky in a plume of color against the darkness. The shockwave, originating at least four blocks to the west, slammed through the winding buildings of the area. Windows shattered. Brick and mortar crumbled. Siding and gutters sheared from the surrounding buildings.

Soriya shot back as the wave hit her in the chest. Her shoulder caught the corner of a nearby property. Upon impact, her body flipped toward the adjacent alcove and into a deep well of rainwater.

Soaked, her body dripping as she stood, Soriya slowly regained her footing. The wave dissipated, the shock of the explosion all but a memory except for the still rising flames in the distance.

Without a second thought to the pain coursing through her body, Soriya raced across the Knoll for the source of the flames. Blocks rushed by in her haste. Cries of confusion sparked from dozens of people in the neighboring area. Sirens picked up in the distance.

Soriya didn't stop until she circled the corner outside the Portents Commerce Bank. The entry doors hung limply from their hinges. The fire within shot out in spurts. Debris covered the sidewalk and the street.

Standing among the massive blocks of stonework and broken glass were two figures. One danced among the destruction. The other merely stood proud at the feat.

Soriya's fists clenched at the very sight of them. "Why am I not surprised?"

At the sound of her voice, they spun in her direction. Comedy immediately threw her hands in the air. "See? She wasn't surprised. And after all my hard work."

Tragedy shook his head, hand to his chin. "What shall we do about it, my sweet?"

Even through the mask, Soriya noted the deep tenor of Comedy's voice change. The petulant joy faded behind malice of the worst intent. "If comedy doesn't suit her..."

Tragedy smacked his forehead playfully. "Ah. Of course. Where is my head tonight?"

He reached into his right pant leg. Fingers dug deep, awkwardly fumbling within the denim of his jeans in his searching. When they returned, he carried a pistol with a barrel the length of his leg. Tragedy held the weapon out, a second hand required on the extra-long barrel, and took aim at Soriya.

"Oh no, you don't," Soriya shouted. She leaped at him before his finger hit the trigger. "Not this time."

She kicked the gun away. It skittered down the street, coming to rest beneath the debris from the bank's edifice.

"Your favorite toy!" Comedy yelled in dismay.

"A real tragedy, my sweet," her companion replied.

Comedy nodded. "So true. So true."

Tragedy drew a knife from his belt. Blood dotted the blade and dripped from the tip. "Let's share the sentiment."

"Let's not," Soriya answered. She raised her fists. The Ribbons of Kali danced to her left, ready to strike.

The pink strands shot out at Comedy, who danced around them with ease. Soriya, though, launched at Tragedy with a driving punch aimed for his left cheek. Her momentum carried her through the punch, which missed by a wide margin. She landed firmly on her feet once more and glanced down.

Blood ran in a thin stream along a cut on her arm. Tragedy cocked his head to the side, the knife covered in fresh crimson. With his free hand, he beckoned her for more.

Soriya was happy to comply. She kicked out for his midsection. The blow connected with nothing but air, yet pain shot across her right shin. Another cut tore through her jeans and into her flesh.

"How did you—"

Comedy laughed. "She seems overwhelmed, dear."

"Confused and lost," Tragedy confirmed. "Tell her a joke, my sweet. That will bring a smile to her face."

Soriya seethed. They were playing with her. "I'll bring something to your damn face. Stand still."

Blow for blow, she drove Tragedy back on his feet. Yet with each one, Soriya failed to connect. He was a ghost, shifting from her grasp at the last second as if he read every single movement before it happened.

"Keep up," Tragedy chided.

With another empty strike, Soriya staggered forward. A kick to her backside by the still-waiting Comedy drove Soriya to the side-walk down the block from the burning bank. Skin sheared from her palms as she caught herself.

"That's it," she said. Their strength and speed were too much for her. She needed an edge. Her hand shot to her hip. "I—"

Her pouch was no longer attached to her belt. Soriya spun to face her attackers, with sudden fear in her eyes.

Comedy waved the pouch before her. "Tut-tut. No toys allowed, remember?"

The grinning ghoul carried Soriya's Greystone without even realizing the power in her grasp. She passed the potent weapon between her hands, gloating with glee.

Soriya screamed with rage. She leaped for the stone. Comedy snatched the pouch in mid-air, then did the same to Soriya, grabbing her by the neck. Her laughter filled Soriya's ears.

Comedy lifted her up, then launched Soriya through the air. Powerless to resist, Soriya soared away from the masked pair. The world faded to a blur, and she struggled to find some sense of her position and that of the ground itself.

Soriya crashed atop a red pickup truck. Her body bounced off the bright chassis and she skidded across the hood to the ground behind the vehicle. She lay there for a long moment, unable to catch her breath.

She was on the outskirts of the CostSmart parking lot. Her attackers had shifted the fight to the still open business in the heart of the commercial district of the Knoll. Soriya staggered to her knees. A group of onlookers pointed in terror at the approach of Comedy and Tragedy in the distance, then fled for their cars.

Grabbing the hood of the truck for support, Soriya stood. Comedy continued to bounce the Greystone between her palms without care. With the stone in their possession, they held the upper hand and no amount of training could swing the fight in Soriya's direction.

She needed an edge, and there was only one place to go. In desperation, Soriya stumbled along the parking lot for the front doors to the CostSmart.

CHAPTER FIFTEEN

The automatic doors slid open and Soriya stepped inside the department store. Shoppers milled around the exit. Kids made plans for their next get together, and couples fretted through the self-checkout terminal to see which coupon failed to register this time.

Soriya shuffled forward, the cut along her leg pulsing with pain. She reached out to swipe her hand against the inner door frame to the shop and ended up smearing a stream of crimson from the slash on her arm. Looks drawn her way shifted from cautious to outright disgusted, but she continued on with no regard to them.

A gangly gentleman, wearing a black t-shirt and a nametag which read Walter, approached Soriya. He raised his hands defensively.

"Hello there," he said in a high-pitched voice. "We're about to close for the night."

Soriya ignored him, scanning the banners along the ceiling, which denoted each section of the massive store.

Walter, however, finally noticed the small drip of blood that followed her every step, and his eyes widened with concern. "Is everything all right? Do you need—"

"Move."

Her hand jutted out and caught the gawky employee in the chest. Walter staggered back from the sudden blow, then tripped over his own feet in a failed attempt to regain his balance. He crashed into a nearby display of pool noodles.

Laughs arose from those loitering around the registers. Walter fumed from his heap on the floor. Soriya, however, turned back to the entryway, which chimed with new arrivals.

Comedy and Tragedy had joined the party.

"Everyone, move!" Soriya yelled. She rushed through the store, her head start all but wasted.

Cries from the entrance trailed her movements, including the words of the fallen CostSmart greeter, "What the hell is that?"

The masked pair swung their hands in the air. Tragedy continued to clutch tight to his knife. The blood-stained blade drew all the attention, though Comedy did her best to garner her own fans by greeting each fleeing customer with a handshake and a wave.

"Pardon us, folks." Tragedy pushed aside the terrified clientele.

"Nothing to see here," Comedy chimed in. "Just a friendly neighborhood murder."

"Don't worry," Tragedy assured them in a calm, collected tone. "We'll get to you soon enough. All of you."

Shoppers screamed in terror. They ran in every direction to escape. Their frantic movements and the sheer number of souls within the bottleneck of the exit created a barrier. Soriya used the time to rush down the aisles of the sporting goods section.

Baseball equipment hung in rows from the walls of the aisle. Soriya scanned through the different balls and bats, looking for the perfect tool.

"Come on, come on," she muttered in a frenzy. When her eyes landed on a pair of metal bats on the upper rung, Soriya snatched them in hand and gripped them tight. "This will have to do."

She ran out of the aisle, swinging the bats against her palm to get a better feel for them. Shoppers continued to race away in swaths. Angered by their delay, Tragedy moved to swipe at them with his shining blade.

"Hey!" Soriya shouted. "Are we doing this or not?"

Comedy and Tragedy left the frantically fleeing crowd and stalked to her position. The grinning woman held up the still closed pouch. "You dropped this outside. I thought about keeping it." She positioned it against her hip and posed for her partner. "What do you think, my dear?"

"Fetching."

Soriya raised a bat at Comedy. "Hand it over, and I'll make this quick."

"And spoil my fun?" Comedy tucked the pouch close, then launched at Soriya. She ducked under the swinging bats, slamming into the stone bearer's midsection. The blow lifted Soriya from the ground and tossed her against the end-cap display of the sporting goods section. She crashed against helmets and gloves until the entire section collapsed beneath her.

Soriya grimaced as she jumped to her feet. Comedy's laughter filled the air, echoing through her head like an endless drumbeat. She drove her twin metal bats hard at the grinning fiend to quiet the sound.

Tragedy blocked the blow with his arm. "Tut-tut," he said. "We're not through yet."

"You two are on my last nerve," Soriya said.

"Don't worry," Tragedy knocked aside the bats and raised his knife. "You'll lose all feeling soon enough."

The blade swung down hard. It was all Soriya could do to raise the bats to block the blow, but even then she was driven back three steps by the force. Strike for strike, Soriya ducked and dodged. Tragedy stuck too close for the bats to be much use and when his knife was out of play, his fist more than made up for it. She took a punch to the gut with little more than a grimace, but the backhand that connected with her slashed arm sent her crashing through the aisle.

The wall fell away beneath her. Soriya hit the floor at the base of the basketball cage. Orange and black balls spooled loose from their holding pen to scatter across the floor.

Comedy lifted one up and tossed it at Soriya, missing her head by a hair. She closed in quickly, hands gripped like claws in front of her, with Soriya's stolen pouch tucked haphazardly in her pocket.

"My turn, my turn!"

Soriya could barely stand. Her head felt lost in a cloud and her vision blurred. The cry of her attacker was her only saving grace. Soriya, with the last of her strength, tightened her grip on the bat in her left hand and swung at the charging woman. The arc of the bat added to its momentum, and it crashed against Comedy's mask.

A small piece, less than an inch in diameter, chipped off and clattered to the dirty tile. Comedy howled in pain. Hands clutched the gaping hole in her mask.

"My dear?" Tragedy called from the end of the aisle.

"You bitch!" Comedy railed.

Soriya smirked, holding the bat toward her foe. "Want some more?"

Comedy flinched at the sight of the bat. Holding tight to her wound with one hand, the other snatched the threaded pouch from her pocket. "You want your stupid bauble? Take it!"

The pouch soared overhead and Soriya immediately moved to track its fall in the next aisle. Aware of its position, she took a second to glance back at her attackers.

Tragedy lifted the chip from the floor. "I have the piece. Let's go."

Comedy continued toward Soriya. There was no more joy in her movements, only the rage of a beast. Tragedy, however, grabbed her by the arm and pulled her away. "We're leaving. Now."

The pair fled for the exit without another word. Soriya, her chest on fire, crawled toward the pouch tucked beneath the shattered display in the next aisle. Lifting it free, Soriya removed the stone from inside and held it close. A wave of comfort flowed through her as she took what felt like her first breath of fresh air in hours.

Sitting up, Soriya caught one more glimpse of the masked pair before they disappeared into the night.

"Yeah, you better run."

The metal bat served as a cane to prop her into a standing position. The stone was already doing its best to help her various wounds. Slow steps gave her the time to regain some control over her fatigued frame and Soriya made her way toward the exit.

Walter stood in her way, hands wide to block the doors. "Hey. You can't just leave. After what you did? And where are you going with that bat?"

"Huh?" Soriya looked down. The bat still in her grip had somehow escaped her notice. "Here."

She jabbed the bat at the man, who was caught unaware by the force involved in the exchange. Walter fell to the floor once more. His head slammed against the tile.

No one moved to help him. The only reaction from the few still present in the store was more laughter.

Soriya felt bad. She certainly never meant for him to fall— twice—because of her. But her focus remained on the masked pair, and what their presence truly meant for the city.

"What do we tell the police?" one of the other employees called after her as she reached the exit.

"Tell them there's a cleanup needed in sporting goods." Soriya slipped back into the darkness of the city without another word.

CHAPTER SIXTEEN

He couldn't let the humiliation stand. It had been another day full of hateful people offering nothing but their worst to their fellow man. From the pushing and shoving, to the outright rudeness in their speech, they added nothing to society. It didn't matter the color of their skin, their financial status, even what car they drove. They came from every walk of life to spread misery wherever they went.

It was enough to drive the shadowy figure mad. Worse, it was enough to bring back the compulsion—more powerful and fierce than ever.

All thanks to the woman with the pink ribbon and the torn jeans.

The shadow managed to suppress his anger, to drum away thoughts of physical violence to the morons perpetuating stereotypes around him. He gave the ignorant and the blind no afterthought. Their time was coming, but not this day.

But her? The woman who had done everything in her power to beat him down, to make him appear foolish for all to laugh at? She had crossed his ethical line from the start and deserved every ounce of pain he planned to bring to her for her misdeeds.

Luckily, she had provided the means of her disposal. His previous victims had been spur-of-the-moment decisions when it came to the murder weapon, but not her. She had handed him his weapon, daring him to strike her down.

Without bothering to clock out from work, the shadow departed after the stony-eyed woman and trailed her from the parking lot down to King's Lane. He kept his distance, his eyes locked on her proud stride. She may have been injured from the fight, but she continued to show her arrogance even in the simple act of walking.

It was a confidence the shadow had never known. He had always been a nobody, struggling in the world day after day without success. His home had been inherited from the dead. His job had been the only one where no one had bothered to look too closely into his background. Formal training and education eluded him—another gift from the dead. Their negligence had left him with nothing but a shadow of a life, one he glided through unable to make an impact.

Until the itch.

The shadow couldn't recall when it had started. One day he had been nothing, and the next the world had opened up for him. For so long, the shadow had merely passed through life unseen. His very existence had been hollow and his presence instantly forgotten by those around him.

In the blink of an eye, however, he experienced sensations undreamed of. Feelings burst forth—joy and sadness. Most of all was rage, one at those who did nothing to benefit those around them. They simply hated and brought the worst of themselves out to build up lives that held no true meaning.

The itch had given him the resources and the confidence to act finally. From out of nowhere, the shadow took what he wanted from the world—to show them they could no longer walk all over him. There was a penalty for treating people poorly, and he carried it out as often as he could.

He had lost count of the dead by his hands. The papers labeled it at eight, but the shadow knew the truth. There were the neighbors who beat him and the relatives who abused him. The cats who hissed at him and the dogs who bit him. All the pain in his life was repaid in kind, and the bodies buried deep behind his inherited home filled a cemetery all their own.

The woman with the pink ribbon would satisfy his urges for another night. She didn't stand out in any way, and he noticed nothing about her that distinguished her from the other rude people he encountered. She had debased him for nothing more than a laugh, and he would see to it such behavior never bothered another poor soul again. He was making the world a better place.

At the corner of King's Lane, the woman turned. Her stride lengthened, and she crossed the way. Evans was only two blocks away. The patrols were heavier there, with the Central Precinct so close. The shadow saw his opportunity slipping away, and he bounded closer to catch up to his prey.

When she reached Elam, a block staggered with alleyways, the shadow closed the gap. His eyes grew hungry. Licking his lips in anticipation, he raised the weapon over his head.

The bat swung down hard.

Spinning around, the woman caught the metal in her hands. Fire sat in her eyes and a wide smirk on her face.

"Well, hello there."

CHAPTER SEVENTEEN

It was him. After all Soriya's searching, all the frustration and the endless waiting for some sign of the killer, here he stood in front of her. Veins ran deep red through his eyes, crazed and manic, yet his grip remained controlled along the bat.

The bat she had handed to the Kindly Killer of all people.

He hadn't appeared to be anything more than a common greeter. His gangly frame held no power and his demeanor portrayed nothing but weakness in their earlier exchange.

All had covered up the truth, however. None of the weakness noted at CostSmart was present any longer. Rage filled this monster, a deep-rooted fury that gave the man named Walter a strength that caused Soriya to second guess the smirk on her lips.

"You made a fool of me," he said with a changed voice. A booming undertone replaced the high-pitch nasal tone from earlier. He reminded her of her other playmates—Comedy and Tragedy— with a mask of his own, though his was a face of innocence quickly dropped when scouting out his prey. "I tried to help, and you threw me aside. Rudeness like that has no place in the world."

He pulled the bat from her grasp and drove it back down with a frantic swing. Soriya sidestepped the arc, then punched out with her right fist. The blow was weak, her own body still aching from her struggle with Comedy and Tragedy. Walter dodged with ease. Confidence overtook him, and he backhanded her across the cheek.

Soriya staggered into the alley behind her. A hand rose to her lips to wipe a dot of blood. "Tell me how you really feel."

"This isn't some joke," Walter scolded. The bat slammed into the wall next to him. Another swing cut the air in front of Soriya and she backpedaled deeper into the alleyway's shadows. "I am not some joke!"

She had handed him the weapon of her own destruction. The rage, however, came from somewhere much deeper than her sleight against him.

Walter chopped the air between them until, at last, she came to rest at the back of the alley with nowhere left to run. She pictured the same scenario played out a dozen times before with the killer. Had he stalked each victim similarly? Had they been dumb enough to trust him with the weapon that ended their own lives?

Calm washed over him. The anger remained, but Walter clearly found his center the moment Soriya was trapped and cut off from any potential rescuer. He raised the bat high once more, his eyes commanding her to prepare for the end.

"Do you know who I am?" he bellowed into the night. Walter brought the bat down. Soriya caught it once more, though the blow forced her knee to the ground. His eyes widened, willing her lower. "Do you have any idea who I am?"

Soriya squeezed the barrel of the bat. Her hands blistered beneath the blow, but held firm. "I know exactly who you are," she replied.

Pushing for her feet, Soriya tightened her grip on the bat. She struggled to remove it from his grasp. With each pull, he followed, and the dance took them around the alley in a wide arc, circling each other repeatedly.

For every kick she attempted toward his legs, Walter countered, pulling the bat with him. They ducked and dodged, bounding around the tight quarters for control of the weapon between them.

Every passing second added to the man's fury. His teeth were clenched and saliva ran from the corner of his lips. He wanted her death more than he wanted anything in the world at that moment. Soriya saw her demise playing behind his eyes and she fed into it by holding tight to the bat.

Clutching it between them, Soriya dug her feet into the pavement. She pulled him in closer, vying for the bat. He refused to relinquish control and yanked her right back. With all his weight on his back leg to support his pull, Soriya did the only thing left to her.

She let the bat go.

Walter flew backward. Two staggered steps and then he crashed to the pavement with a loud thump. The bat remained in his hands, but did little to save him the embarrassment of the fall.

When he looked up again, Soriya loomed over him. "The papers call you intelligent. They consider you conniving, a hunter—always stalking your prey. That's not you at all, is it?"

Walter struggled to stand. The impish greeter returned for a brief second before being subsumed by the killer. "You know nothing. Not about me. Not about the world. People like you tear down the good in the rest of us. Your rudeness infects this world. I've had it."

Soriya nodded. "So have I."

From her hip, she opened the threaded pouch. The Greystone slipped against her palm and cooled her worn hand. She held it before her.

Walter failed to take her meaning in the slightest. To him, she had let her guard down completely. He took the moment to jump to his feet and charge with the bat in hand.

"I'll kill you!"

The Greystone ignited. All her willpower channeled through the stone and light washed over the alleyway. It bathed Walter in deep white, yet he continued his charge toward her.

Three steps away, the bat high in the air and ready to strike, a stiff wind slammed into Walter. His feet skidded back slightly, but he pressed forward. In the next step, another wave slammed into him, this one stronger than the last.

There was no reprieve this time. Funnel after funnel of charged wind stemmed from the Greystone's power over the elements and the stone directed all at the man known as the Kindly Killer.

He lost his footing. His body ripped from the ground and soared across the alley. The bat fell from his grasp, rolling out from under the torrent. Walter, however, found no such reprieve and collided head first against the corner of the brick edifice at his back.

Soriya waited until his body crumpled in a heap along the ground. The light dimmed, and the wind died down to a single wisp of a breeze. The bat rolled across the pavement, coming to rest at her feet. She loomed over Walter once more. Her eyes washed over him. As much as he might have surprised her, she knew him very well.

"You're a scared little man who deserves to suffer for what you've done," she said.

She raised the Greystone toward him again. Light flickered along the surface as thoughts spun wildly through her mind. She wanted nothing more than to summon the lightning down from the heavens and wipe the Kindly Killer from the earth. For all the pain he had caused, Walter deserved nothing less.

Images of Loren suddenly filled her thoughts. He brought Soriya back to reality, and she realized the bitter truth. The stone fell away. The light faded to a cold black.

"But that's not my place," Soriya said. "Not tonight."

Walter grimaced. He revived from the blow, a hand rubbing at the cut along the back of his head. Soriya didn't hesitate. Her foot jutted out and caught him on the chin.

The Kindly Killer collapsed before her.

"Lucky you."

CHAPTER EIGHTEEN

Words blurred on the page. The same report he'd read through ten minutes earlier ended up in his hands again, yet he'd failed to recognize it until after his second read-through. Or was it his third?

Loren dumped the file off the side of the desk into the open box on the floor. It joined four others, the total of his so-called work for the last two hours. Nothing registered. Every word floated through his wandering mind, and he wondered if he would ever escape the nightmare that had become his life.

Ruiz expected him to care about the work, about the proper procedure required to close every file in the makeshift storage closet. Caring, though, was a stretch for Loren. All he wanted to do was hit the streets again. There were new leads to follow, new victims to obsess over, in his never-ending efforts to find the Kindly Killer.

Beth's murderer.

Why did no one see the value in his perspective on such a case? He had been the lead from the start and had spent hours upon hours working through the bevy of evidence left in the wake of each victim. He understood the scene of the crime better than anyone—or so he rationalized in his own mind. Loren, however, remained clueless about much of the case. From common motive to the random choosing of victims, there were far more questions left unanswered.

Ruiz had been right to bench him, even more right to give him the worst punishment available. It was completely warranted after what he had put the captain through.

Loren groaned audibly. He ran his hands through his hair and across the stubble decorating his cheeks. He needed a cigarette desperately. Patting his jacket pocket, Loren found a lump nestled within. He reached inside, practically salivating at the smoke wait-ing for him to enjoy. Instead of a cigarette, though, Loren found a pack of gum. Mango peach.

Another groan escaped his lips. Ripping open the pack, a stick of the detestable gum fell into his palm and he jammed it in his mouth. It cracked beneath his teeth, the flavor offering none of the relief of his former addiction.

Filthy habit.

Another file slipped from the stack and he opened it angrily. Details ran together. Witness testimony on a busted burglary at-tempt identified a woman as responsible for catching the culprit. Dark skin. Young. Torn jeans and a purple blouse, with some kind of ribbon hanging from her arm.

"Wait a second," Loren mumbled. He bent over the side of the desk to retrieve the files summarily ignored earlier. "Wasn't there another statement about some strange woman being involved?"

He thumbed through each. At the third, he almost gave up the hunt as nothing more than a daydream. "Which one was…"

The file fell open on the statement in question. Loren read through it quickly. The desk sergeant had written the report and referred to a witness' description of a fight at a construction site on the corner of Tamerlin and Andrews. The dark-skinned woman was involved against, and—Loren read this part several times—a beast of mammoth proportions. When asked to explain, he went further to call it a minotaur.

Loren rolled his eyes. He slammed the file shut and dropped it soundly on the floor. "Right. Another reliable witness. Just like the rest."

Pushing away from his desk, Loren stood to stretch. Two hours in, and it felt like ten to his bone-weary body. His ankle still pulsed with pain, but the heavy dose of aspirin helped keep him on his feet. Home sounded nicer than ever, despite the emptiness waiting for him inside, and Loren grabbed his coat from the corner of the room.

Ruiz wouldn't mind the delay in the work. For all his bluster, he cared too much about Loren's state of mind, a concern the detec-tive had relentlessly abused since losing his wife.

Footsteps outside drew him to the door. He opened to see sev-eral detectives rushing for the stairs. Loren eyed them curiously. A few shot him a look, but none bothered to explain the mass exodus for the front of the Rath.

"What's going on?" he asked a departing group. They didn't bother to halt their conversation to answer his question. Loren wanted to press, but faltering at their names caused him to keep quiet until they were already at the steps. They had all been considered friends at one time, pushed away and berated by a grief-stricken Loren. Their dismissal of him was not unexpected.

Finally, a friendly face arrived. Loren snapped his fingers, the man's name already in place for a change. "Dickie?"

Delmar's eyes lit up at the sight of Loren. He waved the detective over toward the stairs. "You're not going to believe this."

Loren glanced back at the ridiculous testimony in the files littering his temporary office. "Seems to be a lot of that going around."

Delmar waved him on. Loren hesitated, then followed. His steps were slow, especially when he hit the stairs. He wondered how long his ankle would hurt like hell, then pushed the injury aside when he saw the crowd milling about the lobby and out on the front stoop of the Rath.

Gates held the door for him as he made his way through. She wore a wide grin with hair matted down from the rain.

"Gates?"

"I didn't know Santa Claus made visits in July," she said.

"What are you—"

Loren stared up at the lone streetlight adorning the sidewalk in front of the Rath Building. Hanging from the light was a half-naked man. Someone had hogtied him with a thick rope that bound his hands and his feet behind his back.

Stepping closer for a better look, Loren noticed a sign pinned to the man's bare chest. A note in thick black marker read: *I smile at killing nice people. Please lock me away and throw away the key. Sincerely, Mr. Kindly.*

Loren stared in disbelief.

Gates stepped over, a hand to his shoulder. "It's him, isn't it?"

Delmar pumped his fist. "We finally caught him."

Cheers erupted up the stoop and through the lobby. Screams of joy and elation drowned out the pounding rain, but not the thought that caused Loren to laugh under the man dangling like a Christmas ornament.

"Someone certainly did."

CHAPTER NINETEEN

The entire building came to life in the wake of the Kindly Killer's arrival at the station. Officers worked to process the man quickly. Calls were made to every stationhouse in the city to spread the news, despite the lack of confirmation. Patrols needed to be reassigned, priorities switched to the chaotic masked predators that continued to plague the city.

Loren walked through the chaos of the lobby in a cloud. Their elation was nothing compared to his own. Whoever had brought Kindly to them deserved a parade in Loren's eyes. The arrest brought everyone together. No matter the division, or the politics of the work, they all stood in solidarity at catching the worst killer Portents had seen in quite some time.

Conversations floated through the personnel. Loren picked up the details during his travels from the rain-soaked front steps of the Rath Building through the lobby.

"ID says Walter Shriff."

"Worked at CostSmart," a detective said with the shake of his head. "He was a damn greeter, of all things."

"Doesn't look like much," an officer shared with her partner.

"We sure this is the guy?" the desk sergeant asked anyone willing to engage. It was the question Loren most needed answered, but others fell into place as they did for the rest of the precinct.

"Where did he come from?" someone called out from the water cooler.

"Who gave him to us and why?" another asked at the far end of the hall.

"Loren!" The name stirred the wandering detective from his travels through the station. The desk sergeant held up a phone and waved Loren down. "Call for you!"

"What?" Loren shook his head. "Take a message."

"Says it's important!"

"Who says it is?"

The sergeant shrugged, then laid the phone down on the desk. Loren sighed and cut through the lingering crowd, their excitement almost tangible. He lifted the phone and put it to his ear.

"Hello?"

The words were muted due to the throng of people passing through the station. Loren barely made out the voice, though it sounded like a woman.

"Come again?"

"Parking garage."

"The parking garage? What about—"

The line went dead. Loren held the receiver for a long moment before passing it back to the sergeant.

"Who was it?"

"Damned if I know," Loren said, and put the call out of his mind. Forgetting his pained ankle, quick steps took Loren away from the jubilant lobby and down the hall toward Interrogation.

Kindly—Walter Shriff—already sat inside the room. Quinn and Messick, however, waited outside. They discussed tactics for their questioning; the debate appeared heated until they stopped at Loren's approach.

"Hey, Greg," Quinn said.

Messick spun on his heels, hands to his hips. "You really think this is the guy, Loren?"

The passing detective paused at the monitors. They had given Walter a shirt, though it laid two sizes too large over his wiry frame. A towel was draped over his shoulders to warm him from the rain. The precinct was certainly amenable, considering the gift they had been given. Now all they had to do was seal the deal, hopefully with a full confession to put the murderer away for a lifetime.

To Loren, though, he didn't look like the killer. Shriff appeared to be nothing special at all from the onset. Yet, there was something in his eyes when they passed the camera in the room's corner. A malevolence filled deep blue irises, sharp with fury.

"I..." Loren fought to find an answer for the waiting detectives. He shook his head. "I have to find Ruiz."

Loren dashed up the back stairs to the second floor. He cut across the break room, ignoring the commotion within as everyone tried to describe the hanging man outside to those who had missed the unveiling. Even the closed door to the captain's office didn't deter Loren, who opened it upon arrival without so much as a knock.

"Ruiz?"

The captain stood behind his desk, phone to his ear and impatience in his eyes. "Yes, I'm aware the media will want a statement. As soon as we have one, we'll give it."

He glanced up. Catching Loren's presence at the door, Ruiz waved him in. Loren took a single step, then closed the office from view.

"Public relations is your department," Ruiz shot back through the line. His disgust was clear. "That's not my problem. Deal with it."

Ruiz slammed the phone down.

Loren sighed, hands in his pockets. "Sounds like word is out."

"How could it not be?" Ruiz shouted. "The guy was dangling in front of our building like a damn fish on a hook. This is the last thing we need."

"Why? If he's—"

"If!" Ruiz said, a finger in the air. "That's the issue. We don't know anything!"

Loren shifted closer to the desk. He kept his voice calm. "We'll do this right, Ruiz. We've collected plenty of prints. Forensics can put this guy at the scene."

"Maybe." Ruiz moved for a bottle of water at the corner of his desk, then paused. "Hold it, Greg. *We?*"

"Yes, we." Loren pointed toward the door. "He's in the building, Ruiz. You have to let me—"

"I don't have to let you do anything, Greg," Ruiz answered. Loren's mistake remained fresh in his mind. "You're a liability."

"I have to know the truth, Ruiz," Loren said. He caught the man's eyes and held them in his own.

Ruiz turned toward the window. "You'll get your chance. After we nail this son of a bitch."

"I appreciate that," Loren said. "Really, Ruiz, I…"

The phone rang. Ruiz squeezed the air in front of him with frustration, then reached for the call. "Appreciate me somewhere else."

Loren nodded, backing away for the door. Ruiz's hand hesitated over the receiver, but his words followed Loren out into the hall.

"What a goddamn mess."

Loren let out a long breath after the door shut. It felt like his first true breath in months. A mess was the last thing he saw with the arrival of the killer he had been after for so long. Miracle fit the bill better, and that sentiment carried him out into the parking garage off the back of the building.

Loren slipped away from the jubilant officers of the Central Precinct for the peace of the night air and the soft dripping of the rain. He looked out from the thick ledge that overlooked Heaven's Gate Park, a smile on his face.

"We got him, Beth. We..." A shadow shifted along Loren's periphery. He spun toward it. A woman stood in the darkness. Ripped jeans and a thin jacket were all he could make out. "Hey. You can't..."

Her fierce eyes met his.

"Wait," he said. "Was that you?"

She nodded.

Here she was: the person who had gifted them the Kindly Killer. Not only had she brought them the elusive murderer, she also matched the description from the files Ruiz had forced him to review. So much of his life snapped into focus, and with it came more questions.

"Why would you help us? Who—"

Loren took a step closer to learn more about the woman. As he did, the door to the station opened and a pair of officers stepped into the garage. Loren glanced away for only a second, but when he turned back to the shadows, the woman was gone.

Loren searched the length of the garage frantically. There was no sign of the woman, like she had never been there. Loren, though, knew better.

He settled along the ledge once more. "Who are you?" he whispered into the stormy night. "And how can I ever thank you for this?"

CHAPTER TWENTY

Loren rubbed at bleary eyes. He tore through file after file with a devotion he had not shown the previous night. New connections fell into place with every glance. He scoured through endless reports, witness testimony, and forensic evidence to peel apart each circumstance.

Almost all mentioned her: the shadowy woman from the parking garage. In some cases, she saved a potential victim. In others, she prevented some dipshit thief from his or her prize. The victims spoke in awe of her presence. The thieves, less-so.

Sipping at his coffee, and cursing each cold sip, Loren noted another instance of the woman's intervention.

"Who are you?"

He pulled a fresh pile from the stack at his side. A loud thump boomed through the cramped office at its arrival. Loren moved for the topmost report, careful to keep his ankle from turning. The damn thing still stung. When he settled down with fresh work, a shadow crept over the desk.

"You're blocking the light, Pratchett," Loren commented out of habit. He was used to the officer's ability to steal every light source with his enormous height. What he wasn't used to was the sound of a woman's voice coming out of that shadow.

"Were you here all day?"

Loren dropped the open file. He blinked hard, waking to the room. It was not Pratchett at all, but another tall figure—that of Melanie Gates.

"Oh," he muttered. He chugged the remaining coffee down in one last gulp. He was happy to see an end to the frigid beverage—happier still to have company in his personal Phantom Zone of paperwork hell. "Didn't realize it was you, Gates. Sorry, I…"

"It's all right," she said with a slight wave. "I take it as a com-pliment."

Loren offered a small nod. He pushed away from the desk. "That's right. Pratchett is an old friend or something."

Gates leaned against a precarious stack along the wall. "Some-thing. We grew up together just north of the Knoll. They called it Haymarket District for a time. Sounds like you've been asking questions about me."

"It seemed like the right thing to do after I…" Loren let out a long breath. "Well, let's just say I'm sorry for being—"

"Yourself?"

Loren ran his hand roughly over his cheek. "Unfortunately."

Gates laughed. "Accepted. Now what's kept you from a good day's sleep? And, can I say, a necessary shower?"

His hand immediately went to his two-day-old shirt and lifted it for a clear whiff. The coffee had muted the odor, but it was defi-nitely pungent. Loren grumbled under his breath, wondering how the day had slipped away from him, before he realized the reason surrounded him on all sides.

"Too much," he replied.

Gates shifted to the far side of the desk. Her hands gripped the edge, and she leaned over the open file. "Shriff?"

"No. Not Shriff." The Kindly Killer would have made perfect sense. He remained in the building, downstairs in the interrogation wing. There had been a chance for him to clean up, with meals of-fered as needed and rest given in a solitary cell away from the rest of the rabble.

Loren had fought the urge to visit him on several occasions in the wee hours of the morning. There were questions that needed answering. Loren needed to know the truth about what happened to Beth. However, he knew better than to insert himself into the interrogation. Rather than upset Ruiz further, Loren kept his inter-est on someone else entirely.

"Her."

He shoved the report toward Gates, who took it in hand. She scanned the documents in the file, and Loren could see her mind at work. Gates was a quick study, absorbing relevant details and dis-missing extraneous information in seconds. She picked at another folder without being prompted, and then a third, until she was ready for answers.

"What is all this?"

"Closed cases for review," Loren said. "Only, I think someone else did all the heavy lifting on them."

"Purse snatchers, rapists, and kidnappings." Gates filtered through the files. "These aren't ours?"

"Oh, we certainly took credit for them."

Gates' eyes widened at another case in the stack. "Jimmy Machlin? I remember reading about him."

Loren nodded. "Second-story man out of Riverside. Ended up hanging by his toes from a flagpole outside the Newton Building."

Gates realized the connection at once. "Like our friend last night."

"He claimed a black woman with a serious attitude did it to him. His words were slightly different."

"Thanks for keeping it PG." Gates continued to paw through the work laid out throughout the room. "All of this is from the last couple of years, from the looks of these dates."

"They are all connected to our friend, it seems." The woman from the previous night. Who was she? Why was she doing all this in Portents? And why would she help him the way she had? She had called him to come to the parking garage. If he had listened in the first place, his open queries would have been handled already. Now he stewed in his ignorance.

"Maybe Mom was right," Gates whispered under her breath as she read the files more.

"Mom?"

Gates tossed him another wave. Loren forgot how young she truly was until she grinned.

"I always thought of this place as home," Gates said. "It wasn't full of shadows and darkness. It was the place where I played as a kid. Where I kissed a few boys without my parents finding out. Where I stayed up all night watching movies and dancing with friends. Maybe it's always been this, though."

"Every city has its story," Loren said. "Some people prefer the lighter side to the whole truth."

"That your experience with Portents, Detective?"

"No." He leaned over his knees with his hands clasped tight before him. "I think this place has always been a nightmare, waiting to swallow me up. My wife tried to show me a better side to Portents."

Beth had always been good with that, pulling him from the darkness and back into the light. It never lasted, but it surely helped for a time, and that had been what he needed most from her.

Gates read the memory playing behind his tired eyes. "She was quite the woman, wasn't she?"

"More than I can ever say."

Gates sidled close. "You really think he did it?"

The question startled Loren. He glanced up in confusion. "What?"

"Shriff," Gates said. "He…"

A knock at the door cut her off. Both turned at the sound. Ruiz stood against the frame.

"You ready?"

Loren gripped the desk tight as he stood. The exhaustion fell away, as did all the open questions about the woman from the parking garage. There was only one thing he needed to learn now.

"Guess it's time to find out, Gates." He headed for the door.

It was finally time for the truth.

CHAPTER TWENTY-ONE

Loren followed close beside Ruiz down the second-floor corridor. His ankle struggled at the pace, but Loren ignored the rising pain. The captain's gaze flitted from side to side like a never-ending scanner searching for signs of life. He hesitated with every approach and every drawn glare, but refused to make eye contact with them. If someone came into view, Ruiz tucked his head down and continued on his way with Loren in tow.

The ostracized detective read the situation clearly. Despite his experience in the department, their faith in him continued to falter. They knew the score with Loren these days, how to avoid him at all costs for the betterment of their own careers. It did little to instill confidence in Loren, however.

Neither did the pep talk from Ruiz. "I'm taking a chance on you. You get that, right?"

The captain's nervousness was palpable. He worried about giving Loren an inch, let alone the room, with Shriff. Loren's hand went to his heart as they rounded the corner for the stairs.

"I do, Ruiz," he said sincerely. "I do."

Ruiz paused to read Loren's face. Then he pressed on down the steps, the echo of footfalls ringing throughout the space. "Shriff has been playing with Quinn and Messick all day. A one-word answer here and there, but little else besides that damn grin on his face."

"His attorney here yet?"

"He doesn't care to call one," Ruiz admitted with surprise. "Doesn't care about much from what I've seen."

"That's the only card he has left," Loren said. "Shriff has to know once we match his DNA to what we have on file from the murder scenes, we've nailed his ass to the wall. Why not play the legal game? Why wait for the inevitable?"

Ruiz nodded, hands on his hips. "It's almost like he wants to be here." They entered the interrogation wing. Few people lingered about. Ruiz kept Loren's focus squarely on the task ahead and the man waiting inside. "I'm not sure about this, Greg. The DA is already looking to have him evaluated. He doesn't want an insanity plea keeping this guy from a long stint at Caldwell Correctional."

"Four padded walls and a lifetime of mind-numbing drugs would sound appealing, compared to a bunkmate with a penchant for grab and tug, and the constant beatings from every side of the law once they hear his record."

Ruiz glared at him, a comment on the tip of his tongue to respond to Loren's more-than-colorful description of a prison stint at Caldwell. Before he could, a young man in a plaid button-down shirt and glasses approached in a run.

"Captain!"

"Nolan," Ruiz said, waving him down. Loren was grateful for the namedrop. He had never remembered it, though they'd crossed paths several times. "You have it?"

Nolan passed along a file. "We do," he said. "Prints match those taken from the key at the last scene. Want me to grab Quinn and Messick?"

"In a few," Ruiz replied. He scanned the intel before him, then snapped it shut. The file passed to Loren's chest with an icy stare from the captain. "You sure you're up for this?"

"He's the one, Ruiz."

"For this." Ruiz tapped the file. "But there were no fibers at the scene of your apartment building. No prints. No way to tie him to Beth except—"

"I need a confession," Loren confirmed. "I know."

He moved for the door. Ruiz's hand fell on his arm. "Tread carefully. Don't play his game."

Loren entered slowly, giving himself time to adjust to the dim light within the enclosed space. Ruiz held the door for a long moment, then let it close without another word. Loren didn't need to hear them, anyway; they would have carried a lesson he'd learned well over the course of his career.

Interrogations were always dangerous. For every detail gleaned that led to a conviction, there was just as much ammunition given to the crook for his pending trial. Loren had seen many cases falter because of detectives who overstepped in the interrogation room. Criminals might have been dumb enough to get caught, but that didn't mean they didn't know how to play the system.

Shriff, though, appeared to have given up the game completely. He sat hunched over the table. He stretched his hands to feel the length of the chain afforded him by the cuffs at his wrists. They snapped to, and he let them settle before him again. When he looked up to greet Loren, his eyes were tiny black holes that sucked every ounce of light from the room.

"Mr. Shriff, I'm Detective Loren." He sat as he spoke, sliding the chair against the tile. "I'd like to ask you a few questions, if you're up for it?"

Shriff swayed his head slightly from side to side, weighing the notion. A grin escaped him, his teeth white and pristine. "And if I'm not?"

Loren didn't answer. The question was rhetorical and they both knew it. Shriff, though, understood the situation and intuitively read Loren with a single glance.

"Manners only go so far, Detective." The way he held out Loren's title sent shivers up the detective's spine. Cold, so cold, yet there was malice behind it. "Especially when they ring false."

Loren inched closer, his elbow to the table and the file on his lap. "Which you can detect? Is that part of the training program at CostSmart? Has to be better than their background checks, am I right?"

"Humor," Shriff said plainly. His grin faded in the face of Loren's. "The dullard's tool."

"Work with what you've got, I always say."

Shriff huffed. He rattled the chains along the side of the table. "Ask your questions, Detective. With some respect."

Loren settled back against the chair. "That's what it is with you, isn't it? Respect? Politeness?"

"We live in an overcrowded cesspool of inequity. We should at least be respectful of our neighbors."

"Says the guy murdering people," Loren shot back with a smirk. Shriff's eyes thinned at Loren's tone. The anger flared brighter than before, and his muscles tensed under the oversized shirt. "Oh, too rude for you? How about this one? How do you respect yourself knowing what a pile of crap you are? Sure, the greeter gig has to be a kick in the nuts self-esteem-wise, but at least it keeps you in

Wendy's fries and anti-psychotics. Oops. You must have doubled up on the fries."

Shriff's hands balled up into fists around his chains. He started to stand, before pulling tighter to the table. "You're like the rest. Rude to a fault. Rude to boost yourself up at the cost of everyone else."

Loren was more than happy to let Shriff rant. He wanted him angry. Angry meant a slip-up was more than possible. All Loren had to do was wait for the information he needed. In the back of his mind, he imagined Beth in the room with him, anticipating the truth to come.

Shriff beat his hands on the table. "Scowling and miserable at your own pathetic existence, you pull down all those around you. You want them beaten and ashamed, when we should all rise up, with a smile on our faces and joy in our hearts."

"Is that why you do it? The smiles?" Loren watched the man closely. Shriff hesitated. Thin eyes glanced at the camera, and then back at the waiting detective. Loren edged closer, pressing the issue. "You can tell me, Walter. You'll have to tell us eventually now that we have you for murder. Come on. Share with me. Help me rise up with my fellow man."

The fire dimmed in Shriff's black, beady eyes. A long breath filled his chest, which he let out like the drag of a cigarette.

"The smile?" The coldness returned. His methodical words boomed through the room. "Like the one on the Giles woman? Or do you want to know about the twins at the warehouse on Jessup? The papers have me down for eight, don't they?"

Loren's gaze fell. "That's right."

"What do you have me down for?"

The detective looked at the door. "We—"

"Not we," Shriff said, drawing Loren back. "You."

"I don't—"

"The way you asked. About the smiles. Has that question been gnawing at you, Detective?" Shriff's words echoed through Loren's ears. With each one, Loren felt his heart skip a beat, then race to catch up. Sweat filled his palms and matted down his hair upon his forehead. "Have you been wondering about the smiles, or a particular smile? One that's haunted you for such a long time?"

Loren shifted uncomfortably against his chair. He squirmed with each look to Shriff's content face, smug in his arrogance.

"Loren, wasn't it?" Shriff continued. "The name is familiar."

"Is it?"

"Yes." Shriff pointed to him. "You had a wife, didn't you?"

"You know I did," Loren murmured through clenched teeth. He pulled at his collar, heat rising in his chest.

"Did I?" Shriff asked, aghast. "Now how would I…" He stopped and his grin widened. "Did she die with a smile on her face, Detective?"

"You know damn well she did," Loren snapped. "Now, how about the truth? You're going to rot in a cell, Shriff. Just tell me what happened to my wife."

"Why, I can only speculate, Detective, on the point of her smile. But having been in your presence for mere minutes, I can tell you I would also smile at never having to be near you again." Shriff laughed, and the sound rattled through Loren's ears. The image of Beth faded, saddened by Loren's inability to obtain the truth. Or was it because he had been sitting across from her murderer in conversation rather than acting to stop him once and for all?

"She must have been quite content to never have to deal with your belligerence," Shriff spouted with joy. "Your dumbfounded ignorance with the world. Yes, her passing must have come as quite the blessing. For her."

Loren leaped to his feet. He was around the table in a flash, fist cocked high in the air. "You bastard! Admit it! You killed her!"

The door opened before Loren reached Shriff. Ruiz raced into the room, a pair of officers at his side.

"Detective!" Ruiz called.

"Say it!" Loren bellowed, lost to his grief. "Say the fucking words!"

Shriff simply laughed. His hands spread wide to greet Loren's assault, though he did not seem to care to defend himself. He didn't need to. No one else heard the sound, yet it was all Loren could hear.

"That's enough!" Ruiz shouted. The officers grabbed Loren by the arms and dragged him toward the door. "Get him out of here!"

"You took her from me!" Loren yelled. "You killed her!"

Shriff found his way back to his seat. He laid his cuffed wrists before him, hands clasped tight together. "We're the same, Detective," he said in a calm, rational tone. "You see that now, don't you? Both so filled with rage in our hearts at a cruel world. We're connected, you and I."

His joy echoed down the wing. As the door shut, Loren realized his last chance at answers was gone.

CHAPTER TWENTY-TWO

Gates watched the entire procedure unfold. From start to finish, the second Loren pushed Shriff, he fell into the same trap that had tripped up Quinn, Messick, and every other visitor to the deranged killer. Loren had pushed too hard, laid in too many jokes about Shriff to ever truly hope to connect.

It was a painful experience, not only for Loren, who continued to scream at the top of his lungs for the truth, but for all those who witnessed the proceedings. After their earlier conversation, Gates thought he was in a better place mentally. He had seemed sharp with the files and the mysterious connection between them. But once inside the interrogation room, Shriff bullied him to act. All had been preventable. Many methods existed to prompt a different reaction from the killer, but Loren had insisted on getting an answer to his solitary question.

Now, he probably never would.

Ruiz had had enough. Shriff had encouraged Loren to take action. The rage and utter disrespect Loren had shown for protocol, however, caused the shouting match with Ruiz at the other end of the hallway. Their friendship meant little in the face of what stood between them at the moment: Loren's need for an answer and Ruiz's commitment to the law. Neither was compatible when considering the sheer emotional stake of one and the cold calculation of the other.

Gates hated to see it. The passion both men displayed showed their dedication to the case. Loren's personal duty outweighed his common sense. After months of pushback from the obstinate detective, it was easy to understand why cooler heads no longer prevailed.

Meanwhile, Shriff remained in the room alone. The monitor

continued to show his grinning demeanor, the malevolence that sat dead center of those black beady eyes. Gates stared at them, wishing she could figure out how such evil could exist. There was no place for it in her reality. To her, Portents held nothing of the like, and stood as a place of hope and light.

Shriff took such notions away.

Gates kept a close eye on the screens. Shriff's grin faded and his head lowered toward the table. When it lifted, the eyes softened. The twitching of his hands against the chains ended, and all anger fell from his body like it had been exhaled and released from his being.

Wide eyes glanced around the interrogation room. Concern and sadness filled them. His shoulders slumped and his hands rose to catch his cheeks and hold them in place. Fingers dug nervously along his skin, scratching at his flesh.

None of the anger or malevolence that had appeared in the man only seconds before remained. Something changed in him. It pulled at Gates until finally she peered over the screens at the arguing pair at the end of the wing.

"Detective?" Gates called. "Captain?"

"I'd let them finish, Mel," a voice replied from her side. Dickie stood next to her, munching on some vending machine chips. She hadn't realized he had stayed with her. Gates continued to point at Loren. Dickie shook his head. "Getting between that is asking for trouble."

She wanted to speak up, then returned to the monitor. Shriff's head was buried in his hands, his body rocking lightly back and forth in the metal chair.

"What is it?" Dickie asked.

"Did you see that?" she said. "Were you watching after Loren left the room?"

Dickie cocked an eyebrow. "What was it I was supposed to see?"

"Shriff," Gates tried to explain. "I… He changed."

"How?" Dickie shifted closer to her. Gates gave him room—the smell of his breath from the onion-flavored chips offered plenty of incentive—and Dickie leaned in for a better look at Shriff. He shrugged after a moment. "Looks like the same murderous scumbag he was when we brought him in."

"Does he though? There's something strange about him. The

way he looks at times. The way he acts."

"He's a murderer, kid," Dickie said with a pat on her shoulder. He caught the time on his watch and his eyes sparked. "We should roll."

"I'll be there in a second."

Dickie took off without another word. He didn't notice anything, yet something continued to gnaw at Gates. Shriff, the one currently on the screen, looked nothing like the man she had seen interact with Loren.

Where there had been anger and manipulation, now there appeared to be only a withered and broken man. Murmured words ran under his breath, lost to the feed. He shook his head vehemently, as if arguing with someone else in the room. Hands slammed on the table, then relaxed with fingers spread before him. A deep breath brought his attention back to the camera, and with it came Shriff's knowing smile—malicious with intent.

The monster returned. Gates, though, witnessed more, including the tears clinging to the man's cheeks.

"I know I saw something," Gates said. "I just need to figure out what it means."

CHAPTER TWENTY-THREE

Ruiz had kicked Loren to the curb for the night. Harsh words had passed between them, screams about protocol and the right to the truth fell on their deaf ears. Their two disparate agendas had failed to mesh from the word go on the case, yet Loren realized he'd crossed the line during his questioning of Shriff.

Somehow, the little bastard had gotten into Loren's head. He'd pushed every button to garner the reaction Loren had only been too pleased to share with the killer. It had been unprofessional and wildly idiotic. His chance at answers had come and gone, leaving him cold and empty in the aftermath.

Loren found solace at a neighborhood pub. McDuffie's was known as *the* cop bar in the city, and the proximity to the Rath made it the watering hole for much of the precinct. Of course, drinking brought its own cycle of guilt to Loren. He cursed his dependence on the stuff, hated his weakness at wanting nothing more than to drown away the evening with a bottle or ten.

He added it to the list of mistakes on the night. Not that it deterred him from downing the first pair of double bourbons in a matter of seconds. Immediately buzzed from the lack of sleep and nourishment over the course of his long day, Loren nursed the next drink. His reflection scattered throughout the dingy mirror behind the bar, Loren slumped on his stool and agonized over his error in judgment.

Shriff had killed Beth. That was a fact in Loren's eyes. Every second of the last six months had built to that ultimate truth, yet when it came time to hear the words, Shriff had played him for a fool. The Kindly Killer had listed off several other murders, all matching the detailed records Loren had studied endlessly at work and at home. He had tried everything to get in the mindset of the murderous S.O.B. to no avail. No, it took the killer himself to bring to light his rationale for his crimes.

Rudeness.

Loren nearly spilled his drink at recalling Shriff's aggravation at the behavior of others. Their shortcomings had led Shriff to end their lives, the ultimate punishment for the smallest of misdeeds. Shriff believed himself to be superior, that it was the world at fault because of their poor behavior.

Yet, if that were true, how did Beth fit into the pattern? Shriff had been happy to sound off on the nastiness of CostSmart's clientele. They had treated the greeter with nothing but disdain. That wasn't Beth in the slightest. Even on the worst of days, she had never turned her anger or frustration out on others. That hadn't been her.

But Shriff had to have killed her. The smile, the randomness of the act itself, all pointed to the Kindly Killer above all other scenarios. Truthfully, Loren was left with only the one option, having dismissed Ronne's assessment of suicide. He had found no other signs of foul play to suggest another assailant.

Had Loren been wrong the whole time?

Loren finished his drink when a hand settled on the bar. He turned to see one of the guys from the precinct—his name escaped Loren though they had served together for years.

"Rough night, Greg?" The officer was Loren's contemporary in age. He wore a wide grin and carried a full mug of beer.

Loren huffed. "You could say that."

"Feel like joining us?" He pointed to the table in the corner with three others sitting. They joked and laughed as if the world no longer affected them once their shift ended. Loren envied them. "Some of the guys—"

"No," Loren replied much too quickly. It set the officer back a step. The last thing Loren needed was the pity of his colleagues. He had stomached that for far too long. "I'm good. Thanks, though."

"Greg—"

"Appreciate the offer," Loren said, turning back to the mirror. He caught the offended look on the man's face. "I'm good."

The man stalked off. Loren tried to place his name. It was yet another failure on the night, with more guilt heaped on him for his rudeness. It wouldn't surprise Loren to find himself on Shriff's kill list for his behavior. Maybe he deserved it, too.

Loren caught glances from the table of uniforms in the corner. It was clear he had burned yet another bridge with those still willing to work with him, let alone talk with him. That number had become few and far between in recent months.

"Your friends were trying to help," the bartender commented. He held up the bottle of bourbon.

"What are you, my priest or my bartender?" Loren snapped. "Pour the damn drink."

He did so, cursing under his breath the entire time. Loren placed down more cash, which was snapped up before the bartender walked away.

"What an ass," he murmured as he headed for another customer on the far side of the room.

Loren stared at his disjointed image in the mirror. "Yeah," he muttered, the glass back in his hand. "Yeah, I am, aren't I?"

Emptying the glass in a single swallow, Loren contemplated another. His blurry vision answered the question, and he shuffled off the stool. His foot almost gave way, his ankle unable to carry his full weight yet. Still, he stayed standing and made his way to the front door. No waves were thrown at him during his departure.

The storm met him outside. Sheets of rain sprayed him like a cold shower, and woke him to the night. Loren, as alone as he had ever felt, staggered down the block toward home. He patted his pockets, desperate for a smoke only to find the half-empty pack of gum waiting for him. Disgusted, Loren shoved the pack away.

Filthy habit.

At the corner, he stopped. Leaning against the lamppost, hands in her pockets and a smirk on her face, was the woman from the parking garage the previous night.

"You."

"Hey."

"Who…" Loren closed his eyes tight, struggling through his drunkenness. "Who are you? Do you have any idea what you've done by bringing that maniac into my life?"

The woman saddened at the accusation. "I was trying to help."

Loren gave a sharp laugh. "Yeah, well, that didn't work out."

He moved for the street away from her. The woman spun on her heels. "Look, if I could just…"

Loren swiped at her reaching hand. "Not a chance," he said through slurred speech. "In fact, what I should do… the right thing to do… is arrest you."

He grabbed at the cuffs in his back pocket. He bobbled them between his hands until they fell and clanked loudly along the ground. Loren stumbled after them.

"Oh, this is going well," the woman remarked.

"Vigi… Vigila…" Loren kicked at the cuffs instead of picking them up. His chase continued, as did his struggle for words. "Strutting like a superhero is against the law, lady."

She rolled her eyes. "And we've added lady to the conversation. Yeah, I was hoping our first chat would go better. Sorry it has to be this way."

"What way?"

Loren looked up, cuffs finally in hand. He barely saw her fist connect with his cheek. One second he was on his feet, the next he met the ground with a thud. His head rested next to a puddle at the curb. As the world went dark, the woman's last words rang through his ears.

"I have a feeling you'll be more approachable when you wake up."

CHAPTER TWENTY-FOUR

That definitely could have gone better.

The thought followed Soriya as she lifted Loren from the literal gutter. She carried him away from the torrential rains to a third-story fire escape two blocks over. An overhang off the top of the building covered the metal grating, which gave her and her unconscious guest a reprieve from the elements.

Soriya sighed. She had built up their first true meeting for weeks in her mind. Months of watching over him, of keeping him safe from the dangers in the city, had led to their momentous introduction. First, he'd completely ignored her call to meet in the parking garage following Shriff's arrest. This time around, Loren's drunkenness ruined everything.

She needed this to work and thought—after hearing his thanks carried on the wind the previous night—now was the best time to connect with the man. Her need had nothing to do with proving something to Mentor, though that would have been a bonus, to be sure, but to fulfill her promise to Beth. Everything she'd done of late had been in memory of her lost friend.

Loren's legs dangled off the edge of the fire escape. His upper body lay along the metal awkwardly, and she stayed close to keep him from falling backwards. His breathing was labored and the smell of booze was powerful on his clothes. This wasn't supposed to happen anymore. The capture of the Kindly Killer should have brought Loren back from his constant need to self-destruct.

Or so Soriya had hoped. Something had gone wrong, horribly and demonstratively wrong, with her plans. She tried to figure out what as the wind battered the railing. She sipped at her coffee. Another cup for Loren waited at his side.

Slowly, the detective stirred. His eyes struggled to open, and he swiped at the drool running from the corner of his mouth.

"What hit me?"

Soriya smirked. "I did."

His eyes sparked at the sound of her voice. Loren shot up and his knees slammed into the bars of the fire escape ledge. Pushing back, Loren settled along the ledge of the stairwell and stared at Soriya.

"You?"

"We went through that already," she said. Putting her coffee down, Soriya stretched out her hand for him. "Soriya. Soriya Greystone."

Loren eyed her cautiously. "Yeah. That sounds legitimate."

Her hand fell away. Soriya stood, maintaining a distance from Loren, who shifted tighter to the wall. He pawed at his forehead to stretch his eyes wider, then smacked his temples. The alcohol was clearly still in his system, and he struggled to push through the cloud overtaking his every sense.

"When am I ever going to learn?" he murmured.

"Here," Soriya said, the extra coffee in her hand. He hesitated to take it. "It's coffee. Three sugars."

Surprise took over, and he accepted the gesture. A long satisfied sip brought with it a measure of humanity in the detective. He took a second gulp before lowering the cup.

"Who are you?"

"I already answered that."

"Fine," Loren said with a dismissive wave. "What the hell do you think you're doing in Portents, and how are you connected to the Kindly Killer?"

Soriya wondered how much information to pass along. The buildup for their meeting continued to run through the back of her mind, but his reticence worried her.

"I'm helping the city, Loren," she said. "Like you."

"How you know my name is next on my list, la——"

"Soriya," she interjected, not needing to move backwards in the conversation. Loren returned to his coffee and gave her the floor. "I stumbled on your smiley murderer during another case. He felt I was rude, and I was."

Loren nodded. "You pushed him. I read his statement."

"Did it mention two monsters in masks tearing up the joint?"

Loren shot upright at that missing detail. "What? Like those kids from the paper? The ones that have half the cops in the city running around like chickens with their heads cut off?"

Soriya stared at him in disbelief. "You think they're kids?"

"You think they're monsters?"

Soriya grumbled. She turned away from Loren and peered over the railing. "This city and its blindness."

"To what?"

She wanted to answer immediately. There was so much to share with the man. Wanting to bring Loren into the fold made her realize more than anything, more than fulfilling a promise to a dead woman, Soriya desired a connection. She needed someone to trust—a confidant and a believer, like Beth had been. Something in the way Loren looked at her made Soriya hold back, though.

"Did you get to talk to him?" she asked instead.

"Who?" He stopped himself, then nodded. "Yeah. Yeah, I did."

"Did he tell you what you wanted to hear?" Soriya pressed. She wanted the answer as well. "Did he kill your wife?"

"How did you—" Loren didn't bother to finish the question. Everything about Soriya's presence obviously overwhelmed him, and she did little to help him settle down. Still, he held back the question of her knowledge when realization washed over him. "I… I was so sure it was him."

Soriya fell back a step, eyes wide. "And now?"

Loren looked away, saddened. "He couldn't have done it. Much as I want to continue to believe differently, just so I can have some damn closure. Just so I can know she's resting more peacefully. I so wanted it to be him, but after talking to him, after being in the room with him, and hearing his words follow me all night?"

"He didn't?"

Loren shook his head. "He detested rudeness. Sounds like you can verify that much. And Beth? My wife never had a rude bone in her body. She never would have triggered his rage."

Soriya's hands squeezed the bars of the fire escape railing. She had been sure as well. They both had been looking at one man for the crime they desperately needed answered.

"I'm sorry," was all Soriya could muster under her own frustration.

"Months of searching," Loren said under his breath as he fought to stand. He kept his back against the stairs and away from the ledge. After taking another satisfying drink, he swiped the remnants from his lips. Determined eyes met hers. "You gave me an answer, at least. Unfortunately, I don't see another solution."

"Maybe you need to open your eyes more, Loren."

"To what?"

Soriya showcased the city at her back. "Other avenues of investigation."

"Like monsters?" Loren said with a scoff. "Not likely."

"You don't have to take my word for it."

Alarms rang out into the night. Soriya couldn't help but smile at the timing. She knew they would come eventually, the same way they had during her last visit to the Knoll. Loren trailed the sound, then jumped at her touch. Soriya took him by the hand and led him toward the stairs.

"All you have to do is follow me."

CHAPTER TWENTY-FIVE

What the hell was happening? The entire world seemed to spin around Loren as he was pulled from the fire escape landing, down the steps, and deeper into the Knoll. He tried to form a question, but every attempt at a full thought was interrupted by the sudden jerk of the woman's hand, who continued to clutch tight to him.

Who was she? There had been answers given. None were to Loren's satisfaction. This woman—kid was more appropriate though, since she looked to be eighteen or nineteen—exuded a confidence the likes of which Loren had never seen. She knew what she wanted and went for it with more enthusiasm than Loren had probably ever displayed.

Just her presence made Loren feel lost, both in terms of physical location and his very sanity. When the night had started, everything had seemed much simpler. Loren had been hunting for answers—first about the woman dragging him through the streets like a rag-doll, and then about Shriff's involvement in Beth's fall.

Had Loren truly accepted the fact that Shriff had nothing to do with the incident? Part of him had, the rational part of his brain that had for the last six months been suppressed by the emotional core of his being. Holding onto Shriff as a suspect offered no satisfaction anymore. Nothing did, not even the booze he cursed himself for falling back into. He was better than that, or so he had imagined. Before Beth and the elusive answers to her demise. The goalpost had moved, and Loren no longer saw an end to his quest for an answer.

All thought fell away when they rounded the corner for Davis. A large SUV rested halfway inside an electronics store. The back tires spun, suspended in the air, and the SUV rocked precariously along the window ledge that served as the front of the store.

The woman moved for the shattered glass, but Loren—waking to the world around him for the first time in what felt like days—held her back.

"Hold up." He slipped his hand from hers with some effort. Loren looked at her, the name lost on his tongue. "So… Sorino… Lady, wait!"

"Back to lady?"

Loren sighed. "Is it my fault your name is, let's say, unique?"

"No," she remarked with a grimace. "It's your fault for not remembering it. Now come on."

Loren shook his head. "That's enough."

"Loren?"

"I've humored this long enough," he continued. "You want to pretend you're some urban legend taking down bad guys from the shadows? More power to you. But if you think for one second I'll believe there's more to what you do, you don't know me that well."

"Why do you think I didn't bother with words?" She took another step toward the store. Loren held his position firmly. "And maybe I don't know you as well as I should…"

"How could you?" That bothered him more than anything. She knew his name, where he worked, and how many sugars he preferred in his coffee. He couldn't even remember her name, and she'd mentioned it twice in the last hour.

"My point is," she said, ignoring his question. "There is a crime in progress. Are you going to stand aside and do nothing?"

"And if I said it's not my concern?"

"Then maybe you don't know yourself that well, either."

Loren stood in silence. He tried to refute her assessment. He wasn't on active duty and could barely consider himself sober, yet he couldn't walk away. Not when there were questions to answer. Not when he could help.

"Fine."

"Thank you."

They started down the block side by side. Loren ran a hand over his mouth, muttering, "I did forget the name, though."

"Soriya."

"Right," he said. "Soriya Purplepebble."

She held him up with a hand. "Greystone."

A smile ran across his lips. "That was a joke."

"You should workshop it more." Light laughter accompanied

them to the corner of the electronics store, where the sign read Walt's Games and Toys. Soriya stopped Loren before the broken glass. "Hold up a second."

Loren shot her a confused glance. "I thought—"

She put a finger to her lips, then ducked low to give him a clear view of the inside. The shop was in disarray. Shelving toppled on its side. The items broken from the impact of the SUV at the front of the store only painted a partial picture of the ruined shop. Boxes had been ripped apart with products removed. Some sat twisted and shredded as if played hard with for a second before being discarded like trash.

At the heart of the storm were two people: a man and a woman. Both wore elaborate masks, not the dollar store variety with a rubber-band string around the back. These were carved from something much thicker, like wood or metal—it was difficult to determine. One bore a grin, though her mask was marred by thick strands of glue along the chin. The other carried a frown from cheek to cheek. On their necks, both bore a tattoo of the masks side by side, as if they belonged to a gang.

Neither of them made a move for the cash register on the counter or the safe in the back of the shop. Nor did they seem interested in robbing Walt's of the many expensive products littering the ground. Their entire motive appeared destructive instead of committing a lucrative heist.

Soriya caught his curious gaze. "These clowns have been at it for too long. They've been creating chaos and spreading pain throughout the city for months. Almost begging for attention."

"And getting it," Loren said. He recalled the diverted manpower from multiple precincts. They had been assets that could have caught the Kindly Killer much sooner had they not been needed in the hunt for these two. "But why?"

"Let's ask them."

Soriya was already in the shop before he could stop her. He needed to call it in, to bring the proper authority of the police department to bear on them. Soriya didn't have the same restrictions, it seemed.

"Dammit…"

His ankle begged for relief. Every other sense did the same—not only from this situation, but from Soriya herself. Ignoring them all, Loren stepped forward. Glass crunched beneath his sneakers.

They made it six steps inside before they drew the attention of the masked pair.

"Company, dear," called the smiling woman.

The frowning man dropped his toy helicopter, then stomped on it for good measure. "Without an appointment?"

"You ruined our party before, spoilsport." The woman pointed at Soriya.

"Looks like you've more than made up for it," Soriya shot back, fists at the ready. She glanced at Loren, who hesitated to draw his sidearm. "Say hello to Comedy and Tragedy, Loren. My playmates from the CostSmart, and the cause of that bank explosion."

"So you're thieves?" he asked, confused.

Comedy shrugged. "A trifle. A pittance. A moment of creative output."

"Thieves are mundane," Tragedy summarized. "We are artists."

"Ah, gotcha," Loren replied. "You're just a couple of assholes."

Soriya nodded in agreement.

Tragedy sighed. He pushed the nearest shelf over and joined his partner in the center of the destruction. "Shall we play some more, my sweet?"

"She spoiled my fun already, dear."

"How true," Tragedy said. "There will be pleasure in her death."

"Most definitely."

Loren leveled his Glock at the pair. "Sounds like you have a way with people."

"People is a misnomer," Soriya said. She launched into the fray without another word. Comedy dove out of her path and allowed Tragedy to take the brunt. He fell back a step at Soriya's strike, then caught her wrist. A swift blow sent Soriya crashing into the fallen displays.

Comedy laughed as she spun to greet an overwhelmed Loren.

"Bonnie and Clyde look human enough to me," Loren said. He ducked under a punch from the grinning woman.

"They aren't," Soriya repeated. Tragedy's foot stomped down at her. She rolled before impact and his boot got stuck in an open crate of miscellaneous cables. Soriya jumped to her feet. A blistering kick connected with the side of Tragedy's head, but failed to budge him. "See?"

"Then wha—"

"Comedy and Tragedy are nicknames, at best." Soriya continued dodging the frowning man's rebuttals to her blow. "They prefer Thalia and Helpomene. The masks are vessels of their spirits imprinted on an unknowing host and held in place through the mark on their necks."

"Spoilers!" Comedy exclaimed. She lifted the box to a thirty-two-inch flat screen and tossed it at Loren. "No one likes a know-it-all."

Loren dove to the ground, his elbows slamming against the metal shelving. Every word spoken went over his head, yet he stared in amazement at the masked pair. "You mean she's telling the truth?"

Comedy dropped her arms and cocked her head to the side. "He's quite thick, isn't he?"

"It's his first night on the job," Soriya said. Tragedy grabbed her by the arm and batted her away toward the other side of the shop.

Comedy loomed over Loren. The black chasms in the mask for her eyes offered no hint of her face. "We've been wearing these skins for months. They stumbled on our masks by pure accident, if you can believe that? We had been in the dark for so long, locked away in some storage unit. We called to them. Their curiosity took care of the rest. They did well in a pinch, but time wears on everyone. You see, Officer, eventually the meat rots."

"What are you—"

The grinning woman lifted the bottom of her mask ever so slightly from her chin. From underneath, flesh fell loose in thick clumps. Worms and roaches scattered from behind her exposed bottom lip.

"What the hell?" Loren muttered. He wanted to throw up at the sight. "They're—"

"Dead?" Soriya interjected from a heap at the far end of the shop. "Yeah. The masks burned out the hosts. We need to—"

"That's enough of that," Tragedy interrupted. He slammed his fist toward Soriya's lap. She spread her legs and his knuckles crashed hard along the metal of the shelving. Lifting herself up, Soriya tried to get some breathing room, but he rebounded from his failed strike. His arm swung wide and caught Soriya along her left side. Her body sailed into an undisturbed section of the store. Shelves and products alike crashed under her.

Comedy clapped her hands with enthusiasm. The masked pair

turned toward the lone opposition.

"He looks quite fetching," Comedy beamed.

"If you say so, my sweet."

"What do you think?" She reached for Loren. Her mask filled his entire vision, as if preparing to envelop him whole. "I believe it's time for an upgrade."

CHAPTER TWENTY-SIX

Soriya rubbed at the fresh cuts dotting her arms. She tired of the abuse laid out by the hands of Tragedy, yet he countered her every move to perfection. It disgusted her, the feeling that her years of training meant little in the face of her enemy.

Disgust, however, turned to fear in a flash. Comedy closed in on Loren. Her fingers were tucked tight under her mask, ready to relinquish it to a new host—a more comfortable body to continue her campaign of destruction on Portents.

"Loren!"

She had been a fool to involve him in this. Throwing him in the deep end without a single care to the threat at hand was just the level of stupidity Mentor had warned her against every day of her life. All had been to prove the true nature of Portents to a man she desperately wanted to help. More than that, Soriya hoped to give him something to focus on and fight rather than continue his never-ending spiral.

A quick leap brought Soriya back to her feet. She raced for Loren's position, all thought to her own safety forgotten in the interim.

Tragedy happily reminded her. He barred her path with his burly frame and wagged his finger at her. "Oh no, you don't."

Soriya cocked her fist back and launched at him. Tragedy shifted aside in a blink, the movement so fluid Soriya barely noticed until he stood at her side with a rich gleam in the black holes of the mask's eyes.

Grabbing her by the throat, Tragedy lifted her from the ground. "You know, we don't ask for much. Fun and chaos."

Soriya struggled against his tightening grip. "Ending with death and loss, right?"

"It's the proper way of things."

"Not this time," she snapped. Digging beneath his fingers, Soriya snapped them back. Her body fell into a crouch before him and she bounded up with a knee to the chin of the staggering foe.

Tragedy, though, quickly rebounded and caught her follow-up strike. A toss sent her hard against a nearby display and Soriya crashed to the floor in a heap.

"There is nothing you can do about it."

Soriya snatched at her hip. The pouch was lost in the fray, and with it, the Greystone. She searched around in desperation, hands pawing at the ground in the mounds of debris left by the masked pair. Her hand came to rest on a sharp shard of metal cut loose from one of the broken shelving units. She gripped it tight, a plan forming in her mind.

"We'll see about that."

Comedy closed in on a reeling Loren. Desperation kicked in as Loren leveled his weapon on the decayed corpse strolling after him. He fired a wild shot, his hands shaking uncontrollably. Comedy's laughter unnerved him. It echoed through his mind and his thoughts lingered on another laugh he'd encountered earlier in the night.

Anger took hold. There had been enough pain, death, and manipulation from all those around Loren. He tired of it all. He steadied the pistol, a finger wrapped along the trigger.

The shot cut through the grinning woman's thigh. No blood streamed from the wound. Only rotting flesh fell loose to the ground. Worms squirmed from the gaping hole, joined by insects and roaches that scattered in all directions. Some crawled up the woman's chest and danced along her arms. Others fell to the floor and made for Loren, who backed up against the front-end of the SUV. Still, she continued for his position.

He was trapped. Disbelief set in over the entire affair. Monsters existed in the world. True and terrible horrors lived in Portents, yet he never realized the truth.

Comedy reveled in his terror, her laughter growing with each step.

"Back off," Loren said. He raised the gun again, this time higher against his foe. The shot clipped her in the arm, with no effect. Just more joy from the grinning ghoul.

"It doesn't hurt, if that's what you're worried about," she said. "The transfer is instantaneous. Your mind simply retreats into a warm memory. Like a party with all your favorite people in the world. One that never ends."

"I'm not real big on parties."

She loomed over him. Her foot shot out at his wrist. His gun sailed from his grip. "I'm not real big on stubborn fools. We all have our crosses to bear. All is necessary, though. It's a play, you see. A great production."

Comedy crouched before him. Her fingers slipped under the mask and began to peel it loose. Bugs sprayed over Loren with each shift. This was the end. He felt it in every bone of his body.

"Hey! You know my favorite part of a play?" a voice called from the other side of the store. Both turned to Soriya, who knelt among the debris with a smirk on her face. "The curtain call."

Comedy never saw the metal shard until it was too late. Soriya hurled it like a javelin. The spear connected with the cracked portion of the mask, which spread upon impact. Comedy's hands jumped to her face to hold the broken pieces together.

Shards faltered under her frantic grasp. They fell free and clattered to the ground like tinkling glass. Cries of pain, torturous and booming, filled the air. They rang out from the fallen crumbs of the ancient obol instead of any type of mouth on the dead flesh of the once-grinning woman.

As the last piece slipped from her hands, Comedy's body gave way. Crumpled flesh crashed to the floor and spread like putty. Insects burrowed out from inside, spurting forth and spreading over the decayed corpse. With a massive heave, they collapsed and died.

Loren stared in utter horror. He blinked hard, trying to understand what had happened and why. He bent over the dead thing. His stomach roiled at the drips of flesh smeared across the floor. Then he doubled over and threw up.

"No! What have you done?"

Tragedy spun towards Soriya. There was no more playing around, no more games and chaos and all the crap he had spouted previously. He was a man over the edge and Soriya had put him there—right where she wanted him.

"Your turn, sad clown."

Tragedy charged at her. His strikes held none of the confidence from earlier. He merely lashed out with every ounce of pain and rage buried beneath his meatsuit.

Soriya ducked and dodged, dancing with him through the store. Soriya dove under his punch and circled around. She backed up for the front, always with Tragedy before her and always keeping his fists in view. She didn't want him to look away for a second, not with what she had planned for him.

Tragedy's punches swung wildly through the air with enough force to shatter bones. Without that connection, though, he sailed along with each strike. His emotional outburst served nothing, yet he failed to center himself. All he wanted was Soriya dead.

"You've spoiled everything!"

"You're spoiled all right," she replied with a laugh.

Tragedy screamed and leaped at her. Soriya ducked out of the way.

Loren stood in her place. He launched his fist at the surprised Tragedy. His knuckles crashed against the side of Tragedy's head and the frowning figure fell.

Loren shook the pain from his hand. "I don't think we had anything to do with the spoiling, though. Did we?"

Soriya shook her head. She joined him, patting him lightly along the arm. Even Loren offered a grin at the exchange, and the enemy at their feet.

He reached for his phone. "I'll call this in. He shouldn't bother anyone again for a long time."

Soriya wasn't listening. She surveyed the debris in the conflict's aftermath. The threaded pouch sat atop a pile of bargain DVDs, the sewn loop frayed during the fight. She opened up the pouch, and the Greystone fell against her palm. She turned it to the fallen Tragedy.

"Step aside, Loren."

"Excuse me?" Loren looked up, shocked and confused at the object aimed at the subdued figure. "Whoa. What are you doing?"

Loren stepped between her and Tragedy, hands in the air. "It's done. We got him."

"He's too strong," she said. "The mask is too dangerous to leave out in the world. The Greystone will—"

"That's what you do?" Loren asked with clear disgust. "Kill people?"

"Not people," Soriya reminded him.

"It doesn't matter. Not here. Not like this."

"You don't understand."

Loren covered the stone with his outstretched hand. "So help me figure things out. Isn't that why you wanted our little chat?"

It was. Soriya immediately regretted it, just as Mentor knew she would.

Loren looked her deep in the eyes, his resolve strong. "I won't let you do this."

Soriya held firm for a moment, then relented. The stone slipped back into the pouch. "Okay. We'll do it your way, Loren. For now."

CHAPTER TWENTY-SEVEN

Blue and red lights washed over the entire block. Four patrol cars sat in front of Walt's where officers escorted a cuffed Tragedy from the premises. The still-masked perp said nothing. Icy stares washed over each of the officers, but Loren held the brunt of Tragedy's unspoken anger.

Loren and one other, of course.

When Tragedy's gaze flitted away from the shop to the shadows at the end of the block, Loren stepped in to push the crook toward the nearest squad car. Warnings passed between him and the officers on the scene about the man's mask and the need for it to remain in place for now. He didn't offer specifics, only that there was a danger to them if Tragedy attempted to remove it, so restraints were ordered for all times.

Everyone involved demanded more information—Loren included. The truth of the matter remained elusive to Loren as well. He sold the story as best as he could, with a few flourishes to deflect from the lack of an honest answer to the cause of the entire conflagration.

There was no way to explain how Comedy's body fell apart right before his eyes, or why so much vomit was found at the scene. His colleagues, though, had a few guesses on that front thanks to the odor emanating from Loren.

The stalwart detective didn't let their prejudice sway him, and continued with his tale until all parties were satisfied enough to call it a night. After the patrol car departed with Tragedy in the back seat, trapped and broken, Loren let out a long sigh of relief and retreated to the shadows.

Soriya waited for him. She sat, at ease with everything somehow, with her legs dangling off the side of a city dumpster. Her entire existence staggered the exhausted officer. How had she dealt with the situation of the masked pair without even blinking at the terror of it all? Loren knew he wasn't likely to sleep for weeks because of the affair.

At his approach, Soriya kicked off the dumpster and landed at his side. She showed none of the wear and tear he did, though bruises and scrapes covered her exposed skin.

Loren rubbed at his neck as he circled her. "I don't know what I'm supposed to think about all this."

"This is Portents, Loren," she replied. "The true city."

"What do you—"

"Myths and legends live among you," Soriya continued. "Some want nothing more than to live out their days in obscurity. Others?"

"Like our masked friend?" Loren asked, a thumb toward the departed car.

Soriya nodded. "There are dangers in Portents beyond anything from your worst nightmares. Threats that want nothing more than the ruin of everyone and everything."

"I've seen monsters before."

"Not like this."

Loren read the hard look in her eyes. Despite her youth, he could tell the truth in her assertion. Years were buried within her deep brown irises, with experiences Loren could never—and *would* never—understand. It went well beyond murder and mayhem.

"No," Loren said. "Sometimes that makes it worse."

"Tragedy is still dangerous, Loren," Soriya said. "Too dangerous for your people to handle."

"I've done all I can." She huffed loudly. Loren held out his hand in defense. "We have to try, Soriya."

She wanted to say more. He felt her frustration at not being able to put an end to a beaten foe. She wanted him to fall in line, to understand her position. He couldn't. Never in that regard.

"I'm still a cop," he said. "Some lines shouldn't be crossed."

"They'll become blurred, Loren." Soriya left the comfort of the shadows for the street. She leaned along the lamppost, the pink ribbon at her side dancing in the wind. "Against what's out there? I'm talking about monsters of unspeakable evil and power beyond imagination. Let me show you."

She held out her hand. Hope sat in her wide eyes.

Loren, though, took a step back. "I… I can't. I'm sorry."

Her gaze fell to the street, and she kicked off the post hard. "I understand."

"Do you?"

"Unfortunately, I was warned how this would go."

"Yeah? By whom?"

She shook her head. "That's a story for another day. But I want you to know, Loren, I won't give up on making this work. I'll be there when you're ready, truly ready, to face the real Portents."

"Myths and all?" Loren said with a laugh. He rubbed at tired eyes. "And how do I get in touch with you when that miraculous day arrives? Do I just call you, or should I start carrying a signal watch set to a specific frequency only you can hear?"

He spun around, his hand falling from his eyes and down to his side. The street was empty.

"Soriya?"

She was gone.

Loren fell silent, listening for any signs of life. Not a single footfall hit the ground in any direction. He witnessed no evidence of Soriya's departure, no matter how hard he looked or how quietly he stayed.

Eventually, Loren surrendered to the loneliness of the night. "Now that was cool," he muttered. "Rude. But cool."

CHAPTER TWENTY-EIGHT

Loren went to work early the next evening. His sleep had been troubled. Dreams of rotting flesh and maggots had made his skin crawl. Even the light of the television screen hadn't been enough to drive the fear away.

Worse than the nightmares had been the endless stream of unanswered questions left in the wake of his experience. Soriya's revelation to Loren had opened doorways undreamed of, and he needed time to process that information to the best of his ability.

The files were the place to start. Loren rummaged through boxes at a frantic pace. The reticence displayed on his first review was no longer present. He took every word, every witness testimony, and every verbal flourish at face value—from minotaurs to blue-skinned maniacs to a trio of witches. Every incident held a new meaning for Loren, though what that meant for his future he couldn't rightly tell.

Soriya stood at the center of them all. Her actions saved lives, yet Loren continued to resist trusting her. Their meeting had not been random chance. She had sought him out, studied him for some time before approaching. Why him? And why now? She refused to share some key piece of information with him, and it gnawed at the back of his mind with every page turned and every report examined.

Loren's entire world spun out of control. With each incident, he wondered more and more about what might be waiting to leap out of the shadows in Portents.

A knock at the door thankfully snapped him from his spiraling thoughts. Ruiz entered slowly, holding tight to the door. "Got a minute?"

Loren pushed the file away and took a sharp breath. He settled deeper into his chair, then waved Ruiz in.

The captain eyed him curiously. "What are you working on?"

"Remember the Frank Domingo bust?"

A call had come in about a warehouse owned by the famed gangster. Loren and Pratchett had found Domingo and a bunch of his crew hanging from the rafters. Below them were crates of laundered cash. Domingo had been untouchable until that point. Loren always wondered who deserved the credit for the criminal's fall.

"Your guardian angel theory?" Ruiz asked, reading Loren's thought.

"Not a theory," Loren said. "Not anymore. I think I met her last night."

Standing, Loren stretched. His body still ached from his fight the previous night. He started for the window, staring out into the rain as it fell in droves over the downtown area.

"Loren?" Ruiz clearly waited for more about the Domingo case, on everything going on with Loren, yet the detective hesitated to share.

With a deep breath, Loren said, "Do you think there are monsters out there? True monsters we can never hope to understand?"

"I'm having trouble understanding *you*. What is this all about?"

"I've always felt there was more to this city. A darker side. I think I glimpsed it last night." Loren glanced at his superior and dear friend, only to see the confusion on his face. Loren smiled. "Sorry. You didn't come to hear me ramble."

"Definitely didn't expect it," Ruiz replied. "Or the smile."

"What?"

"I haven't seen one in quite some time," the captain continued. "Not a real one, at any rate."

Loren rubbed at his chin as he paced around the stacks of boxes in the office. The dull throbbing of his ankle fell to the background behind his swirling thoughts. It felt leaps and bounds better than even an hour earlier. His spirits followed suit. The thought of the true city filled him with a mix of dread and wonder at the same time: dread at the danger involved, and wonder at the possibilities.

"I found out some things. I'm still trying to make sense of it all, but it was… I don't know how to describe it yet." Loren threw his hand in the air, unable to make sense of anything, it seemed. "Listen to me. What I do know is you were right to put me here. Right to take me off active duty. I should have walked away a long time ago."

Ruiz fell back a step at the statement. He recovered quickly and reasserted the stern look on his face. "Yeah, well, what happened in the interrogation room with Shriff last night—"

"Was out of line."

"It was."

Loren nodded. "You gave me a shot, and I blew it. Seems to be a pattern of late."

"Stop."

"What?"

"Agreeing with me," Ruiz said with frustration. "I'm pissed at you. I want to stay that way."

"Feel free."

"You ruined it." Ruiz sighed, then leaned on the desk. "What the heck happened to you last night? I heard about the robbery you broke up, but—"

"It's... hard to explain."

"More complications you don't need." Ruiz started for the door. "I won't keep you."

Loren settled into the chair once more. He pulled the Domingo file in front of him, then closed it once more. "Ruiz?"

The captain stopped at the door, a quizzical glance back.

"He say anything new? Shriff?"

"About Beth?" Ruiz's gaze fell to the floor. "Greg, I don't think—"

"Neither do I."

Shock spread across Ruiz. "You don't?"

"No," Loren said. "He didn't do it, but someone did. I won't give up the search. The way I've been doing it, though? I... Like I said, you were right to put me in here. After I finish with these reports..."

He hesitated, unable to look his friend in the eye. The thought had stuck with him since he realized the truth about the Kindly Killer's lack of involvement in Beth's fall. For so long, he had been blinded, unable to see any other solutions to what had happened to his wife. Now, there was nothing but possibilities. He feared where they might lead, as well as what he might be forced to do if he followed those paths into the growing shadows of Portents.

"What is it, Greg?"

Loren removed the badge from his pocket. "It might be time to rethink some things, is all."

"You don't mean—"

"I don't know," Loren said. "I really don't, Ruiz. Not yet. There are still some questions I have to answer, but…"

"Like Shriff?"

Loren wasn't sure. Shriff was a big question mark. His rage made no sense, considering the precision behind the killings. "Did he say anything else?"

"Not much," Ruiz answered. "Maybe he'll open up to his shrink."

"Shrink?"

"The DA's request was approved," Ruiz said. "Shriff is being evaluated at Castlemere Institute."

CHAPTER TWENTY-NINE

Castlemere Institute stood in the deep recesses of the Grove, away from the bustle of downtown Portents, and along the western border that ran against Rose Riley Forest. Built in the early 1920s, the institute worked hand-in-hand with her sister facility, Caldwell Correctional, as the medical wing for Portents' prison system. Those inmates suffering from mental illness and those prisoners deemed unstable by the law were placed in Castlemere to serve out their sentence.

The hope was always rehabilitation. The institute allowed for more personal interaction with staff and doctors. Private and group counseling sessions gave each patient the time and attention necessary to work to find a path back to society.

So the flyer read, at any rate. Loren had known little about the place and had made it his mission in life never to visit. While Beth had been more than happy to educate him on the history of the city and her favorite landmarks, including the creepy insane asylum, Loren had kept his personal promise to stay away. It was yet another failure added to the long list of late.

Castlemere, to Loren, was the great boogeyman of the city. Patients were regarded as vicious lunatics rather than ill. The view stemmed from the origin of the institute, and the brothers who built it: Frederick and Felix Castlemere. Wilbur Caldwell himself had brought the brothers in to construct the institute. They had worked together previously on the penitentiary, which sat half-an-hour's drive to the north.

Frederick was an astute businessman. His brother, Felix, though, was the creative genius of the pair. All had marveled at his designs in the city. He'd put together the Newton Building, the Franklin Center, and a dozen other architectural wonders that continued to stand tall and proud within the spires of Portents.

Felix, unfortunately, had the honor of being the institute's first patient. Madness had taken him during the late stages of construction. Stories of the time, those that passed to hearsay and legend, relayed a young man at the prime of his life. Felix had been betrothed to a wealthy heiress, who he'd loved more than any of the projects he had worked on. She had been the true marvel. Many had thought the same, including the foreman who had been working nights at Castlemere. Felix had caught wind of the man's affection for his bride-to-be.

Though explanations had been offered and apologies rendered, Felix had spiraled at the mere thought of a man wanting to be with his woman. Even Frederick, his brother, could not reason with him as work on the institute slowed. Mistakes had been made. Flaws in the designs had been listed as the cause, with the foreman at the heart of these allegations. Felix had lost control. He'd murdered the man in cold blood by flinging him from the top tower of Castlemere.

It marred the place after that. The woman had eventually married Frederick, and the pair had moved on from Portents for the rest of their days. Felix had lived his out in a cell, amid the high gate and concrete walls that surrounded the Castlemere facility.

Those walls stood to this day. As the cruiser passed the wrought-iron gate from the main road, Loren noticed the emptiness of the grounds. They kept all outdoor activity for the inmates confined to a small courtyard locked in the middle of the wings of the building.

Trees dotted the matted and swampy lawn. Most were lifeless, with dead branches swaying in the stiff breeze. Another rainy day brought with it thickening clouds and a foggy haze that accompanied Loren the entire way from the city.

The gloom wasn't the only thing to accompany the detective, though. Gates sat behind the wheel. Idle chitchat fell away upon their departure. She had, thankfully, read his need for silence as they took the RDJ to the Grove, then exited the massive turnpike for Hennessey Road, which ran the entire length of the western border.

What am I even doing here?

The question plagued Loren's every thought. He owed nothing to Shriff, yet something sat in the detective's gut over their time together. The man's grin continued to follow him when he closed his eyes. So did the booming laughter that chilled him to the bone. Shriff wouldn't leave him alone. His last words about their supposed connection haunted him. Loren felt obligated to do the same for the murderous madman.

The car cruised along the single lane up from the outskirts of the compound until it came to rest around a loop which circled the front of the institute. Statuary decorated the loop. A figure offering a helping hand to another dominated the landscape, though who they were had long since been lost to time. The faces had eroded, the helping hand more like a mass of stone than fingers. Surrounding the work were, or what had been, flowers of multiple colors. The rains had drowned them thoroughly, their colorful array yet another gray shadow on the ground.

Gates slipped the car into park and glanced past Loren at the facility. "Here we are. The site of every horror film that still haunts my nightmares."

Loren stared at the pitted walls and the cracking brickwork. Twelve wide stairs carried visitors and staffers alike into the building, which spread in both directions for hundreds of feet. Offices for administration appeared to occupy the second floor at the front of the building. The cell blocks and medical wings were no doubt tucked to the rear. A parking lot sat to the left, filled to the brim.

"Detective?" Gates called out. He turned and noted the nervous look in her eyes.

"Let's try to keep your visits to the day, Gates."

They stepped out. Gates held up at the driver's-side door, a hand on the frame. "Hey. You're not upset I tagged along, are you? The captain said you needed a lift, and I—"

"Eagerly volunteered, as I understand it." Loren tried to read her approach. Gates was an anomaly to him, someone who believed in Portents through and through. Even during the gloomiest of days, she carried a hope that would not quit. "What has you curious about this guy, Gates?"

"I don't know," she replied, taking to the stairs. "Yet."

"Questions can get you in trouble."

Gates grinned. "You would know. Sir."

"Yeah. I would." He waved her on. His ankle no longer hampered his movements thanks to the painkillers taken that morning. They finished their ascension and Loren held the door for Gates—

more out of habit than obligation, though the officer appreciated the gesture.

The reception area opened before them. Lush carpeting ran the length of the space. It fed under a pair of shut doors where a staircase could be seen ascending to the offices upstairs and the more presentable portions of the institute. Security personnel monitored the cameras positioned around the compound from a station in the left corner of the room. A welcome desk stood in the room's center and wrapped in an arc to limit access to the storage rooms visible beyond the security station.

Two women worked the desk, one on the phone and the other offering a smile to the newcomers. Loren let his badge do the work for him.

"Detective Loren to see Walter Shriff."

The woman, a nurse by the looks of the scrubs hidden behind the desk, threw a glance at her companion, who shook her head while on the phone. "I'm sorry. He's with the doctor in his room at the moment. If you'll wait—"

"I'd rather not," Loren answered. He continued around the desk, leaving the stares of the open-mouthed nurses behind for the connecting wing. Guards moved for his position, but were once more greeted by the badge. Too young to stonewall him, they lifted their radios to call their superiors about Loren's infiltration.

At the door, Loren peered back. Gates stood before the desk, aghast at his belligerence.

"Detective?" Gates asked.

"Well? Are you coming or not?"

Gates muttered an apology as she passed the women at the desk. The pair exited reception for the adjoining wing, which carried them away from carpeting to the stone floors of the prison wards.

She continued to look at him with growing concern. He brushed it off. "And make it Greg, would you?" he said. "Hearing Detective makes me think of Shriff, and not in a good way."

"Okay," she replied, drawing out the word. "But don't you think they would have given you a tour if we'd waited?"

"I prefer to see things for myself."

Their travels took them by a community room sparsely populated. Inmates worked on activities in silence, or shuffled around the place without direction. Rooms for counseling sessions dotted both sides of the wing. There was little activity at the moment, and their swift travels soon brought Loren and Gates to the cells.

Gates stopped at the door, obviously amazed at the design of the facility. They kept the inmates of the ward in glass houses, state-of-the-art, to allow for constant observation. Some pounded and screamed as the pair passed through. Others stared curiously at the newcomers. One such inmate caught Loren's attention, and the detective turned to face Tragedy.

The frowning figure crooked his head to the side. Black holes from the mask bore down on Loren, who couldn't help but tap on the glass obnoxiously before throwing him a wave.

"Friend of yours?"

Loren glanced at her. "One of the questions I told you about." When he peered back at the glass, Tragedy stood in front of him. His hands were spread against the surface. The masked man pulled them back and slammed them hard against the glass.

Loren jumped away from the cell. Then he stuck his tongue out at Tragedy before moving on from the ward.

Gates ran her hand over her heart. "Maybe don't antagonize the violent ones," she said. "Or, you know, anyone?"

"I have to take my fun where I can get it." Loren pointed ahead at the neighboring wing. Large windows brought in the dreary gray from outside. The wing connected to the next ward, which circled the back portion of the institute. "I think it's this way."

The cells of this ward no longer contained the glass and security hardware of the previous one. They were iron barred, though open. The inmates stayed within the confines of each one. They appeared content to sit in silence or work through their own sentence through exercise, writing, and other outlets. Near the end of the ward, Loren noted Shriff's name outside a cell. Before he could reach the open door, a man wearing all black and carrying a baton cut him off.

"Can I help you two?" the security guard said. His arms crossed his barreled chest, flexing against the tight material of his uniform. A radio attached to a shoulder holster. His belt carried keys, restraining equipment, and a buckle the size of the state of Texas. The nametag he wore read OLSON.

Loren didn't bother to engage with him. He continued to glance at the open cell. A lone figure made his way out. He wore thin glasses that slid down the bridge of his nose as he walked. In his early-forties, the man had a receding hairline. What remained had already shifted from his natural color to gray. He cradled a tablet before him.

"I have them, Mr. Olson." The doctor appeared slightly shaken at the door of Shriff's cell, but passed it off during his approach to the gathering crowd. His voice was calm and collected, intelligent and warm. "Detective Loren, I presume?" He extended his hand and Loren took it. After a firm shake, the doctor turned to Gates. "And you are?"

"Melanie Gates," she said, and she took the offered hand.

"Welcome to Castlemere. I'm Doctor Arnold Finney. Mr. Shriff is my patient for his evaluation."

"I'd like to see him." Loren's impatience showed, though he regretted his brusque tone in the face of Finney's calm demeanor. "I have a few questions."

Finney glanced back at the open cell. Loren craned his neck to catch a glimpse of Shriff sitting on his bed, head in his hands. Finney cut off his view. "I'm afraid Mr. Shriff is due for some time in the community room at the moment. Mr. Olson?"

Olson snapped to attention. He raised his radio to his lips. "Escort to Wing D-2."

Before any of the party could utter another word, two guards rounded the corner.

Finney nodded to each. "Thank you, gentlemen."

They entered Shriff's cell. No cuffs were at the ready, no sidearms prepped to take down the hostile killer. They walked in and helped the despondent Shriff to his feet. He tried to lift his head to greet the others in the corridor, but faltered from the effort. The guards pulled him along, down and away from Loren and Gates, who both looked on with curiosity.

Where was the killer who had manipulated Loren so well two nights earlier? What happened to the man who had eluded police for seven months during his rampage through the city? Where was the Kindly Killer?

Loren said nothing aloud, though his thoughts were clearly picked up by Gates, who jutted her thumb after the departing patient.

"I'm going to join them."

Loren caught her worried stare. "Have fun, Gates."

"Mr. Olson?" Gates asked, hoping for an escort of her own.

Olson waited for confirmation from Finney, who certainly ran the show. The doctor offered a nod.

"Right this way," Olson said, and the pair disappeared out of the wing.

Loren and Finney stood alone, their gathering all but dissipated. The detective moved toward the still-open cell. Inside was a bed and toilet. A small desk sat in the corner. Nothing else drew his attention. No markings signaled the shift in Shriff's behavior. The emptiness provided no evidence at all for Loren's unending questions.

He spun around to face Finney. "I only needed a few minutes."

"Which may have set me back many hours or days." Finney fixed his glasses on his face. He tucked his tablet tight to his side and started down the corridor. "Come with me. We can talk, and perhaps I can relay your questions at my next session. With less physical violence, let's say."

Loren's jaw tightened. Finney had obviously heard about Loren's last foray in questioning Shriff. "Ruiz ratted me out."

"Your clenched fists didn't help. Or the strain in your voice that came with the patient's name."

Loren shook his hands loose, then joined the waiting Finney at the door to the adjoining ward. To the right was the courtyard. Gardens and wildflowers filled a field that stretched between the wards. Benches were positioned around the perimeter for what appeared to be quiet reflection, while a trickling fountain provided background noise.

The left offered an overlook of the property and the far wall. The corridor snaked into another series of cells and wards branching off into the distance. Finney, though, kept moving forward along the path of the courtyard until they came to the end of the hall.

Carpet returned. Loren could see reception through the closed double doors. Rather than loop to the beginning of his travels, Loren and Finney climbed a tall staircase to the second level and the administration wing. The cool climate of the wards faded behind them. No more shuffling feet accompanied their travels, only the curious onlookers that staffed the institute.

Loren acknowledged none of them, his focus firmly on the swift pace of the doctor at his side. He tired of the silence between them, as well as the doctor's obstinance in the face of the threat

Shriff presented.

"He's a murderer, Doc."

"I'm well aware of the man's crimes," Finney replied. He stopped short of his office.

"Then you understand my feelings toward him."

"Your lack of control doesn't make you any better than Mr. Shriff in some regards," Finney shot back.

Loren balked at the comment. "I'm not the threat here."

"Not according to my patient."

Finney unlocked the office behind him by scanning an ID card over the keypad next to the frame. It beeped, and the scanner shifted to green. He inputted a four-digit code, and the door clicked open.

Pushing inside, Finney left the door for Loren, then proceeded into the office. Bookshelves were boxed in by two windows overlooking the front steps and Gates' parked cruiser. Plaques were hung from floor to ceiling on the right wall. A desk was positioned before the shelves, a small laptop in the corner and little else on the neatly kept surface.

Finney settled his tablet down on the desk and came to rest before the chair. He leaned hard on the edge. "This institute was built to protect those who have lost their way. Who no longer connect with the world in a rational manner. Most of our work centers on criminal cases. You most likely passed some of our violent offenders during your ill-advised tour of our facility."

Loren met his hard gaze. His eyes fell low.

"They are a rarity compared to the rest," Finney continued. "Most simply need a helping hand back into the world. Castlemere provides that in the form of long-term rehabilitation within the penal system."

"Looks a little too cozy for some of them."

"They reflect on their crimes, Detective." Finney held the title long and hard. It echoed through Loren's ears, but he shook it off. "Daily therapy sessions. We have some of the best behavioral doctors in the country. Doctor Deckart, the head of this facility, has always had an eye for talent."

"Like you, Doc?" Diplomas, awards, and other credentials spoke to the man's qualifications. Loren passed the desk for the bookshelves. He found several tomes with Finney's own name adorning the spines. "A little too experienced to be working in a place like this, don't you think? Hell, the books alone should keep you on the lecture circuit instead of cooped up in a dreary office in Portents."

One book grabbed his full attention. The title read, *The Secrets Kept in Dreams.*

"I had my own practice long ago," Finney said in a distant voice. "My license was revoked for a time. I grew a little too close to my patients."

It surprised Loren to hear the man's honesty on the subject. Most held back the dark secrets that haunted them, or pretended they never existed at all. "I'm surprised Deckart brought you on at all then, let alone made you head of such a high-profile case."

Finney smiled. "The good doctor has been kind enough to overlook my indiscretions. We are all capable of learning from our mistakes."

Loren wondered if that was true. He certainly hadn't felt capable of much since losing his wife. His hand crept back to the shelves and the book at the end of the row. He lifted it up for a closer look at the contents. The description discussed the messages hidden in the dream world humanity could only tap into when they were open to listening.

"Interested in dreams, Detective?"

A shiver ran up Loren's spine. "Please, make it Greg."

"Something wrong with your title?"

"I've just been hearing it too often and from all the wrong people."

"And the book?" Finney asked, drawing closer. "You find it interesting?"

"The treatise," Loren said. "You believe there are messages to be gleaned from dreams? Seems farfetched."

Loren moved to put the book back, but Finney stopped him. "Take it. Read it. Then we can talk."

"About Shriff?"

"Walter is deeply disturbed. There is no denying it. But where his anger resides is something I have yet to discover."

"Yeah, well, be polite when you inquire," Loren commented.

"I always am." Finney offered a slight bow of appreciation. "Feel free to leave your questions."

Loren didn't have any to give, none that could be called fully formed at least. Everything was intuition, and Loren's gut said there was more to Shriff. What that meant, however, remained a mystery.

"He's not a specimen to study, Doc," Loren said on his way to the exit. "He's dangerous."

Loren winced at his words. He heard Soriya's same warning echoed back at him, yet how much had he listened?

Finney grinned politely, a gleam tucked behind his lenses. "We all are when we have to be."

CHAPTER THIRTY

Gates trailed behind Olson around the corner. The wing branched in four corridors like a massive X, and Olson kept to the upper right. Signs indicated wards occupied the other halls, with security guards stationed at each entrance.

In fact, Gates took the time to count the number of guards since their arrival at the institute. A pair stood at each checkpoint and monitor station. All were armed with non-lethal weapons, including mace and some kind of taser from what she could tell at a distance. Constant radio contact kept the teams in the loop with Olson at the center of each decision.

By the time they arrived at the community space, Shriff was already inside. The pair of guards helped settle him at a table in the far corner. Crayons and markers were positioned around him, and a blank board was placed on the table for him to use. Olson went to join them at the entrance.

Observation glass gave Gates a clear view of the entire room. No security personnel occupied the space. The doctors clearly designed it for patients only. It was a place for them to interact and feel connected without oversight—or as little oversight as was possible within the penal system.

Shriff made no eye contact with any of the others in the room. They didn't pay him much attention either, truth be told. All were solitary in their doldrums, tinkering around or, as Gates viewed it, killing time.

Gates couldn't believe the shift in the so-called Kindly Killer. The malice had vanished, and with it, so had the man's spirit. He appeared to be a frightened waif instead of the cunning killer. Only a shell remained somehow.

Olson's reflection caught in the glass at her side and he settled next to her. Gates subtly shifted a step away from him to give herself some personal space. Olson failed to notice and leaned heavier on the glass.

"You run a pretty tight ship, Mr. Olson," Gates said, unwilling to make eye contact.

"Brent," he replied with a cocksure grin. "And I try to. The docs are good about listening, which helps. Two guards for every patient. Non-lethal ordinance to subdue. They care about these wackos. Don't ask me why."

Gates tried not to take offense. She had a feeling it was a common reaction with the head of security. Instead, she pointed to the frail figure on the other side of the glass. "Any problems with him?"

"Shriff? Mr. Kindly Killer?" Olson said with a scoff. "Why do you ask?"

"Has he been given any drugs yet?"

"Maybe something to help him sleep." Olson rubbed at his chin thoughtfully. "Finney and the rest always hold off until after evaluating before prescribing."

"Hence the two guards per patient."

"Exactly," he said with a wink. "They figure things out quick for a bunch of lunatics."

Gates nodded. "But no problem with Shriff?"

"Not a peep." A guard approached slowly. He waited for Olson's attention, then waved him over. Olson tucked his fingers in his belt loop. "Excuse me."

Gates appreciated the quiet that came with his departure, yet her troubled thoughts continued to circle her. What was she doing at Castlemere in the first place? She wondered if Loren had a legitimate answer, but given the looks they had shared earlier, she thought she knew the answer.

Shriff stared into space, mindless of the world around him. Hands needled at the crayons at his side, but never fully reached for any of them. He simply sat there, completely lost.

"He was so angry," Gates muttered under her breath. "Where does all that anger disappear to?"

Inside the community space, a walking behemoth of a man took notice of Shriff's position at the art table in the corner. His eyes widened, fists clumped at his sides, and he stomped over in large strides.

"Uh, Brent?" Gates called. Olson didn't flinch at the sound of his name. Gates spun from the glass. "Olson!"

The security chief patted his companion on the shoulder and rushed to the officer's side. Inside the room, the giant stood over Shriff. Angry words went unheard through the glass.

"What is it?"

"I think there might be a problem," Gates said.

"Goddamn Saprowski," Olson grumbled. He snatched the radio from his shoulder and brought it to his lips. "I need a team in the community room. STAT."

It was too late for Shriff, unfortunately. Saprowski's fist slammed down upon the man's face. Shriff fell to the floor, only to be lifted again by his screaming attacker. The giant man's fist crashed down in an endless series of blows. Shriff made no move to defend himself in the slightest.

Gates held a hand to her lips and whispered, "Oh, God."

Guards swarmed the room, rushing into the community space with tasers charged and ready.

"Move! Move!" Olson commanded before joining his team. Gates followed, but remained near the door. Security surrounded Saprowski in seconds. "Saprowski! On the ground!"

"He took it," Saprowski wailed. His voice was a high-pitched whine. "He took it from me!"

Olson inched closer. "Get on your knees, big guy. Last warning. You know what happens next."

Saprowski's eyes saddened with realization. Tears welled up and fear took over. He dropped Shriff to the ground. "Not the violent ward again. No. You said—"

"Listen to what I'm saying now," Olson said. "Okay, big guy?"

Saprowski wavered for a long moment. He weighed his options with the temperament of a toddler. A second glance at the art table and the decision was made.

"He can't have it!"

Saprowski lifted his fist to strike again. As he did, Olson fired, joined by four others. The raving giant shook as electricity jolted through his entire body. He crashed hard to the ground, his legs twitching involuntarily even after the tasers had been deactivated.

Olson helped Shriff to his feet. Blood ran down the frail figure's nose and right cheek. Olson quickly escorted him from the room.

"Shriff, are you all right?" Gates asked as they passed. The beaten man's murmured reply was muted by his bleeding lips. "What was that?"

Shriff looked at her with wide eyes. "I deserve it. I deserve it all."

"What?"

Olson continued to rush Shriff away. "I need to take him to medical."

Gates wanted to stop him so she could question Shriff further. The beaten man, however, ducked his head low and shuffled clear of the room and down the hall.

"Right," Gates said as they left. "Good idea."

Shriff's words lingered in the air. They were not the words of a remorseless killer and left Gates with nothing but more questions.

"What happened to the Kindly Killer? Where did he go?"

CHAPTER THIRTY-ONE

Finney watched the cruiser depart from his office window. Loren stared out blankly at the passing trees, lost to the world. Something about the detective stuck with Finney. His drive, for sure, but a deeper connection resonated with him.

After the car reached the gate and fell out of view, Finney moved for the door. He locked the office tight and started for the steps leading deeper into the institute. He passed Deckart's private wing during his travels, not bothering to check in with the head of the facility. The Shriff situation fell on Finney alone. He had to clean up the mess.

Medical resided through the branched corridors at the very rear of Castlemere. Two members of the security team guarded the entrance at all times. Even then, the keypad at the door barred unauthorized entry. Every precaution was taken for the safety of the patients under the institute's care.

Finney swiped his card, inputted his code, and opened the door to a small reception room. A pair of desks were positioned on either side. Only one was occupied. Stephen Mayer jotted down a few notes, then stopped at Finney's arrival. He greeted the man, whom he had worked with for years, with a soft smile.

Finney left him behind for the treatment area. Olson stood at the end of the occupied bed within. At Finney's approach, the guard shot him a stony glare, then returned his attention to the bruised and bloodied patient in the medical bay.

"How is he?" Finney asked.

Mayer stood to join him at the glass barrier separating reception from the treatment area. "A few bumps and bruises, Arnie. He'll be fine."

Finney's eyes thinned at Olson. "You were supposed to be

watching him."

Olson raised his hands defensively. "Whoa there. I warned you about putting Saprowski in the room with people. He's not ready."

"That was Doctor Deckart's determination to make, not yours."

"If I could station a team inside the community spaces—"

"Absolutely not," Finney shot back.

"But—"

"The patients come first."

Olson swallowed the argument, one they continued to have since his appointment as head of security. He raised a good point, one that Finney had trouble debating against considering the danger some of their patients presented. Yet, the doctor knew treatment only came from the fleeting sense of free will afforded the inmates at Castlemere.

Olson cared little either way. If the patients killed each other, it didn't faze him in the slightest.

"Right," the security chief muttered. He backed away from the glass and moved for the door.

Finney waited until they were alone. Once the door slammed back in the frame, he turned to Mayer. "Can I speak with him?"

Mayer shrugged his shoulders. "Don't see why not. Though he's not much of a conversationalist."

Finney grinned at the comment. That was one of the few things he knew about his latest patient. "I'm trying to change that."

"Then I'm sure you will," replied Mayer. "Want the guards?"

Finney shook his head.

"I'm here if you need me." Mayer returned to his desk and the required report to document the incident. When Deckart heard about it, the fun would really begin for Finney.

Rubbing at his eyes, Finney entered the medical bay. Shriff rested uncomfortably on the middle of five beds. A half wall separated each bed to give the illusion of privacy, but helped the staffers maintain a clear view of all when fully occupied.

Finney sat down in a chair positioned next to the bed. "I apologize for Mr. Saprowski's aggression, Walter. He'll be dealt with. How are you?"

Bandages covered much of his face, but the eyes remained visible. They stayed locked on the bed. "Fine."

"No injuries?" Finney asked. "You can tell me."

Shriff tucked his legs in close as he sat upright. "I deserve them."

"What?"

"I killed them," Shriff said. His hands hugged tight to his legs, and he stared off distantly. "They made me do it. I didn't have a choice. The way they behaved... someone had to punish them. Now *I* have to be punished."

Finney pulled a small pad from his breast pocket. He jotted a few quick notes, surprised at the man's words. "You remember them, Walter?" Shriff nodded. "You understand what you've done?"

"I was so angry," Shriff said. Clarity changed to confusion. "I still am, can still feel... all of it. But how could I... Doctor, I..."

Finney reached out and placed his hand over Shriff's. "We'll get there, Walter. Acceptance is the first step. There is plenty of time to figure out the rest."

Shriff's attention shot down to the doctor's hand. "You..."

"Is something wrong, Walter?" Finney pulled away and stood from the chair.

Shriff screamed. He flailed with his hands, trapped by the restraints on his wrists. He tried to grab Finney, his words barely audible through the yelling. "It was... It was..."

Mayer rushed into the room. "What happened?"

"I'm not sure." Finney backed away, giving the doctor room.

"Why?" Shriff bellowed. He kicked his legs at them. "Tell me!"

Mayer grabbed a syringe from his pocket. "He's losing it. Hold him down."

Finney nodded. Blocking the flailing hand of Shriff, he moved for the patient's shoulder. He locked the arm down and held firm. Mayer did the same from the other side, then slipped the sedative into Shriff's arm.

Shriff immediately calmed. His body slid to a resting position on the bed. His eyes became heavy.

"He should rest, Arnie."

Finney slowly retreated from the patient. He wondered what Shriff saw and what he meant. His hand grazed the end of the bed as he left.

"We'll talk more tomorrow, Walter," Finney said to the sleeping inmate. "Everything will make sense soon enough. I see great things coming for you."

CHAPTER THIRTY-TWO

He should have been thinking about Shriff. Not so much sympathy for what had happened to him in the community space at Castlemere, but about the questions still unanswered from their time together in the interrogation room.

Loren had traveled to the institute in the hopes of closure. Shriff, for as much time as he had taken from Loren during the seven-month-long investigation into his murder-spree, had had nothing to do with the one death that mattered most to the detective.

Beth's murder remained unsolved.

Yet, instead of heading back to the precinct and getting to work on finding the at-large killer, Loren couldn't care less. All he saw with work was what it had taken from him. The missing moments with his wife because of the long hours on the job. The muted conversations, or worse, the angry ones he'd had over the dangers of Portents when all Beth had ever seen was beauty in the city.

He felt lost, but somehow the book in his hands grounded him. Maybe there was a message waiting for him—an answer to all his questions.

Glancing up from the book Finney had given him, Loren noticed the car pass familiar sites. King's Lane crawled by, the traffic snarling in the late afternoon race to get home. Loren pointed to his apartment building a block out.

"Right over there."

Gates nodded, her mouth agape. "You're kidding."

He cocked an eyebrow at her. Gates pulled the car in front of the building, then set it in park. "My mother's apartment is two blocks down on Cambridge."

Loren let his attention lapse back to the book. "Hmmm."

"Good book?" At the question, Loren tucked it under his arm. "You've been studying it the entire ride. Does it have anything to do with Shriff?"

"No." He reached for the door handle. "Thanks for the lift, Gates."

He stepped out into the drizzling rain. Gates called after him before he could move toward the building. "Detective..." she stopped herself at the wince he gave. "Sorry. Greg. I just wanted to say I could help with the case. I think something is going on with Shriff. Something about the way he's changed since his move to Castlemere."

Loren felt it as well. Every instinct told him more was going on with the Kindly Killer, yet when Loren faced the prospect of pursuing that line of inquiry, he shook his head instead.

"Let it go, Gates," he said. "Shriff is going away for the rest of his life. Don't waste yours on someone like him."

"He's a question that needs answering," Gates replied. "Aren't you curious?"

Of course he was. His entire life had been one curiosity after another. What had they brought him in return? For all his work, catching bad guys and protecting the people of the city, Loren had nothing to show for his efforts. His apartment was devoid of life, his friendships dwindled to a handful, and even those were precarious at best.

"Well?" Gates said, pulling him from his thoughts.

"Not anymore," he said. "I'm just tired now."

"How about I dig up—"

"Take the hint, Gates," Loren snapped. "I don't want or need a partner. Not on this. Not on anything."

He regretted the sharp words immediately. He tired of trying with her, though. Shriff had consumed too much of his life already. He wasn't about to give up more.

Gates was clearly upset. She gripped the steering wheel of the cruiser tight, her gaze on the dash rather than face him directly.

"What happened to you, Greg?"

"Life happened." Loren leaned close, the rain picking up and the storm settling over them all for another long night. "Go home, Gates. Live yours while you can."

Without another word, Loren left the cruiser behind. He didn't bother to look to see Gates depart. There was no need. Her questions were her own and had nothing to do with him any longer.

Loren headed inside his apartment building. All he wanted was some decent sleep and to forget for a while.

CHAPTER THIRTY-THREE

The shadow stalked the wide corridors of the institute. Lightning illuminated his presence in bursts, then the darkness took hold once more and hid him from view. A few lights within the massive complex fought to remain active, flickering in a struggle they were destined to lose.

His distraction worked to perfection. The surge at the heart of the generators powering Castlemere brought down not only the electricity to the building but also the entire security array. Defunct cameras forced all security personnel to man the wards directly to keep the prisoners locked down for the duration. Every other available hand rushed toward the generators to attend to the problem or call in more help as needed.

It left plenty of time for the shadow to pay a brief visit.

Of all the systems taken down in his strike, only the violent offender's cells continued to function normally. Their state-of-the-art systems ran off a separate grid to feed constant attention to the locking mechanisms. The locks, of course, were controlled by specialized keycards, which had been the last piece to his infiltration of the ward.

The shadow swiped the card at the designated cell, the four-digit code memorized for such an occasion. He quickly typed it in. When the door clicked open, the shadow stepped inside.

Ronald Saprowski lay curled up on the floor. He hadn't bothered with the bed. His size made any hope of comfort impossible and clearly found the floor more to his liking. Sobs rocked his body, quiet tears over the events from earlier. At the shadow's approach, Saprowski silenced. Slowly, he rolled to face the door and the figure who loomed over him.

He immediately raised his hands in defense. "I'm sorry, I'm sorry. I shouldn't have done that. Shouldn't have been bad again. I—"

"It's okay," the shadow said in a whispered tone. He leaned closer, a hand reaching for the behemoth's cheek. "Shhh. Calm yourself, my friend. You did the right thing, you know."

"I did?" Saprowski asked in astonishment.

"Yes," the shadow replied. "You simply didn't take it far enough."

The giant sat up and pulled away from the visitor. He rocked his head. "No. No, that's bad. I'm not bad anymore, I'm good. I don't do the bad things anymore."

"But you want to, don't you?" His words echoed through the room, catching a glint of light in the eyes of the teary giant. "You want to make the truly bad men pay. They need to pay, remember?"

"They… the bad men?"

The shadow knew the inmate well from his file. Saprowski, because of his limited intelligence, had lived a lifetime of abuse by relatives who hated his very presence. He had been seen as nothing but a burden to them after the death of his mother. They had beaten and humiliated him, not only in the privacy of their own homes, but in public as well.

The beatings had turned more and more violent, culminating in the burning of his flesh by matches, cigarette butts, lighters or whatever else had been available. The lumbering boy had said nothing during all this, believing every mean-spirited word spoken by those who purported to love him most in the world.

As Saprowski grew older, he developed an obsession with flame from his years of torture at the hands of it. He obsessed over its power and, when his deep-rooted anger sprouted, he burned his abusers while they slept in their beds.

With his primary trigger gone, Saprowski continued to burn those he viewed as the bad men of the world. He'd targeted rapists, dealers, wife beaters, and more. After pummeling them into submission, he had burned them all for the pain they had brought against others.

"He is a wicked one," the shadow said. "You see that, don't you?"

Saprowski stared deep at the shadow, then nodded. "He took it from me. They all know it's for me, but he took it anyway. Always trying to hurt me."

"Hurt them back," the shadow pressed, a fist in the air before him. "Make them pay. Make *him* pay for putting you here."

The shadow retrieved the image from his pocket and placed it before Saprowski. The mugshot of Walter Shriff was clear, even in the dim lights of the cell.

"I... I..."

"You need to finish what you started," the shadow commanded.

"They'll punish me. Lock me away forever," Saprowski pleaded. His childish fears overwhelmed him.

The shadow reached out once more, consoling the behemoth with a gentle touch on the shoulder. "No. I'll take care of you. Haven't I always taken care of you?"

Saprowski rested his head against the hand. "Y... Yes."

The shadow smiled. His hand fell away. He retrieved the image of Shriff and tucked it in his pocket. When the hand returned, it carried something new.

A lighter.

The shadow flicked it on. Saprowski's eyes widened at the flame dancing before him. The lid snapped shut, and the shadow held it out for Saprowski's waiting hand.

"All you have to do is this one little favor for me."

CHAPTER THIRTY-FOUR

Loren dreamed. His entire world was nothing but a black void. No substance formed within his vision. No scents or other stimuli. He simply wandered through the dark, hopelessly lost.

"Hello?" he called out to the emptiness. He walked on, his hands before him for some sign of life, some faint trace of existence anywhere in this shadowed plane.

Sounds arose far behind him. It came in thin whispers and the tinkling of steps along the ground. A shadow billowed in the darkness, with eyes aglow in a fierce red.

"I've been waiting for you, Detective," it said.

Loren cowered in terror. He recognized the figure immediately as Walter Shriff, only this wasn't the frail figure from Castlemere. Shriff lorded over Loren, his power clear in his prominence within the dreamscape.

"No," Loren cried. "You can't be here. This isn't real."

"This is more real than you know, Detective," Shriff said in a booming tone. "We're connected. We've always been connected. Accept it."

Tendrils snaked from the hovering form. They shot out like thick vines of black, oozing ever closer toward Loren. They snatched at his hands and looped around his ankles to ensnare him. Shriff reeled Loren in like a fish. His savoring grin became brighter and brighter in scope through Loren's beleaguered eyes.

The detective struggled endlessly with every ounce of his strength, only to find he had none left to give.

"See?" Shriff exclaimed. "This is what you want. This is what you've always wanted!"

Loren shook his head and closed his eyes. The tendrils snapped around his neck, then ripped open his lids. There was no escaping the clutches of the void and the beast at the heart of his nightmare.

He waited for the end to embrace him when a new sensation fell upon his senses. A scent carried on the wind, swirling around him like a gust of fresh air.

Lilacs.

Their presence rejuvenated Loren. The tendrils weakened under his struggle. He fell to the ground to find it no longer black and vacant like the rest of the void, but solid and in the shape of the steps outside his apartment.

"Don't fight this, Detective," Shriff railed against the onslaught of the lilacs and the forming of the world. "We're connected."

Loren wheeled around sharply. The stairs continued to form right in front of his view, bending at the end of the corridor for another flight up.

"Greg…"

A voice penetrated the void, so clear and so strong, it brought him back to his feet. He took his first step away from the darkness into the light.

"Detective!"

Loren refused to look back at Shriff. Tendrils shot out, but he pushed through each attack. He had to hear the voice again, had to see who it belonged to, like a distant memory calling to him. The rooftop door stood before him. He grabbed the knob and twisted.

"Greg…"

Loren woke with a start. He jerked upright, a hand over his face as he shook loose from the dream. Shriff's cries continued to follow him and he peered around the room frantically in search of the demented killer. The apartment, though, was empty.

The dream had felt so vivid, so real.

Struggling to sit up, his body aching from the stress of the dream, Loren's gaze fell on the open window nearby. Rain poured in through the screen. The curtains and shade beat against the frame. The storm brought with it gusts of blistering wind that chilled the entire room.

Loren groaned in frustration. He thought he had shut it before he'd dozed off. Shuffling to the window, Loren closed the sash. The whistling wind continued to rush along the frame.

"It wasn't Shriff," he muttered under his breath. Loren sighed and rested heavily against the wall. "It was only the wind. Not him."

Finney's book sat on the coffee table near where he had fallen asleep. It was a dense read, though Loren had found himself enthralled with the subject.

Was there something to it? Was that the path he was meant to travel for the answers he sought?

Shriff's screams continued to beat against the walls of his mind. They called to him, begging him to connect. Loren struggled to push it aside.

"It was the wind," he repeated like a mantra. "It had to be."

The question remained, and Loren lifted the book once more. Finney's card sat inside. Loren ran his thumb over the cell number on the business card, then retrieved his phone from his fallen jacket.

Part of him knew it was a foolish thought. It had been a nightmare and nothing more. Yet, he clung to the card and to the belief of something more. As he started to dial, his cell rang loudly.

"Hello?" Loren answered. "Ruiz?"

"There's been another murder."

CHAPTER THIRTY-FIVE

The gloom held even as night faded over the city. Rain lessened, and the wind died down, but still the sun made no appearance in the sky, leaving the city with nothing but a haze of light at the dawn of another day.

Loren wanted nothing more than sleep. His troubled dreams followed him from his apartment toward the Riverside District. Cordons were in place, officers at the ready to handle any traffic diversions from the modestly busy area that fed from residential neighborhoods to the businesses of downtown.

Along one such stretch—on the eleven-hundred block of Griner—stood several small businesses. Medical offices covered the left-hand side. A pediatric facility stood at one end. At the other end was a psychiatric firm, the entrance barred by a crowd of uniformed officers.

Loren displayed his badge, a wordless greeting offered to the officer at the door. None was reciprocated and wasn't expected. Loren slipped inside and headed for the stairs, where he found signs pointing to the office of Dr. Simon Raynor.

Ruiz stood at the landing. He clutched the railing, like his entire body might collapse from exhaustion without some support. Loren understood completely after his own long night.

"I'm surprised you called," Loren said upon arriving at the top of the steps.

"Trust me, I didn't want to." Ruiz led him through the building. Three other offices—partners to Raynor, it seemed—were closed. Raynor's was left open. "I needed your opinion."

"On the tie?" Loren asked, pointing to the yellow and red striped monstrosity over Ruiz's chest. "It clashes with the shirt."

Ruiz stopped him with a glare. "It's going to be one of those days, eh?" He lifted the tie to look it over, then let it fall back against his purple shirt. "Michelle bought me this tie."

"She should know better."

Ruiz ushered him into Raynor's office. It was a sprawling space with a desk to the immediate left upon entering and two couches to the right for what Loren assumed were patient sessions.

A team of forensics worked diligently on all sides. They dusted every surface and scanned for any trace evidence. None took notice of Loren and Ruiz as they stepped between them.

"What are we looking at?" Loren glanced around for signs of the body. "You said a murder, but—"

It wasn't until he rounded the desk that Loren saw the dead man. An older gentleman, pushing sixty if Loren had to guess, lay on the carpet. His head and shoulders leaned along the base of a bookshelf with his legs sprawled out. Bloodstains ran in circles around the deceased. The trail started at the top of his bald head, where a deep blow had been struck by Raynor's attacker.

None of that mattered to Loren. They were necessary details to tell the story of what happened, but spoke to the victim, not his attacker. The one detail that locked in the killer, though, screamed for attention.

Simon Raynor's lips had been twisted into a smile.

Loren wheeled to face Ruiz, panic in his eyes.

Ruiz nodded. "Yeah. That was my reaction as well."

"It's… It's not possible."

"Yet here we are."

Loren stepped away from the body. He ran his hands through unkempt locks of hair, trying to rationalize the situation. "The Kindly Killer? Shriff is in Castlemere."

Ruiz's gaze fell to the floor, and he shifted away from the pacing Loren. "Then how?"

"Any prints? Fibers? Hair?" The questions fired rapidly at everyone in the room. No one offered an answer. Most didn't even bother to glance in his direction. All felt defeated at the return of a killer they believed to be behind bars.

Loren moved for the closest tech, looking for more information. Ruiz stopped him, a hand to his arm. "Hold up, Greg. This case is still Quinn's and Messick's."

Loren's brow furrowed. "You're kidding me. Why did you call?"

Ruiz escorted him back to the body. "You know more about this killer than any of us. You've spent months chasing this son of a bitch. I wanted your insight."

"As an obsessive, not a detective," Loren replied. "Thanks, Ruiz."

"What do you want from me?"

"That's what *I'm* wondering," Loren shot back. Ruiz didn't want him back in an official capacity. He merely wanted to bleed him dry of insight before kicking Loren back to the curb where he belonged—where he had been before Ruiz called him to the scene. This wasn't what Loren needed anymore. "I thought this was over. I wanted this to be over."

"A copycat?"

Loren sighed. He surveyed the scene. A single blow committed the murder, the same as the previous victims. The metronome next to the dead man was clearly the weapon used, most likely picked up at the last second in this very room. That act spoke to the same confusion presented by Shriff's murder scenes. Each could have easily been labeled as crimes of passion with no pre-meditation, but the methodical strike always threw that theory into doubt.

Everything lined up with Shriff. Everything pointed to the Kindly Killer being in the room at the time of the murder. A copycat, no matter how precise, could never deliver a scene so exact, could they?

"No," he said, in answer to his own thought. "Much as I would like it to be a copycat. Every detail matches the other scenes we've investigated. A single strike, the weapon definitely found here." He pointed to the bare spot on the middle shelf behind the victim. "And that damn smile…"

Ruiz didn't reply. He had clearly already reached the same conclusion. His old friend had simply needed a sounding board and a direction to take the investigation. It was a way to keep Loren informed without jeopardizing his position at the precinct. For as much as Loren appreciated the effort, it was unnecessary. He tired of the dead.

Loren stepped away from Raynor's body. "Let Quinn and Messick work the scene. I'll talk to Shriff. He has to know who this is. A partner, maybe." Ruiz refused to meet his eyes, causing Loren to groan. "Look, I know I messed up, but if anyone has a clue about this new killer, it has to be Shriff."

"I agree."

"Then you'll let me talk to him?"

Ruiz shook his head. "I'm afraid that's not possible."

"Dammit, Ruiz, listen—"

"You listen, Greg," Ruiz said. All eyes in the room turned to them. The captain's hands fell to his hips, his head to his chest, and he let out a long breath. When his eyes met Loren's, the exhaustion was back along with something new: desperation. "You can't talk to Shriff. I called Castlemere before you got here."

"What aren't you telling me, Ruiz?" Loren, though, already realized the answer. It made things much more complicated.

"Shriff is dead."

CHAPTER THIRTY-SIX

Tucked alongside the Raynor office building, Soriya spied from the shadows. She was pushing her luck. The muted sun offered enough light to give away her position, straddling the corner of the brick edifice, to the officers who ran back and forth below.

Traffic picked up; the detour caused snags along Griner, which spun off into the Riverside District. There were better ways to get around, though all had their drawbacks when it came to rush hour.

Those were petty distractions—the stresses of a normal life—compared to the nightmare within Raynor's office. Soriya couldn't believe what she had witnessed or overheard from Loren.

A copycat killer?

Loren had been right to dismiss such a theory. The second he had, Soriya left the discomfort of her position for the rooftop. She slid down the side of the ledge and pulled her knees in close. The roof was cold from the rain, but she ignored the elements—the entire world—to find some answers to the latest death.

How had the scene been replicated so perfectly? The single blow, the position of the body, the random weapon, and, of course, the smile all followed the strict rules set by the Kindly Killer.

The Riverside District was new hunting ground, however. Was that the key insight to pull away from Raynor's murder? Soriya didn't know what it meant, or how the clue might connect to Shriff's string of killings, or if it did at all.

No, something else was at play here. Soriya felt it in her bones, like an itch she couldn't scratch. Portents never offered a simple solution to any problem. Complications always presented, and Soriya knew this would be no different. This was something more, something far worse than a serial killer stalking the streets.

"Loren's going to need my help."

Their initial outing might have overwhelmed him, but Soriya could only give Loren so much time to figure things out. This was bigger than Loren's fears, more dangerous than her guilt over Beth's fall. He needed to understand, and quickly, before things became even worse.

Loren wasn't the only one who needed help. Realizing that, Soriya groaned into her open hands. Her questions about the latest murder, and the killer behind such an act, came with no immediate answers. Open questions meant research, which meant spending more time with Mentor… and his books. His many, many books.

Soriya rolled her eyes. That was the cost of being the Greystone.

She stood and shook away the damp air that surrounded her. With fleet feet, she took to the ledge and jumped to the adjacent roof. Hurried steps carried her away from Loren, toward home.

Every thought turned back to Loren, and with each one came more concern. She needed him to trust her, to see the city for what it truly was. After dealing with Tragedy and Comedy, Soriya hoped to give the detective time to acclimate to the new dynamic. This new killer made such a delay impossible. If Loren chose to go it alone, there was every chance he would end up like Beth.

The guilt would swallow Soriya whole if she lost Loren, too. It was too important to have him by her side in this.

She just had to show him why.

CHAPTER THIRTY-SEVEN

Rain returned in the afternoon. The soaking deluge permeated everything and everyone within the city limits. It washed over the car and chilled the occupants. They held their silence, the sounds of the storm taking over any need for conversation between them. The drive was slow and plodding with the growing traffic out to the Grove and Castlemere Institute.

Loren eyed the facility with dread. He didn't know what had brought him back. The news of Shriff's death haunted him. So did the body of Simon Raynor and the implications that came with his demise. The Kindly Killer was back somehow, yet dead at the same time. The situation made about as much sense as Loren's desire to return to Castlemere.

Gates joined him for the journey. Shriff's death affected her as well. Her unanswered questions lingered, though this time she kept them to herself. She was merely an escort, using her personal car—a dark blue Kia Forte—rather than a police cruiser. Neither had a leg to stand on in terms of the official inquiry into Shriff or the Raynor case.

Their curiosity simply won out over common sense.

Ruiz had fought him on the trip. His worry for Loren had pulled him from the case and from the obsessive life that had consumed much of the detective's existence. In the end, though, despite wanting nothing more to do with the murder and mayhem of Portents, the journey was Loren's to make.

Gates opened an umbrella upon exiting the car. Loren, having no foresight, let the rain wash over him in buckets. His soaked sneakers squished under him with each step. Gates tried to share the small shield from the elements, but Loren pressed on ahead without a word of gratitude.

Stepping through the main entrance, both stopped to see the heads of Castlemere. Finney and Olson were joined by a third gentleman who wore a button-down shirt and khakis. A thick auburn beard covered much of his face, accompanied by wide-framed glasses. Loren didn't need to read the nametag pinned to his chest to know it was Clyde Deckart, the head of Castlemere. The doctor's angry, booming tone made his position at the institute crystal clear.

"I want answers, Arnold!" Deckart yelled, a finger to the chest of his colleague. "Another mistake under your watch and there won't be a thing I can do to save your career. Not again."

Finney gazed down at the aggressive finger digging into his shirt. "Clyde…"

"Don't sing me a sob story," Deckart railed without concern. The eyes in the room didn't dissuade him from airing out his grievance in public. If anything, the presence of so many staffers provided Deckart with the audience he seemed to desire. "I've put my life into this institute, and I won't have its reputation tarnished. Or my own. Find my access key. Get Olson's people on it. Hell, get the cleaning staff and the kitchen detail on it as well. If we can't control what happens in our own house, we might never—"

Loren cleared his throat loudly. Even after the first wave of coughs, he continued to draw out the sound until Deckart's finger fell away. The focus of his anger shifted toward the door and the pair of newcomers to the institute.

"Can I help you?"

Loren opened his mouth to answer, a thousand clever replies ready to spout. Gates held a hand out to his arm, a look of concern in her eyes. Loren offered a nod of understanding, then took a step toward the intimate gathering of Castlemere officials.

Before Loren could introduce himself, Finney intervened. "It's all right, Clyde. I have this."

Deckart's hand fell on Finney's shoulder. Fingers dug into his flesh. "I'm serious, Arnold. Fix this mess."

The head of Castlemere pushed off Finney before heading through the open double door divider and the stairwell beyond. Finney stumbled slightly from the shove, a hand to his glasses to keep them from slipping to the ground. He righted himself in the next step, then tossed a false smile on his face to greet his new guests.

"Rough day, Doc?"

Finney rubbed at his shoulder. At Loren's glance, he moved the hand up to his head and ran his fingers through what little hair remained. The smile faded and his voice lowered as he drew them near.

"There have already been calls from the state to shut us down. Our own lovely mayor hasn't helped matters."

Reginald Dunn. The man was an idiot, elected by a landslide thanks to the uneducated or those too fed up to care. The way people kissed his ass, Loren wondered if Portents would ever get rid of him.

"You must not have donated enough last election cycle," Loren said.

Finney chuckled, then ushered them for the stairs. "What can I do for you, Greg?"

Something in the way the doctor said Loren's name instantly comforted him. The way he had remembered his preference, like they were old friends.

"I'd like to see what happened."

Finney stopped at the landing, weary eyes unable to meet them. "You really wouldn't." He continued down the corridor, away from Deckart's personal wing, for his office. At the door, he sighed. "Then again..."

They entered. Gates closed the door lightly. Loren followed close to Finney, who circled the desk. He padded the wrinkled button-down along his chest. Sitting at the desk, he pulled the laptop close.

"Nothing appeared out of the ordinary," Finney said as the security camera footage from that morning filled the screen. It was taken from the cafeteria, one of the few areas missed during their previous visit. Shriff stood in line, bent over and hobbled from his altercation earlier in the week. The man who had beaten him, Saprowski, was in the room as well.

"Our patients are well versed in kitchen etiquette," Finney continued. "Mr. Saprowski has helped during meal times on many occasions without incident."

On the monitor, the giant of an inmate moved around the counter toward the back of the kitchen. He grabbed an apron as if to help with the cooking or cleaning.

"So no one questioned him behind the counter?" Loren asked.

"I have a question," Gates interjected.

Loren turned toward her, curious. "Gates?"

She pointed to the screen. "What the hell was that maniac doing in the same room as Shriff after what happened?"

Finney pinched the bridge of his nose. He pushed his glasses back into position. "Mr. Saprowski wished to make amends."

"He certainly wished something," Gates snapped. "I don't think amends made the list."

Loren cut her off with a raised hand toward the screen. "Can we?"

Gates nodded, though her frustration was obvious. He couldn't argue the point. Neither of them could. What happened next only made the mistake worse.

Saprowski, mitts covering his hands, grabbed a tray of grease from beneath the griddle used for bacon. He lifted it over the counter and dumped the contents on a shocked and baffled Shriff. Screams of agony at the still steaming liquid filled the room.

Finney's voice was low and pained. "By the time the staff realized what was happening, it was too late. Mr. Shriff was covered in grease, and…"

A lighter rested in Saprowski's now bare hand. He flicked the flame into position, a mad gleam in his eye. The flame connected with the grease. Fire consumed Shriff in seconds.

"Dear Lord," Gates exclaimed. Her hand shot to her mouth, horror in her eyes. "I… I can't. I'm sorry."

She rushed for the door. Whipping it open, Gates ran out of the room without a second glance back.

Loren hesitated for a moment. He should have followed to check on her. More than that, he should have stopped watching the damn replay of a man's demise. He failed on all fronts.

Shriff burned. His howling screams reverberated through the speakers. Security rushed in, extinguishers in hand, but it was clear they were far too late to do anything to save Shriff.

Loren waited until the man fell to the ground, then he looked away. "Turn it off."

Finney did so. He settled deeper into his seat. "We don't know who gave him access to the lighter. As a man with a history of arson, there were precautions against feeding his mania."

"Your precautions failed, Doc."

"They did, yes."

Loren leaned against the desk. "And Saprowski?"

"In isolation," Finney answered. "He will be permanently kept in the violent offenders' ward. There is no coming back from this, I'm afraid."

Loren nodded, trying to process everything. Shriff was dead. He had been asking for closure, and it arrived in the worst way imaginable. Nothing but questions remained, but Finney's held the most weight in that moment.

"Will she be all right?" He looked to the closed door as if he could see Gates still rushing for the exit.

Loren shrugged. He wished for a better answer. "Gates sees only the good in the world."

"I used to as well, Greg," Finney replied. "But seeing this? Sometimes I wonder if there was any good in the first place."

CHAPTER THIRTY-EIGHT

Loren and Finney strolled through the institute. Images of Shriff's death lingered in their thoughts and halted their pace from Finney's office, down the steps to the reception area.

"You said you didn't know who gave Saprowski the lighter," Loren said, running through the details offered. "Do you know how?"

"Yes," Finney replied with some regret in his voice. He ran his fingers across his forehead. "It was the cause of that unfortunate discussion you walked in on earlier."

"Discussion is one word for it." Loren peered at the private corridor used by the head of the institute with disdain. "Deckart wanted to tear you a new one."

"I was the one running the shift last night. The blame falls on me."

"Not completely," Loren said, to lift the doctor's spirits. No one could have foreseen what happened to Shriff. Loren certainly hadn't. Yet, he felt he should have known something was coming. His dream had spoken to their connection.

Finney stopped at the bottom of the stairs. His voice lowered to keep from being overheard by the staffers moving through the facility. "The keycard used to access Mr. Saprowski's room last night was Clyde's."

Deckart's card? That was a wrinkle, to be sure. It didn't reflect too kindly on the angry head of the institute. "Did you see Deckart last night?"

"In the early evening," Finney said, a hand to his chin. "He typically heads home around six or seven."

"Typically?"

Finney nodded. "He sometimes remains in his office to pull an all-nighter. There is a lot of paperwork involved in running the institute."

That was one possibility—one of far too many. Loren pointed across the room for the security station at the rear. "Can you verify his departure? Security cameras of the parking lot catch him leaving?"

Finney's gaze lowered. He held the corner of his glasses to keep them from falling. "That is where our issue comes from, I'm afraid. Something sent a surge through our security network. All cameras were out for most of the night."

"Including the patient's ward," Loren surmised from the expression on the doctor's face.

"Most of us were dealing with the surge," Finney confirmed.

"Leaving anyone with the stolen keycard access to Saprowski." Loren stared back up the stairwell to the branching hallway and the private access afforded Deckart. When he looked back, Finney stared at him coldly.

"Clyde wouldn't have done that."

"But you can't say for certain."

The doctor's eyes wavered. He recovered quickly, but the doubt held for a second. "As I said, if he decided to hole up in his office for the night, no one would know. He has private facilities, a pull-out couch, anything he might need."

"And no way to monitor him."

Deckart stepped out from the hall upstairs. Loren and Finney caught a stern glare from him before they started for the main entrance.

"Where does he keep his access card?"

"On his person at all times," Finney said. "He used it for our group session in the afternoon, in fact. Sometime afterwards, he noticed it was missing. I can send you a list of the patients involved if you'd—"

Loren held up his hands to stop the man. "I'm not exactly here in an official capacity, Doc."

"Oh," Finney said in surprise. "I can relay the details to your captain, then."

"Probably a good idea."

They stopped shy of the front door. Gates leaned along the railing to the left of the landing. The steep overhang kept her dry from the storm, but the wind plagued her long, dark hair. She still appeared ill from the footage, visibly shaken by the horror that took Shriff from the world.

Finney gave Loren a queer look when he faced him at the entrance. Loren's brow furrowed. "What?"

"I'm simply curious. Why did you come today?"

"Yeah," Loren muttered. He ran his hand through his hair, rubbing deep for a suitable answer. He came up short. "I'm still trying to figure that one out myself."

"It's difficult to disconnect," Finney said with a degree of understanding few others could achieve. "To take a break."

Loren nodded. He stifled a yawn, covering his lips with a fist.

"Having trouble sleeping?"

"I had a helluva nightmare last night. Couldn't rest after." Loren let out a low laugh. "It's funny. I almost called you about the whole thing."

"Really?" Finney leaned along the door frame, intrigued.

"It's silly, Doc," Loren said with a dismissive wave.

"Yet the dream is still following you around. Why?"

"I thought…" Loren let out a deep breath. "It was Shriff. He was chasing me, telling me to embrace some connection between us."

"A connection?"

"Something he'd said during my interrogation with him." Loren closed his eyes. He could feel the tendrils snaking toward him and the deep cold they brought with them. A shiver trailed up his spine. "He believed we were the same."

"Fascinating."

Finney shifted closer, studying Loren like a prize specimen for the psych ward. "I don't like that gleam in your eye, Doc."

"I take it you started my book?"

"Read a bit before I fell asleep. Is that why—"

"Possibly," Finney interjected. "Dreams, though, are a curious medium. They hold power, opening doors to the past and the future. Do you believe there was more to your encounter with Walter?"

"It was a nightmare. That's it."

"Maybe," Finney said. "Or maybe it meant something much more."

CHAPTER THIRTY-NINE

A chill wind bit into Gates. She tucked close to the pillar at the peak of the steps to Castlemere, her jacket bunched around her to keep the rain out.

She couldn't stay inside, not after seeing Shriff burn to death. No one deserved that end. No matter what a person had done in their lives, the terror created and the victims taken from their families, no one should have met their fate in such a manner.

It sickened her. For every ounce of hope she displayed, she received another glimpse of the darkest in humanity. No one else appeared to care about the man's passing, either. The sheer disregard for Shriff frightened Gates beyond the image of death that carried her from the institute to the driving rain outside.

Loren and Finney stood in the entryway. The pair shared a laugh and a handshake. Gates sat in disbelief at how close the two had become in such a short amount of time. None of the hard questions seemed to be asked of the negligent doctor who had allowed Shriff's death under his watch. Instead, there was contented joy.

Gates pushed from the railing when Loren departed the institute. Finney remained at the door. Loren glanced at Gates, concern fading quickly when he clearly noted the anger in her eyes.

"You're leaving already?"

Loren nodded. "Shriff is dead."

Gates huffed. "And his killer…"

"Is in custody." Loren spun to face her. Rain swept the air around him as his arms outstretched. "What do you want from me, Gates?"

He couldn't see it. To Loren, the case was closed. All meaningful inquiry ended with the Kindly Killer's death. He carried no suspicion at the timing of his death: the same morning the first body from a copycat killer was discovered.

Beyond that were her lingering doubts about Shriff as the Kindly Killer. How could a man filled with such rage simply surrender? Where had the rage gone? The second he entered Castlemere, Shriff changed. He was remorseful over his murderous acts. Those were not the makings of the man who had driven the city of Portents into a panic for most of the last year.

Shriff had wanted death at the end. His regret over the nightmares playing behind his eyes was clear. Yet only Gates saw it.

Everyone else had left the case long ago.

Loren, fed up with arguing, continued toward the parked car in the entry loop. Gates rushed after him. She swept her soaked hair back, not bothering with the umbrella thanks to the wind.

"How the hell did that maniac have access to a lighter?"

Loren reached for the handle of the car door. "They're looking into it."

"But not you?" she asked in amazement.

"They'll keep Ruiz informed."

"Not exactly the hands-on approach I'd expect from a seasoned detective," Gates shot back.

"Feel free to dig around, Gates," Loren said with dead eyes. "I'll be in the car."

He opened the door without another word and slipped inside. Gates wanted to scream at him more. His total disregard was unlike anything she could have imagined when discussing the so-called master investigator Pratchett believed Loren to be.

Unfortunately, he wasn't the only one who had given up. Gates stared back at Castlemere through the pouring rain. Deckart and Olson had joined Finney at the entrance. The arguments started again. Deckart was heated, screaming, though his words died on the whipping wind of the storm. Finney bowed his head. He took his berating in stride. Olson, of course, interjected continuously. He surely wasn't going to take the blame for what had happened.

None of them wanted that. Every word said, every argument expressed, showed their true nature to the once-optimistic officer.

"A man is dead and they're too worried about covering their own asses," she murmured in the gloom of Portents. A sickened glance fell on the car and her passenger. "Or they're not worried at all."

Gates rounded the car. Her feet stomped through the deepening puddles of the driveway. She wondered when they would pull her under like they had everyone else around her. None cared about the dead man at the center of the entire affair. They worried for themselves and the fallout to come.

Shriff was dead, and no one was going to figure out why. No one cared except for Gates, who witnessed nothing but apathy surrounding her.

"What is happening to this city?"

CHAPTER FORTY

Another book launched across the cramped living space. The hardcover landed with a thud on the pile, then slid down to join its brethren in an ever-expanding mess that covered much of the floor.

Soriya didn't care. She moved on to the next tome on the shelf, which dealt with multiversal shifts in reality. Even the title was over her head, and she tossed the book away without opening. None followed her train of thought over the latest Kindly Killer scene.

The collected works that occupied the entire right-hand wall of the room featured every iteration of myth and legend passed down from the ages. The Japanese Kojiki sat beside a detailed account of the pharaohs of Egypt who butted against angel sightings in America. All read as more rational alternatives to anything that crossed Soriya's mind when she pictured the death of Simon Raynor.

A copycat killer wasn't possible. The scene had been too precise, too knowledgeable of Shriff's methods, to be anyone but the killer himself. It was another impossibility added to the mental pile which stacked higher than the one on the floor behind her.

How was the Kindly Killer still active if he was in custody? The question carried Soriya from shelf to shelf, no longer content to go in order. She glimpsed titles, removed a book for a quick scan of the contents, then moved on without a second glance. *And where the hell are the answers?*

The sound of another book hitting the floor stopped her. It fell with the same resounding thud, but when it slid to the floor, the cover failed to whistle along the carpet. Soriya lifted her head from her search to see a shadow pass over her.

A sigh escaped her. "I could do without the lurking."

Mentor stood in the doorway, a smile on his face. "I don't

lurk."

"You're lurking right now," Soriya said with an accusing finger. "You're a lurker. It's off-putting."

Mentor leaned along the door frame. "Would it help if I sat during your tantrum?"

"Sure." Mentor stepped over the pile of books for the cot in the corner. Soriya shook her head. "Somewhere else."

Mentor paused. He rubbed at his right knee, the old wound clearly acting up. He would blame the weather, but she knew there was more to it: Mentor was getting older.

Soriya pushed the idea away, afraid of being alone in the Bypass. She had too many other concerns to become focused on a future that was far off. The books took the brunt of her frustration. They offered nothing of value, and she tossed them aside.

"Why can't I figure this out?"

Before she could launch another book across the room, Mentor snatched it from her. "What are you looking for?"

She groaned. He was right to ask, right to be by her side, if only as a sounding board. "You heard the latest?"

"A new victim," Mentor said with a slight nod. "The press believes it to be a copycat killer."

"It can't be." Soriya stepped away from her search for the fireplace at the far end of the room. Her hand rested on the mantel. "You didn't see the scene, Mentor. It was meticulous to the last detail. Everything screamed Shriff's involvement."

"Perhaps there was always a partner involved."

That would have made things easier, yet something about the scenario struck Soriya as wrong. Maybe it was the way his coworkers looked at him with disdain, or how quickly they laughed at his misfortune.

"No," she said with the shake of her head. "Shriff was a loner. Greeter or no, he didn't have a friend in the world. Mostly because he couldn't stomach the depravity of the rest of us."

Mentor's arms crossed over his chest and huffed audibly at her summation. "That sounds more like the detective's insight than your own. You sought him out, didn't you?"

"Mentor…"

"Has it helped?" he pressed. "Has it helped either of you with the guilt?" Her silence offered the only answer possible. "I didn't think so."

"She was my friend," Soriya snapped.

"That doesn't mean he will be," Mentor replied. "This world is not meant for all."

"He'll understand." Soriya swiped at the mantel, then headed back to the shelves. "He'd probably have this solved if he knew the truth."

Mentor held her up with a hand to her shoulder. "Or he may have run away. From Portents. From monsters in the dark. From you."

She forced his hand away, unwilling to meet his gaze. "This isn't about Loren."

"No, I suppose you're right," Mentor said. "For once."

Soriya rolled her eyes. "Nice save. I don't know how I would handle an actual compliment."

She lowered her knee to the ground for a better view of the bottom shelves. She dug through text after text until her eyes alighted at the tomes at the end of the row. Pulling them loose, she carried them to the table and opened each in turn.

Mentor took up a position on the other end, watching her mindfully. He held his tongue as she scanned the nearest works. When his patience waned, he asked the same question she'd struggled to answer the entire time.

"If there was no accomplice, how was the murder committed?"

Soriya held out the book in her hands. "Astral projection?"

Mentor took the tome, his hand upon the pages. "It's possible, yet very difficult to maintain for such a violent act. Besides, who might carry such an ability?"

"Shriff," Soriya answered. "He—"

"Walter Shriff is dead."

Her eyes widened with shock. Mentor retrieved the paper from his cloak pocket and passed it along with the book on astral projection. Soriya let the book fall away. She scanned the article.

"He's dead," she muttered. Her only suspect was gone. Shriff had to have been the killer. He had attacked her. But if he was dead, how had someone recreated one of his murders so perfectly?

She continued through the paper. A thin column near the bottom of the page focused on the upcoming trial of Tragedy. The image showed a profile shot of the frowning figure, the tattoo of the masks prominent on his neck.

The tattoo…

Comedy's words echoed through her mind. *"We've been wearing these skins for months. They did well in a pinch, but time wears on everyone. You see, Officer, eventually the meat rots."*

"What if… What if it wasn't Shriff at all?"

"I'm not following."

It came to her like a crashing storm. All that anger that welled up in Shriff hadn't been present when she had encountered him at the CostSmart. It had been buried beneath the weak persona he shared with the world—like camouflage.

"Soriya, what are you thinking?"

She left the books behind. The answer wasn't in any of them, not the one that overtook her. She looked at her teacher, hands before her. "Possession."

Mentor straightened at the suggestion. "There has never been an incursion like it before."

"First time for everything."

Mentor grimaced at her cavalier rationalization. He turned to the Bypass and its connection to all worlds. The glowing orb of light served as a bridge to the infinite, but both knew other doors existed and were exploited.

"Think it through, Soriya." Mentor stood, pacing the room. "If an entity escaped the Bypass or from the myriad dimensional planes in existence, they have always regained their physical form."

"How do you explain ghost sightings?"

"From the lucid or drug-addled?" he asked with a wry smirk. She huffed at his response. Grumbling, Mentor continued. "Ghosts, typically, are at a transference point. Building up power to reclaim their form. New arrivals go through much the same thing when, and if, they escape into our reality."

There was no lore to speak of, no historical record anywhere in Mentor's extensive files that confirmed Soriya's theory. Yet, through it all, she couldn't dismiss it. Though everything demanded a more logical explanation for the sudden rise of a second Kindly Killer, Soriya's gut told her possession was the key.

"This is it, Mentor," she said. "I don't know how, but something is loose in the city. And it could be anyone."

Mentor wanted to argue. Instead, he offered a resigned glare of submission. "Then we are in uncharted territory."

Soriya agreed with a silent nod. She closed the tomes on the table and returned them to the shelf. Standing, Soriya started for the door. Mentor barred her path with an outstretched hand.

"I'd advise caution," he said.

Soriya smirked. "Do you know who you're talking to?"

"Why do you think I said it?"

She took his hand in hers and squeezed. Letting him fall away, Soriya continued over the pile of books and into the Bypass Chamber. She gazed at the glowing orb, wishing for confirmation of her theory. The answers were there, but she couldn't wait to unlock them.

The threat was loose in the city.

She left for the stairs, the stone at her side and the Ribbons of Kali stretching along her left arm. If the Kindly Killer had possessed someone, the threat was graver than anyone realized. Through it all, though, only one person mattered to Soriya.

She needed to tell Loren. They needed to work together to find the newest host to the killer before they jumped bodies again.

And before more bodies turned up.

CHAPTER FORTY-ONE

The shadow felt the urge rising in his chest. It had sat there, burrowing deeper and deeper into his very soul, the moment after the first death. *Simon Raynor... the hack.* He had done nothing for the medical community but serve his own interests. Petty rivalries had cost innocent victims their livelihood.

Raynor deserved to die for what he'd put others through over the years. He wasn't alone in that regard.

The shadow didn't realize he was following his next victim until he was already halfway home. He had been wandering the streets, searching for an answer to a question he didn't even know, when Matthew Sinclair left the office for the night. The man had paid no attention to the passing shadow, nor to anyone else in his way.

Sinclair had always displayed a certain arrogance when it came to his position in the community. Not only did this pertain to the medical profession, but as a member of the Board of Trustees for several companies, pharmaceutical research firms, schools, and more. Everything he touched became his and his alone. No one else brought value in his eyes, and he had used his vast wealth to destroy all others who tried to follow in his footsteps.

The walk went quickly. The shadow trailed his target in a haze, as if someone had dropped a veil over his vision and only Sinclair remained. A deep urge burrowed through him like fire in his veins. It begged for release. It screamed for retribution.

Then he was there: Sinclair's home. The estate stood on a corner lot in the Riverside District, close to the man's office. The street was desolate. No one walked the block as the sun waned. The distance between properties afforded more privacy than was necessary, and served the shadow's purposes perfectly.

He waited for Sinclair to enter. Using the tall foliage surrounding the rear of the property, the shadow found a quiet place to hide. With each passing moment, however, the urge increased. Memories of Sinclair slammed into him. The shadow recalled every utterance, every derision, and every spiteful deed.

By the time the shadow snapped out of his spiraling thoughts, night had settled over the neighborhood. The sound of crickets in the trees, the buzzing bugs enjoying an intermission between storm fronts, filled the air. The shadow paused in his hiding place until the last light went out in the Sinclair home.

Taking his time, he crept toward the home. Gloves slipped over his steady hands. The mudroom window shattered under his fist, covered by his jacket to muffle the sound. The lock snapped open and the door followed suit.

The shadow was in.

He scurried through the house, scanning room after room for signs of life on the first floor, but found none. It wasn't until he reached the den that he glimpsed someone. The shadow's reflection stared back at him through the mirror over the mantelpiece. His eyes were harried, his face distraught, like a man possessed instead of the centered intellectual he knew himself to be. Anger sat in those wide eyes, anger he barely recognized. The shadow moved for the mirror and stared deep into those strange eyes.

"I have to do this."

Images lined the wall around the mantel. Family photos included Sinclair with his wife, Darla, on various vacations. From beaches in Europe to cruises along the Caribbean, the couple traveled the world with the money earned off the backs of others.

Rage grew in the shadow's chest. He pulled an image off the wall and gripped it tight. "You pushed me to this. Your arrogance. Your small-minded criticisms of pure genius. You took my future."

He threw the photo to the floor with a crash. Glass shattered, and the frame cracked from the impact. The shadow stomped on it repeatedly while he held back a scream.

The shattered photo echoed throughout the dark domicile. From the den, the shadow heard the shuffling of feet above and then a light clicked on at the top of the stairs.

"Hello?" Sinclair called.

The shadow's fists clenched at the sound of the man's voice. He bent low and retrieved a large shard of the broken glass. "You took mine. So I'll take yours."

Sinclair slowly descended the stairs. Each one creaked under his weight. "Darla? Is that you?"

Sinclair reached the bottom of the staircase. He hugged the wall, unsure of himself in the darkness, then pushed off at the sound of movement in the den.

"Dear?"

The shadow stepped into the dim light afforded by the moon. "Your wife isn't here. I'm afraid you won't be seeing her tonight. Or ever again."

Sinclair staggered back, a hand to his chest. "Who?"

The shadow loomed taller in the room. His eyes widened with anticipation. Light glittered off the shard of glass. "Don't you remember me?"

Sinclair shook his head, but with each passing moment, recognition filled his terrified eyes. "What… What do you want?"

"Control of my life back," the shadow spat in fury. "Control you stole from me."

"Now look," Sinclair said. He raised his hands before him defensively, staggering toward the stairwell. "We can… We can talk about this!"

"No more talking."

The shadow swiped the air once with the shard. The blow caught Sinclair in the jugular and cut clean through. A spurt of blood shot across the room. Sinclair tried to cover it up with his hands, but nothing would stem the bleeding. His life gushed from his body, and he collapsed to the ground with a gurgle instead of a roar.

The shadow dropped the shard to the ground. It clattered against the floor and came to rest in the growing pool of crimson beside Sinclair. Blood ran down his cheek, on the sleeve of his jacket, and on the gloves he wore to conceal his prints.

Sinclair lay with his face to the ground. Carefully, the shadow flipped him over. The body spasmed slightly and more blood spurted before it turned to a trickle. The shadow set to work, wiping the terror from the dead man's lips. He twisted them into a smile.

"No more thinking," the shadow said. "No more agonizing over everything. Just acting. It feels good. It feels…"

He looked back and caught his reflection in the mirror once more. The anger vanished, the urge cleansed for the time being. In its place was a malicious grin. The image nodded to him, content for now.

"Right," the shadow said in the darkness of the Sinclair home. "Yes. It was the right thing to do. I didn't have a choice."

CHAPTER FORTY-TWO

Soriya lifted the sash on the window. She was grateful for the storm's reprieve, though the distant rumble made her wonder if they were simply caught in the calm before the next great push. She stepped inside, careful not to disturb the rotted plants along the ledge.

Dishes filled the sink in the kitchen. Crumbs from sandwiches past were visible throughout the stack. The floor carried a film on it from neglect. Stray dust bunnies piled in the corners and webs ran from the ceiling around the light fixture over the small table next to the fridge.

She should have knocked on the door. That would have been the sensible thing to do. For so long, though, Soriya had had to sneak around Beth's life. Her deceased friend had been so concerned with keeping Loren in the dark over their adventures, Soriya had always used the window to visit.

Old habits.

Loren leaned along the frame of the front window in the living room. He looked out at the street below, his sullen eyes reflected in the glass. Everything weighed on him from the way his shoulders slumped.

This is the wrong move, Soriya continued to think with each passing step. Yet as she crossed the threshold to the living room, she knew it was too late to backtrack. She needed to bring Loren up to speed and quickly. Concern be damned.

The moment she reached the end of the couch, Loren spun on his heels. His gun was in his hand, a finger over the trigger.

"Not another step!" he yelled. Recognizing the intruder in his midst, his eyes widened and the weapon fell to his side. "You?"

Soriya raised her hands sheepishly. "Me."

Loren jammed the gun back in his holster. "What the hell? It's bad enough you seem to know everything about me, but now you think you can waltz in here like you own the place? I almost—" He cut himself off from finishing the argument. A frustrated wave and a sigh escaped him. "Ah, the hell with it. One more thing out of my control. Like this city, right?"

Soriya backed away as Loren approached. He rounded the corner of the couch, then collapsed against the far cushion which sunk almost to the wood beneath him. He leaned forward, his hands clutched tight together between his knees.

"The true city, you called it," Loren said. "How can that be, if I never saw it that way?"

Soriya took a peek around the room. When Beth had been alive, flowers sat in every corner with decorations on every wall. Now there were none. The mantel bore a single image from Loren's wedding day. The wall to Soriya's right was completely bare, except for some stray pieces of tape that once held something to the surface. Sitting near the door by the coat rack was a single box, stuffed to the brim with what appeared to be official police reports.

"Loren…" She pointed to the box. "What's all this?"

Loren trailed her finger. "Everything on Shriff. The Kindly Killer. I don't even know who anymore."

His doubts about the killer were one thing. Loren had taken it to a whole new level, though. "You're walking away?"

Loren stood. "It's not my case. It hasn't been in some time. He didn't kill Beth. You agreed with me on that. So what am I even doing?"

"Looking for an answer."

Loren chuckled. "You sound like Gates."

Soriya's brow furrowed with confusion.

Loren shook his head. "Nothing. Never mind."

He started back to the window and the night outside. Soriya moved beside him. "There's more to this case, Loren. More than a simple killer on the loose."

"You're right," Loren replied. "There's at least two now."

"No. That's not…" She bit her lip slightly. This was it, the moment she had been dreading since revealing her presence to Loren. She didn't have a choice but to take the next step with him, no matter the consequences. "I believe Shriff might have been innocent. To a certain degree."

"What?" Loren exclaimed. "What are you saying?"

She tried to find the right words. None came, so she let out a long breath and let her theory fly. "He was possessed by the actual killer."

Loren's jaw sagged open. He stared at her in disbelief. "I'm sorry. Run that by me again?"

Soriya took a step closer, locking eyes with him. "An entity took over Shriff's body, or manipulated an already mentally ill man into committing murder."

Loren let the words wash over him. He left the comfort of the window to pace the length of the room. On the return trip, he stopped. "Have you lost your mind?"

"Loren, listen—"

"Shriff killed eight people!" Loren bellowed. "That we know of! The department has reached out to old neighbors and colleagues from years past without success, so who knows how many he tallied before we became aware of him? You caught him trying to take your head off with a damn bat. He did all that. End of story."

"How do you explain the latest murder?"

"I…" His response fell away to silence.

Soriya approached him slowly, hands before her. "I'm right about this, Loren. This is much bigger than either of us imagined.

"You saw Comedy and Tragedy. Possession isn't a stretch when it comes to masks able to take over a host body. You saw that, Loren. If the Kindly Killer can do that as well, we need to start thinking about who—"

"No," Loren said. His gaze hardened with his voice. "I'm sorry. I can't go down the rabbit hole with you. I won't."

"How do you explain—"

"I don't have to!" Loren shouted. "It's not my case!"

Soriya fell back a step at the force of his words.

Her reaction caused him to take a breath, hands on his hips. "Look. I… I don't know if I'm going back to active casework. Not for a while. Not until I get things sorted out. I'm done. So go ahead and see yourself out."

He returned to the window and the cold dark outside. Soriya wanted to push harder, to drag him kicking and screaming back to the case—back to her—but stopped herself. This wasn't how it was supposed to happen. Loren was going to join her, to fight alongside her. She was going to save him by showing him the truth about everything.

Now, because of her, he seemed more lost than ever.

"I thought better of you, Loren."

"Well, you were wrong," he said without looking. "This is exactly who I am."

"I doubt that," Soriya said. She held tight to the kitchen entryway and caught his reflection once more. "I'm sure you do as well."

She didn't stay for a rebuttal. A brisk pace brought her to the still-open window, then out into the night.

Disappointment followed her. So did Mentor's warnings. She wished he hadn't been right, but none of that mattered any longer.

Only the killer mattered. Promise to Beth or not, with or without Loren, Soriya needed to end the threat of the Kindly Killer once and for all.

CHAPTER FORTY-THREE

Mentor shuffled the last of the books from the table to the floor at his side. He had spent the better part of his evening rummaging through every text tossed aside by his student to find the solution she had missed in her so-called research. For every theory offered by the library at his feet, holes quickly followed.

Soriya's theory, however, stuck with him.

"Could it be?"

In all his years as the Greystone, from student to teacher, Mentor had encountered nothing like possession before. That something beyond the veil could influence people in the world without a physical form, and to such a degree, was nothing if not terrifying.

With beings like Comedy and Tragedy, there were the masks at least. Obols of power controlled the possession, overtaking the host body in an instant. Nothing in the Kindly Killer showed that level of power.

Mentor stood and stretched. His back cracked and his knees ached, though his right always irritated him after a long day. Soriya had clearly noticed the strain. He tried his best to hide it from her, but the pain was getting worse. Disregarding his discomfort, Mentor left the small domicile tucked in the corner of the expansive chamber.

The Bypass swirled before him. It hovered over the ground like a spinning top. Mentor hesitated when he felt the pull of the majestic intersection of reality calling to him. Slowly, he approached.

"I have to be sure."

He stepped beyond the barrier of the four pillars. Taking his position in front of the Bypass, Mentor sat and crossed his legs before him. He removed his Greystone from the pouch at his side. It lay before him, the surface blank for the moment.

The Bypass was a conduit to everything in the universe. Every now, and every possibility, existed within. The mysteries lay hidden from view, but one could gain insight through the proper methods—and a bit of good luck.

"Hopefully, you're feeling talkative."

Asking the Bypass, though, was not without risk. Look too deeply and suddenly one might be pulled deep into the ether, never to return. He had seen it happen before, though the experience was under much more deadly circumstances.

At the thought of the past, Mentor instinctively ran his finger along the scar on his left cheek. It trailed from his temple to his ear, another in a long series of injuries that marked his time as the Greystone.

More than anything, Mentor preferred to leave the Bypass alone when investigating the dangers that cropped up in Portents. Study was where he excelled thanks to his former life as a professor. It was one he had tried to impart to Soriya with mixed results.

There were times she was as in tune with the situation as he was. She scoured ancient texts for knowledge lost to the ages, unlocking secrets to help those in need. Other times, though, Soriya did nothing but barrel ahead and hope for the best. It had worked out on most occasions, but how long would that last?

The questions, in this particular case, required a more direct approach. Stopping the threat was too important to leave to the random chance Soriya seemed to rely on of late. Mentor closed his eyes and set to work. Before him, the Greystone lit.

"Show me the Kindly Killer."

Within his mind's eye, Mentor was pulled along the surface of the swirling mass of glowing green energy. Shriff's image joined him, though his form appeared covered with shadow. His body shifted from that of a man to a growing darkness and back again repeatedly.

"I do not want the facade he hides behind," Mentor continued. He channeled more will through the stone, and the light grew. "Not the unseen mask of a man. Reveal him to me. The true presence. Peel back the shadows. Show me…"

Shriff faded from view. Mentor was left with nothing in the Bypass. He fought through the resistance of the swirling mass. By the time he realized he had pushed too far, it was much too late.

Darkness seeped into his vision. Sharp flashes of black stabbed at him. The force sent him faltering back to the surface, like the Bypass deliberately resisted his question. More shadows snaked out from the orb; tendrils of darkness reached for him. They flew toward Mentor, whipping through the air like chains.

"Wait! Don't!"

A crack of air from the tendrils snapped Mentor from the Bypass completely. His body flew back, sailing across the chamber for the domicile on the far end. He crashed into the outer wall of his bedroom and rebounded to the floor with a thud.

Mentor struggled to stand. He rubbed at his wounded knee. A staggered step forward almost brought him back to the ground before he steadied himself.

Concerned eyes scanned the Bypass. It had never hindered him in such a way before, never stood in the way of his pursuit of knowledge.

"How?" Mentor collected his Greystone, still warm to the touch from his interaction with the Bypass. Another attempt was ill-advised. He tucked the stone away rather than incur more of the swirling orb's rage. "The answers are there, aren't they? Yet you hold them back. Why?"

It was almost as if the Kindly Killer's murders somehow served the Bypass' plans.

CHAPTER FORTY-FOUR

Loren felt lighter of late. Days after his unfortunate conversation with Soriya, he was no longer bogged down with obsessions and problems.

For as much as he continued to go to work, he spent most of his time on the incomplete reports. The secrets behind each one, and the mystery woman at the center of them all, faded to the background. Instead, Loren focused on closing them out.

With each one completed and sent off for the proper approvals, Loren sensed the end approaching. Where once that idea might have caused him a certain level of dread, now only a calm freedom accompanied it. His burden disappeared, and he came to enjoy the world again. Even Portents, much as it surprised him.

He had the man seated across from him to thank for the newfound joy. Finney had become a fast friend over the last week. They had shared several calls in the meantime, some started by Loren and others by the good doctor. Work never played into it. They enjoyed the other's company, so much so that they had scheduled to meet for lunch at a nearby diner on the Knoll.

The crowd paid no attention to them. There was no drama to their meal, no scene to be displayed. The two friends shared ambitions and hopes. Dreams, though, came up more often than not.

"Any more since we last spoke?" Finney asked.

Loren finished a sip of his soda. He settled the cup on the table, but needled the straw. In the corner, the television continued to showcase the local news. Loren shifted more to keep his eyes from straying.

"No," he said. "The voice that called to me, that saved me from Shriff... it sounded so much like Beth, but..." He sighed. "I'm starting to think it was a fluke—my imagination creating the sound of her voice."

Finney nodded as he picked at the remnants of his meal. "A possibility, to be sure."

"You think it's something more?"

"My opinion holds little weight here," Finney said, a hand to his heart. His smile widened. "You're looking well, though."

"I feel well," Loren replied. "Better than I have in months."

The volume of the television increased at the control of a near-by patron. The banner on the screen made the subject clear, though the image of a bloodied sedan helped in that regard.

It read: KINDLY STRIKES AGAIN.

Loren turned away from the coverage that went into further detail about the victim and the scene. He grabbed a few leftover fries. They slipped between his lips and he chewed loudly to drown out the chatter.

Finney leaned closer, obviously sensing his discomfort. "Any progress on the case?"

"I wouldn't know," Loren said. He kept his eyes on the plate, as if ashamed he didn't empathize more over the murders. In truth, there was little he could do now. Ruiz had removed Loren from the case, after all. Shriff was dead. Loren may have felt free, but a twinge of guilt remained, like a deep pit in his gut.

He shoved the thought away with a false grin. "I've been keeping my head down to finish up some old files. Confirming witness testimony. Filling out proper paperwork. Verifying evidence or forensics. No murders. No new obsessions."

Or wild theories, he wanted to say. Soriya's insane concept of possession had woken him to the truth about her and her view of the city. It was something he never wanted to be part of.

Finney leaned back in his chair. "Good for you."

"It has been," Loren commented. "I've even considered making it permanent."

"Leaving law enforcement?"

Loren shrugged. "What has it ever brought me?"

Finney stared at him with wide eyes. "And your wife's death?"

Loren fell silent. Walking away from the precinct meant never finding out the truth about Beth's fall or who took her from him. Beth had been everything to him. He owed her better than that, didn't he?

"The past never goes away," Finney said in a quiet voice. He read the conflict in Loren's silence.

The detective offered a nod of agreement, then reached for his soda to prolong the silence. Finney immediately understood and let the moment pass.

Once finished, Loren pointed to Finney. "How about you? You mentioned your review was coming up."

"Yes." Finney perked up in his chair. "My appeal to the medical board is finally going through. There were some roadblocks to remove, but they've all been taken care of, it seems." He let out a long sigh. "I would love to start up my practice again in the city. That's where my true passion lies."

"Is Deckart on board with this change?" He nearly spat when he said the name. Deckart had left an unpleasant taste in Loren's mouth from the moment they'd met. It didn't help matters that Deckart's keycard had been used to slip Saprowski the lighter that had led to Shriff's death. His whereabouts that night remained an open question as well. Loren hated open questions.

Finney's response did little to rectify the feeling. With a lowered gaze, he said, "Clyde and I haven't been on the best terms of late. He's..." He trailed off to find the words, always the diplomat and never the complainer. "He's withdrawn from everyone since the Shriff incident. Keeping strange hours. Running unspoken errands. I barely recognize him anymore. Maybe I never really knew him at all."

"Do you think he—"

Finney ended the question with a wave. "I don't. No. How could I? He gave me a second chance when no one else would."

"Right." Loren let it lie. That was Ruiz's job now, though Loren wondered how long it would be before he saw Deckart's face on the screen with a warrant out for his arrest. "Do you think the board will approve your appeal?"

"If you would have asked me a few weeks ago, I would have said not a chance in hell," Finney said with a laugh. "But the past, while omnipresent, should not dissuade us from making the best future we can. I can only hope the newer members of the review board will look past my errors in judgment."

If only it was that simple. Loren knew from experience, but rather than bring the sentiment back down to earth, Loren lifted his glass.

"Here's to new beginnings."

Finney's joined his with a clink. "Indeed."

CHAPTER FORTY-FIVE

The groceries seemed heavier in her hands. Maybe it was the walk up the Knoll for Cambridge, where her mother lived. Maybe it was the lack of sleep from the last few nights.

Gates hadn't had a decent rest since Shriff died. She'd spent hours at the precinct before and after her shift to learn all she could about the latest victims.

No one questioned her. No one cared, which was what it boiled down to. Whenever she'd stopped by the evidence locker or hit up the coroner's office for information, there had been a complete lack of enthusiasm with the case. Everyone had believed it to be over with Shriff's arrest and subsequent death.

Raynor's murder sucked the rest of the energy right out of them. Even the pause in the rain had done nothing to brighten the spirits of those around Gates. The Kindly Killer had won in that regard, and it weighed on Gates more than the three bags of groceries caught in her mitts.

She tried to put aside all her concerns. A false smile spread across her lips, which she eagerly passed along to all those on the sidewalk. Few bothered to look up from the pavement or their cell phones. The ones who did made a point to look away from her quickly or head across the street rather than engage in the slightest.

Her mother would act the same way. Worse, she would see through the false front Gates slapped together. The last thing Gates needed was another lecture about the city. To her mother, Portents would be nothing but a dismal cesspool.

I bet Loren would get along with her.

She ground to a halt in front of a restaurant on King's Lane. Loren sat inside, as if her joke had summoned him. Finney, of all people, accompanied him. They laughed and passed along jokes while they paid for their meals. When they were together, it seemed like the world faded away—like nothing else mattered, especially the case.

It irked Gates to no end. Loren had been presented to her as the golden boy of the department. Not in social graces, certainly, but in raw talent. She saw none of that so-called skill, but plenty of the poor manners he brought to every occasion. Yet, with Finney, Loren looked almost human.

Before Gates could continue for her mother's, Loren and Finney headed for the door. They stepped out to the sidewalk, a hard shake ending the lunch for them. Finney stalked off for his car around the block. Loren patted his pockets, as if searching for a cigarette. A quiet curse escaped his lips, and he started down the Knoll.

Gates called him back. "Greg!"

Loren stopped, clearly confused, when he turned to see Gates at the window of the restaurant. He skirted through a large family gathered outside the entrance. "Gates? What are you doing here?"

She lifted the bags of groceries. One bag started to rip along the handle and she set them back to the ground. "Heading to my mother's for her weekly delivery."

"That's right," he said with a nod. "You said she lived nearby."

"I did." Gates offered a smirk. "What are you doing?"

"Lunch with a friend."

"Dr. Finney," Gates replied knowingly. Her eyes thinned. "During an open investigation into Castlemere."

Throwing his hands up, Loren backed away. "Not my investigation."

Gates stopped him before he could head off. "But why?" He said nothing, unsure about the question. "I've heard the stories, Loren. The case is all that mattered to you. Nothing would stop you from solving the mystery set before you. What changed?"

"My wife—"

"Doesn't get to be your eternal excuse!" Gates shouted. Everyone had one, but Loren's had been dogging his every decision for months. "This guy is killing innocent people. The last three within two weeks. All worked in the medical field at one time or another."

Loren's eyes sparked at the revelation. "They weren't random?"

"There he is."

She waited for more, but Loren shook his head, hands in the

air. "No. Sorry, Gates. I'm out. Talk to Quinn and Messick."

"They won't give me the time of day," Gates grumbled. "And they wouldn't see the connections even if I laid them out in front of them. They aren't Greg Loren."

"Don't give me that." His jaw clenched. "I am sick of living up to everyone's expectations. Let them do their job."

Gates shook her head. He didn't care, couldn't care, about Shriff's death or the new killer adding to the original's tally. Loren had changed since they'd met. Sure, he appeared happier than she had ever seen him. But he was no longer the detective everyone despised, despite his results.

"You know, Pratchett said you were the best in the department." She walked up to him, a finger to his chest. "We need you. The real you, not this self-involved jerk."

Loren bit his lower lip. There was plenty to say on the subject, but he held it back. She wondered if it was for her benefit or for his, but she realized it would always be for him, the way he was now. He backpedaled down the block, his sad gaze held on her.

"I'm not the guy you're looking for, Gates," he said. "Not anymore."

With that, he left. Gates watched him go. Quick steps carried him across the lane and then out of sight as the Knoll twisted. Loren wanted nothing to do with the case. No one at the precinct did. She was the only one who cared about Shriff's murder, and what it meant about the new-and-improved Kindly Killer.

Solving the mystery fell to her now.

CHAPTER FORTY-SIX

The rain started as evening hit the city. Gates had left her mother at the onset, using the excuse to escape another diatribe about the need for more red meat in her diet. The missing dietary component changed from week to week, but the lecture at the heart of it had long since been memorized. Letting it play out again would have been a waste of time for both of them.

Gates needed air. More than that, she needed to let her thoughts roam on her way to the precinct for her shift. Passersby paid no attention to her mutterings. Their rushing steps took them to shops and eateries throughout the downtown area. They had their own lives to live, killer among them or not. Their lives were all that mattered.

Like Loren.

Her exchange with him that afternoon had stung, to say the least. She had none of the experiences of the other officers at the precinct, but to see the man fade to a mere shadow of his potential had been disconcerting. He should have been first in line to solve this case, not that a line existed. Not a single soul was willing to put in the effort.

The latest storm brought with it a new level of misery at work. Her colleagues put forth no energy toward their jobs. They meandered through the station, offering strained greetings to each other. They talked about sports or where to go for drinks after their shift instead of work.

Gates found herself on the second floor of the Rath Building. Dickie most likely waited at their shared desk on the first, but she wanted another crack at Quinn and Messick before they headed out. As she passed Ruiz's office before the turn in the corridor, a scream echoed through the air.

"Find something already!"

Seconds later, Quinn and Messick burst from the office. Messick, the shorter of the pair, pulled at his uncomfortable tie. Sweat gathered under his arms in puddles. Quinn busied himself with a toothpick between his lips. Both stared at the floor, their grumblings following them.

"Guy won't give us a damn inch," Quinn muttered.

Messick let go of his tie and slapped Quinn on the arm. "Let's dig into the latest from Ronne."

"Sure," Quinn said. He flicked the toothpick at a nearby waste-paper can. It missed by a wide margin. "Sixth time has to be the charm, right?"

Gates barely avoided a collision with the pair. She tried to signal to them with a wave before their faces. They paid her no mind. Pushing through, they continued for the stairs to the coroner's office in the basement.

"Thanks for the time, guys," Gates whispered. She wasn't one to give in to despair. There was always hope in any situation. That hope, however, quickly dimmed in her eyes.

So had Ruiz's, it seemed. Standing behind his desk, the office door still open, Ruiz flipped through piling reports without an answer for any of them. He read words he clearly couldn't absorb, given the stakes of late. At the same time, the phone sat tucked on his shoulder while he listened.

Gates held out her hand to knock on the frame. "Captain?"

Ruiz glanced up from the reports. He waved her in. "Get me what patrols you can, Jamie. Right. From Tempest to Broslin. Thanks." He pulled the phone free and returned it to the cradle. He tried to smile, the act too much work to maintain for more than a brief breath. "What can I do for you, Melanie?"

"Do you have a minute?"

He chuckled at the notion, an eye toward the reports on his desk. "I don't think I ever will again." Then he waved her further in. She closed the door behind her. "What's on your mind?"

"It's…" Gates trailed off. She wanted to tell him about Loren, about her experience outside the restaurant that afternoon. There were so many things she wanted to mention. Yet when she looked into his tired eyes, she knew Ruiz didn't need to hear any of them. The weight of the case sat on his shoulders as it did her own. He didn't need any additional concerns.

"It's nothing, sir," she finally said. "Can I get you a cup of coffee or something?"

Ruiz searched around the office. He found a no-longer steaming cup stationed on the window ledge and moved to retrieve it. "I'm set."

"Okay."

"Gates?" Ruiz glanced back from the window.

Gates, heading for the door, stopped and joined him. "Yes, sir?"

Heaven's Gate Park lit up in the distance, obscured by the rising storm. Rain fell in a wave, while clouds rushed by overhead. Ruiz stared out over the city, the spires of downtown nothing but shadows in the night.

"You grew up in Portents, didn't you?"

"That's right," Gates replied, her first genuine smile all night. "Been here my whole life."

Ruiz nodded, a hand over his heart. "Montague by Saint Sebastian's."

"I know, sir."

Ruiz chuckled. He always spoke about his childhood. "It's changed, hasn't it? The city?" he asked. "I remember whole days of fun in the streets. Playing with friends without a care in the world." It was the same as she felt about Portents. She recalled glory days where nothing could go wrong as long as you were out laughing with loved ones. Looking out into the gloom, Ruiz continued. "Laps at the pool at Sanctity Park."

"We always went to Prospect," Gates interjected. "Fewer people."

"Smart," Ruiz said. "Sanctity was always jammed. Like the entire city had taken off from work to enjoy the sunshine. No responsibilities, no burdens, and no damn shadows to wreck the day." The memory of youth faded from him. Concern filled his eyes. "Were we blind?"

"I don't think so, sir. Portents has changed." She hated to admit it. Just saying the words felt like defeat.

Ruiz nodded, lost to the storm outside. "This rain won't stop."

"Maybe the weather heard you."

"Or maybe we don't deserve the light anymore," he said in a weary tone. "Maybe all that's left to us is the darkness."

He was right. Darkness had overtaken their city. That feeling had settled over everyone at the precinct and it centered on the Kindly Killer. He provided the tipping point in her eyes.

The only way to help the precinct, and the city, was to solve the case. That was how Gates could bring the light back to Portents. That was how hope would win the day.

CHAPTER FORTY-SEVEN

The city was quiet. Well, outside of the pounding rain, a few morons busting into a hardware store on Eighth, and a couple of fae on a drunken bender through the Allure Marketplace, things were eerily silent.

Soriya found no sign of the Kindly Killer. The madman was out there somewhere, stalking his next victim. It had been how Shriff worked, though she wondered if that was truly Shriff's method at all, or the thing that had possessed him.

The possession angle was the right one to take. No one could tell her any differently. Not even Loren's inability to conceive of such a scenario caused her to doubt her theory. Mentor had stopped arguing about it as well, which surprised her, though she felt something new bothered her teacher. Whenever he looked to the Bypass, deep concern filled his eyes, and he rubbed at his arm as if wounded.

Whatever had happened remained secret, and Soriya didn't pry. Her focus lay fully on the task at hand. The Kindly Killer needed to be stopped. She was the only one who could do it. She simply had to find the bastard.

Screams cut through the air. Soriya launched down the street towards the sound. The ribbon at her wrist shot out and snagged the nearest lamppost. Pulling taut, Soriya soared into the air and across two blocks before landing in a full run.

"Help!" a kid cried. "Someone, please!"

She rounded the corner at Harlem and Opine to see a family of four cornered at the dead end. Three bearded men wearing leather jackets and carrying crowbars closed in on them.

The father pulled his family close behind him. Rain mixed with tears on their faces. "You don't have to do this."

His wife struggled against his arm. Fire sat in her eyes. She wanted the fight. The kids bit back screams of terror.

What the hell are they doing out at night?

"We haven't done anything!" the wife yelled at the trio. There was something deep in her voice, and Soriya realized the truth. Though they appeared normal, the family was anything but. The rising snout of the wife and the whiskers on the faces of the kids made it clear. They were shifters, though she couldn't tell what creature they manifested.

"Exactly," the closest hoodlum said in a raspy voice. He pounded the crowbar against his palm. "You haven't given us what we want."

"Which is?" the mother replied. Her husband attempted to halt her with a glare, but she wasn't one to be intimidated by anyone.

"Everything," the thug to the left answered. "Don't worry, though. We'll take it when we're done playing."

Soriya leaped over the thugs, flipped through the air with the Ribbons of Kali dancing around her in the wind, then landed between the hoods and the family. She smirked at the thugs. "Playtime's over."

On closer inspection, all three of the aggressors were middle-aged, carrying more fat around their guts than muscle. Beards ran from their chins all the way to their chests, a deep mud brown for the one before her, while the other two had already gone full gray. They were clearly not in the prime of their lives.

"Playtime was probably over a long time ago for you three."

The family stood rooted to the spot. They were even more confused by Soriya's intervention. Unsure where to move or how to act, Soriya took the guesswork out of the situation.

"Go," she exclaimed and pointed down the road. "Get out of here!"

The thug to the right immediately bolted to block their path. Soriya's ribbon shot out from her left side and caught him by the ankle. It lifted him from the ground. His cries echoed throughout the block. The ribbon snapped to the right, and the man went soaring into the brick wall of a bakery.

With their path freed, the family took off in a run. The thugs watched them flee, unsure whether to pursue. They peered back at their fallen comrade, and the decision was made for them.

"She took out Sean!" one said.

"Well?" the other huffed. "Get her!"

The first one tossed a punch. It was slow and Soriya saw it coming. The strain on the thug's face was clear, as was the fact that he had no strength behind the blow. He would have been better off leading with the crowbar, but she assumed brains were even more lacking than muscles.

"Thanks," Soriya said, dodging the blow with a stiff block. "You're saving me the trouble of chasing you down. I'm already at my steps for the night."

"What?" the thug asked in confusion.

Soriya sighed. She knocked his arm aside, then decked him across the face. He fell to the pavement in a heap, and his crowbar clattered by his side.

"I know," she said over her unconscious foe. "Mentor says I need to work on my banter. But he means cutting it out completely, and where's the fun in that?"

The last thug stood in the road. He panted heavily, terrified on one hand and full of vengeful rage in the other. He leaned forward, crowbar raised, then fell back on his heels. His nerves struggled against his anger, yet rational thought never played into it.

"Well?" Soriya said mockingly. "Are you going to *get her* already, or what?"

He ripped off his jacket. Only a stained and discolored A-shirt hugged his bulging gut. Tattoos ran up his arms and across his chest. Demons and skulls flowed like a river from hell on his flesh and flames rose along his thick neck.

Soriya glanced at the other two fallen thugs. They groaned from their beatings. As they rolled around on the ground, their jackets opened to reveal similar markings on their skin. Distinctive body art covered each one. The images reminded her of the masks etched on the necks of Comedy and Tragedy.

Shriff held no such marking. Why?

Her eyes widened as revelation struck her.

Luckily, the last thug's blow didn't. In her amazement over the connection between all of her foes of late, Soriya failed to realize the thug had found his bravery. He closed the distance, a cry of rage in the air, and swung his crowbar with all his might. The tool passed like a stiff breeze to the left of Soriya.

The thug caught a glimpse of the satisfied smirk on her face. Then her fist filled his view. It crashed against his nose and blood spurted like a geyser as cartilage snapped.

He cried out in pain. There was no more room in his heart for rage. His hands shot up to cover his shattered nose. It also blocked his vision as Soriya spun around with a roundhouse kick that connected with his left side. Feet left the ground, and the third hoodlum went headfirst into the neighboring wall. He landed with a resounding thud on the pavement.

Soriya edged close, her eyes on the tattoos once more. Like the brands on her masked foes, they held the key to the Kindly Killer.

A shadow crossed over her. Soriya spun to face the family once more.

"What are you still doing here?"

"We saw what you did," the mother said. "We wanted to thank you."

"Thank me by getting somewhere safe tonight," Soriya replied. "The Courtyard is your best bet."

Shocked looks passed between them. "How did you know?" the young girl behind her father whispered.

Soriya could hear Mentor in her head. "I have my ways."

The two children and their mother departed. The father paused for a moment. "How can we ever thank you?"

"Honestly?" Soriya said. Her gaze lingered on the tattoos once more. "I should be thanking you."

With that, the father was gone, and Soriya stood alone on the street. She knew what she had to do now, and how to prove to Loren she was right about the Kindly Killer.

CHAPTER FORTY-EIGHT

Gates rummaged through the files on Loren's computer. His password had been fairly obvious—his wife's birthday. She didn't work too hard to figure it out. Loren kept the password written on a notepad in the center drawer of his desk.

With each click of the mouse, she worked through his massive archive. She also continued to keep an eye out for any random onlookers. If Ruiz or Dickie found out, she knew she would face a stiff punishment for overreaching.

She let her partner know Soames would take her spot on patrol that evening. She had cleared it with the night shift duty officer, explaining there had been a family emergency at home in need of her attention. Once out of view, Gates had immediately rushed to Loren's desk, hoping to find the clue that would unravel the Kindly Killer case once and for all.

The glimmer in his eyes when Loren had realized the potential connection between the latest victims made it clear something of value was there. No one else seemed capable of figuring out what it might mean. It fell to Gates to solve the case, for the sake of everyone else.

"There's something here," she muttered to herself. Gates left the archive for more recent folders on the desktop. She clicked through each one, scanning hurriedly. "Why can't anyone see it? Why is no one trying to see it?"

Raynor's profile filled the screen. She pored through his work history and his contacts in the medical community. They were extensive for a retired professional. His work, while not daily, had continued.

Raynor had spent time with dozens of charitable organizations, medical firms, and more. The constant meetings had required the use of an office at his former practice, something his partners had been more than happy to provide. The connections buried deep within Raynor's mile-long dossier grabbed her attention. Switching gears, Gates moved onto the most recent victims, Matthew Sinclair and Rosita Castillo. She pulled their information from the shared files on the department's Intranet.

The latter had been found in her home that morning, though she had been murdered at least three days earlier, according to Hady Ronne's team. Gates pushed through the forensics reports from the scene. Images of the deceased were littered throughout, including photos of her gaping chest wound. The murder weapon—a letter opener—laid in a pool of blood at her side. The grin was present for all to see, with crimson smeared across her lips and teeth from the act.

Work histories for both offered much the same as Raynor. All had been pillars to the medical community for their entire lives and had served Portents in multiple capacities. Gates clicked through for some commonalities that Quinn, Messick, and everyone else had missed.

One line jumped out at Gates. She latched onto it like a life-preserver. "That has to be it."

She grabbed the image and sent the information to the nearest printer. The paper whirred from the cartridge. Gates pushed her seat back from the desk. Standing to retrieve the item from across the bullpen, Gates almost ran into an enormous figure rounding the corner at the same time.

Pratchett stepped out of her way and nearly stumbled through the half-wall divider. "Mel?"

Gates jumped back, a hand over her heart. "John," she gasped. "You scared the hell out of me."

"Where's Loren?" Pratchett asked, glancing around.

"Not here."

Pratchett huffed. "I see that." He continued to scan the floor without success.

Gates watched him rub at his neck, his discomfort clear. He didn't want to be found at Loren's desk any more than she did.

"What did you need from Loren?"

Pratchett stiffened at the question. "Nothing."

"But you're looking for him?"

Pratchett's eyes thinned and he raised a finger toward her. "Are you trying to distract me from asking why you're rummaging through his files?"

She matched his movements. "Are you avoiding my question because you don't want to answer me?"

"Maybe?" he replied, his brow furrowed. "I actually have no idea what I'm doing now."

Gates leaned against the nearby wall with a huff. "Sounds like the rest of the department. Including Loren."

"What happened?"

"He's basically washed his hands of everything," Gates said. "I don't know what you ever saw in him, John. Quitting might be the best thing for him."

"Quitting?" Pratchett exclaimed. Looks shot their way from nearby detectives. Pratchett lowered his voice and leaned closer. "He's quitting?"

"Seems to be," Gates said with a downward gaze. She felt bad for pushing Loren so hard earlier that day. He had been through enough, and she had criticized his pain rather than support him. "He lost his wife to an unspeakable tragedy. Who could blame him?"

Pratchett's gaze fell to the floor. "He's not the one to blame."

Gates reached out to her friend. "John? Hey, you all right?"

"Yeah," he said, drawing out the word. "I… I, uh, cleared it with the captain. I'm back in two weeks."

"That's great," Gates beamed. It was the best news she'd heard in a long time. Yet, for some reason, the excitement wasn't shared by Pratchett. "Wait. Is that not great?"

"No. No, it is," Pratchett said. A goofy grin filled his face. He backed away slowly from the desk. "I just have something I need to take care of first."

Gates watched him leave. Pratchett had never appeared so burdened before. All she could remember from their days growing up together was his ever-present smile. Now it faded, like so much of late. She worried for her friend, but her concern for everyone else took precedence.

The printout remained in the tray when she arrived. The information was buried between so much history it was almost impossible to decipher. She stared at the slim connection found, hoping she was right. Gates grabbed hold and started for the exit to the parking garage.

"Yeah," she said to herself in the absence of her friend. "I have something I need to take care of, too."

CHAPTER FORTY-NINE

Blood dripped from the shadow's fingers. It leaked from the tips to the carpet below. His shoes were steeped in crimson, which squished beneath his weight.

He had gone too far this time. There was no going back to the life he wanted—that he deserved to have. After everything he had done to secure his new lease on life, the urge had sent him once more into a maddening rage.

"Why?" the shadow seethed. "Why did you push me like that? Why did you have to open your ignorant mouth and push me like you always do?"

The shadow backpedaled from the corpse at his feet. Bloodied steps carried him off the thick rug to the desk at the far end of the room. A mirror hung along the wall and the shadow caught his distressed reflection upon on the glass.

"He deserved it," the reflection said. "They've all deserved it."

The shadow shook his head vehemently. "No, no, no. That's not true. They were just doing their jobs. I…"

"Made a mistake," the voice snapped. "A little mistake that you paid for. They took years from you for it. And they would have kept taking, like they did for countless others. You did the right thing."

The shadow glanced at the wide eyes in the mirror. He stood up straighter and smoothed his bloodied shirt with his hands. "I… I did. I did the right thing."

"There you go."

"What do I do now?" the shadow asked the mirror. The dead body looked like a massive lump on the rug, bloated and already smelling. "There are too many eyes here. Even with them out of the way like you wanted, I can't—"

"You can do anything," the mirror replied. "No one can stand in the way of your future—the one you've always deserved. The one I have given you. This is your chance at the brightest of futures."

"Yes." The shadow turned toward the door. "You're right. I can make this work. There are ways to make this work."

He felt the grin growing across his lips. It matched the one on the corpse. It had become his signature, passing along joy to those who never appreciated the life they had unless it was at the expense of everyone around them.

Bitterness and rage grew as the shadow unleashed a frenzy of kicks against the dead body. The heaving corpse rolled with each impact, then sank back down to the divot already created by their girth.

"You shouldn't have said those things to me," the shadow whispered in the dark of the office.

The late hour gave him time to act. It might take all night, but he began to formulate a plan to remove the corpse from the office and secure his freedom from the complex before someone found out.

He quickly pushed at the corner of the oak desk to free up the rug tucked beneath. As he rolled the rug toward the dead body, twin beams of light showered the front of the office through the thin curtains covering the windows.

Dropping the rug, the shadow moved for the closest window. He tucked close to the frame, careful to keep out of the approaching lights. A car cautiously entered the loop in front of the institute. The sedan coasted along the road; the driver remained hidden from view. Still, the shadow recognized the vehicle from their earlier visit.

The police.

The shadow cursed. He needed time and no longer had it.

"You know what you have to do," the voice in the mirror called.

The shadow returned to his reflection. Manic eyes stared back at him. Rage coursed through his veins and the urge grew in his chest once more.

There was more work to do.

CHAPTER FIFTY

This is stupid.

The car stopped at the edge of the entry loop. It took Gates a few seconds to realize her headlights were illuminating the completely dark facility. She rectified the situation with a quick turn of the dial to her left. The engine continued to run, her foot still on the brake. She thought about slamming the accelerator and heading back to the city, back to her mom and work and her sanity.

She should have told Ruiz. He would have helped her flesh out her theory or laughed in her face, both helpful in keeping her from making a huge mistake in judgment. Instead, she found herself at Castlemere in the dead of night. What had Loren said to her on their very first visit to the institute? Try not to come at night?

Mission not accomplished, Melanie. Way to go.

The place looked like a nightmare in the shadows. The storm certainly did Castlemere no favors. Trees rattled along the windows. Rain pounded the surface. The clouds blocked all natural light, and the institute offered none of its own. The darkness was a strange sight considering the number of people the place employed as evidenced by the cars still in the lot even at such a late hour.

"Where is everyone?"

Gates put the car in park. She brought out no umbrella this time and opted for her sidearm instead. Gripping the handle tight, Gates exited the sedan. The rain pushed back, but she forced her way out into the whipping winds. The door shut, and the car locked with the press of a button. Of course, the beep echoed throughout the grounds and the headlights blinked twice to confirm, both of which she could have done without.

This is stupid. This is your worst idea yet.

Her thoughts carried her up the steps. A quick glance through the storm toward the parking lot confirmed Deckart's car in the lot, as well as Finney's, among the other staffers on duty. At the door, she took a deep breath. Her fingers slipped from the handle on the first try. With the second, she pulled the door loose from the frame and stepped in from the rain.

The reception area was pitch black. No one was present.

"What are you doing, Melanie?" she asked herself in the dark. Cautious steps took her deeper through reception. The double doors were open and led to the stairs for administration. "You're here. No one else is, but maybe that's normal. Turn around and go home. Walking through the creepy asylum at night is definitely the wrong move here."

Her foot took the first step, then she shot back down again. She sighed heavily, her hands shaking. "No plan. No backup. Why didn't I call for backup? Oh yeah. They wouldn't believe a word. Because you barely believe a word.

"I can practically hear Dickie—sorry, Del—yelling at me." She shook away her doubts. No one else was coming here. No one else cared enough to pursue the lead she'd found. Solving the case fell to her and her alone. "Sorry, partner. I have to do this. I have to see if I'm right. About Shriff. About everything."

The creaking of the floor above ended her musings. She hugged the wall at her back along the bottom of the steps, waiting for signs of life to make themselves known. One breath, then two passed. She tried to slow her heart without success.

After a full minute went by, Gates left the comfort of the wall and took the bottom step again. "Hello?" she called into the night, followed by a silent curse at her idiocy. "Yep. You just let everyone know your position. Get it together, Melanie."

At the top of the landing, Gates paused. Drops ran along the tan carpet runner that extended the length of the floor. They were sporadic but visibly different from the artificial fibers.

"Blood."

She turned down the corridor for Deckart's office. It was out of the way from the rest, his own private wing of the building. She knocked on the door, only to have it creak open under her knuckles.

Gates peered through the dark. "Doctor? It's Melanie Gates, sir. From the Central Precinct?"

No answer. She glanced around but found no one waiting inside. Just the empty confines of an office used much too frequently. Books and paperwork covered every surface and were stacked in the corners.

Gates wheeled around and returned to the hall. Deckart should have been there. By all accounts, he was always in his office. Where could he have gone?

Her steps quickened and took her back through the wing. Standing outside Finney's office, Gates held her breath. The door was open. She headed in before she could talk herself out of it.

The darkness was thicker here, almost like a veil covering everything. Gates inched farther into the office. She whispered, "Doctor Finney?"

No answer came. She continued for the desk, hoping for some sign on the monitors—if they were working. As she did, Gates nearly stumbled on an obstruction in the middle of the floor. Her feet splashed along the soggy carpet, and she struggled to hold back a scream as she peered down at the body before her.

"I…" Gates tried to find the words. "Oh, no. No, no…"

So focused on the dead man, Gates failed to notice the shadow behind her. From the corner of her eye, she noticed a glint of metal rise in the air, then arc for her position. The needle pricked her neck, the injection a wave of heat that seared her skin and pulsed rapidly through her body. In an instant, her entire world blurred.

"What did you…"

"I'm sorry you had to see that," a voice said from behind her, though it sounded distant. "Sorrier still for the cost of your curiosity."

"No." Gates attempted to lash out at her assailant. Her wild swings merely threw her off balance. The drug coursing through her system caused the room to spin. She tripped over the dead man and fell to the carpet. Frantic hands groped for the exit, but her arms felt like lead weights. Her eyes were heavier, unable to stay open a second longer. A shadow loomed over her and the world filled with darkness.

Gates passed out at the mercy of the Kindly Killer.

CHAPTER FIFTY-ONE

Sleep wouldn't come for Loren. He spent hours tossing and turning, trying to find some sense of peace so he might dream once more. Thoughts of his wife carried with him, as did the creeping tendrils of Shriff. The killer was the problem. Every thought of the dead man and his successor brought more questions to the surface.

As the clock in the hallway chimed eleven, Loren gave up on the notion of rest. He sat up along the edge of the couch and placed his head in his hands. He pried his eyes open, then brushed back his overgrown hair. Staring across the room, his eyes fell on the box beside the door—one he should have passed along to the Central Precinct a week ago.

He snatched the television remote from the table. When the screen came to life, the news displayed a weather report of nothing but rain, rain, and more rain, surprising no one.

Clicking through a dozen channels, Loren paid less and less attention to the content on the screen. His eyes flitted from his distraction back to the box. With a loud sigh, Loren turned off the television and tossed the remote aside. He stood, his body aching from the fitful rest of the evening, and headed for the box.

Dragging it across the room, Loren lifted the box up and placed it on the coffee table. The lid popped off and file folders threatened to spill out immediately. He caught the top set, removed them carefully to the side, then rummaged through the rest.

He wanted to scream. Mostly at Gates, if he was being honest. Her words kept repeating in the back of his mind. They pushed him to act, to care about what had happened to Shriff, about the copycat killer in their midst, and what the hell it all truly meant.

Loren collapsed on the couch once more and proceeded to pore through the files. The top ones were recent additions—

dossiers on the latest victims which he had procured without too much trouble. He wasn't familiar with Sinclair and Castillo, but Gates had been right about the possible connection because of their careers in the medical field.

What that connection was, though, eluded him. Loren rubbed his chin hard. "There's a reason I let this go, isn't there?"

He could feel the old tensions rising. His obsession had bought him nothing but pain and misery since losing his wife. Every effort had ostracized him from the world. Yet, the case lingered. Gates had been right in that regard. The case was always in the background.

A knock at the door shook him back to the room. Loren stared at the door as another knock rang out. The clock read 11:18, not the usual time for company.

"Just what I need."

His first thought was of Soriya, but after the way he'd treated her, there was no way she would bother with him again. More knocks resounded through the apartment. Loren grabbed his gun from the holster hanging off the side of the couch and started for the door.

"All right, all right," he announced. "Who is it this time?"

Loren opened the door, his gun behind his back. A towering figure stood in the hall, filling the frame.

"Hey," the man said in a low voice.

"Pratchett?" Loren eyed him curiously. "It's good to see you, despite the insanely late hour."

"Sorry about that," Pratchett said. "Didn't think it could wait."

An awkward silence fell between them. Loren relented. He tucked his weapon away as he shifted to the side of the door. "Come on in. I can't even remember the last time you stopped by."

"I…" Pratchett fell quiet upon entering. His gaze locked onto the mantel to the right and the lone photo there.

Loren lifted it up slightly. "Yeah. She always liked you, Pratchett."

"I… I liked her too," he replied in a solemn tone. "That's kinda why I came."

Loren offered the end of the couch and took his place on the other side. Pratchett slowly made his way across the room. He sat, leaning forward with his knees almost to his chest.

"What's up?"

"Well, you see…" Pratchett fought for the words, his discomfort clear. Loren couldn't imagine what might be bothering the guy. Pratchett had always been good for a laugh. "Melanie talked to me."

"Gates," Loren said with the shake of his head. "That friend of yours has been following me around all night."

"What do you mean?"

Loren ignored the question for the moment and stood. He pointed to his company. "You want a drink?"

Pratchett nodded. "Water is fine, thanks."

"Sure thing." Loren slipped into the kitchen and set to work on the drink. He luckily found a clean glass in the back of the cupboard; the dishes had taken over the sink. Upon his return to the living room, Pratchett was digging through the contents of the box on the coffee table.

"She got you back into the case?" he asked, delight behind the question.

Loren grumbled, passing over the water before joining the officer on the couch. "She reminded me of a guy I used to know. Someone I'm not ready to put in the rearview just yet."

Pratchett chuckled. "Yeah. That's Melanie through and through. Too good for her own good sometimes."

"Well, I appreciated the kick in the ass," Loren said. "Not that I'd tell her that, understand?"

"Your secret is safe with me." Pratchett quickly turned away for the casefiles. "Anything interesting?"

"Too much," Loren said. "Relevance is the key and where I keep coming up short. There has to be something to the change in victims. The copycat seems focused on the medical profession. A retired surgeon. The head of one of the top family practices in the city. And this most recent."

Loren passed along the dossier. Pratchett took it in hand and scanned the opening page. "I read about her. Castillo, right?"

"Rosita Castillo," Loren confirmed. "The woman's made a career on unwrapping the criminal mind."

Pratchett set the file down next to Raynor's and Sinclair's. "Three docs, all in a row. Sounds like a joke my shrink would make."

"Three docs who never worked in the same place at the same time." His frustration showed, and he did what he could to rein it in. Pratchett picked at the files, reading as he listened. "Like I said, the one was retired, so what—"

Pratchett lifted Sinclair's file. "Looks like he was still active in the field, though."

"What?"

Pratchett pointed to a small list of affiliations. Most had been former links to the prominent doctor, but a few remained current. "He was a member of some review board."

"Let me see." Loren followed Pratchett's finger to the relevant section. He skimmed through it, then snatched at Raynor's and Castillo's files. His eyes widened with each word read. "These two were on the same board. They reviewed… Oh. Oh, God."

"What is it?"

Loren jumped to his feet. Papers flew from his hands. He grabbed the holster from the side of the couch and secured it to his waist. He slipped his gun in place before reaching for his coat on the floor next to the hanger.

"Detective?"

A chill settled over Loren. "I need your keys."

"What?" Pratchett asked. "You don't drive."

"I do tonight," Loren muttered. Pratchett tossed him the keys. "I need you to call Ruiz. Tell him I'm going to Castlemere Institute."

Pratchett stood. He hurried for the door. "I'll go with you."

"No." It all became clear to him. He should have seen it right away, should have listened to Gates from the start when she'd complained about the change in Shriff. He'd simply wanted everything finished: the case, the pain, and especially the memories. How many lives could he have saved if he had listened?

"I have to do this myself, Pratchett."

He left Pratchett at the landing. His frenzied steps carried him down the stairs and into the blowing storm swirling up the Knoll. Pratchett's car beeped at the press of a button, and Loren made a beeline for it.

For seven months, the Kindly Killer had plagued his every waking moment and even his nightmares. Loren had to be the one to close the case. It was time to finish this, once and for all.

CHAPTER FIFTY-TWO

"Pratchett, slow down."

Ruiz held the cell phone close to his ear. He could barely understand the man over the sound of the pounding rain and rushing footsteps in the background. The howling wind kicked up nothing but static.

Stopping outside his office, a fresh cup of coffee in his hand, Ruiz pressed the phone as hard as he could against his ear. Words rang out over the storm, and Ruiz nearly dropped his mug.

"Greg's heading where?" he yelled, though it wasn't necessary. All it did was draw looks from the few who remained on the second floor of the Rath Building. "Okay. I'll take care of it. Thanks."

He hung up. The cell slipped into his pocket. Taking a hurried sip of his coffee, Ruiz revisited the information passed along by Pratchett from Loren. It didn't make any sense. What was at Castlemere that Loren deemed so important?

"What are you doing this time, Greg?"

He was supposed to be off active duty. No, he was supposed to be off tonight, period. Loren's continued interference on the case caused nothing but complications, not only for Ruiz and the department, but for Loren himself.

Everyone available at Central was already on the streets. Patrols ran up and down the Knoll and now stretched as far as the docks at Riverside to fit the latest pattern of deaths. Quinn and Messick had coordinated with half the precincts in the city to draw up a search pattern. They were the leads on the case. Yet Loren had headed the investigation for far longer, his knowledge of the case irrefutable.

Ruiz groaned. "What the hell are you doing to me this time?"

He wandered down the corridor. Loren's makeshift office was

shut, but a light shone inside. Curious, Ruiz opened the door.

A young woman wearing a leather jacket and torn jeans stood inside, a hand on the window ledge. Along her back was a weapon—almost like a pipe or poker—strapped to her coat.

"You?"

Rain poured against the side of the building and through the still-open window. The lithe figure left the comfort of the ledge and turned to greet the man at the door.

"I—"

"Don't." Ruiz pulled his gun on her. They had only met once, the circumstances of which hadn't been ideal. Ruiz had said plenty about the recruitment of someone so young into a fight he neither wanted nor truly believed in. To him, monsters didn't belong in his city and neither did Soriya Greystone. "Don't move a muscle."

She hesitated. Defiance filled her eyes for a moment, then she raised her hands into the air.

Ruiz shook his head in disbelief. He closed the door behind him. The gun remained in his grasp when he looked back, reticent to leave himself defenseless against someone so capable. Eventually, he tucked the weapon along his hip.

"Now it makes sense," he said, recalling a conversation with Loren from over a week earlier. "Greg talking about monsters in the shadows. About darkness in the city. That was you, wasn't it?"

"Guilty."

"I told your boss—"

"Mentor," she corrected, hands still over her head.

"Whatever," he replied. He waved for the hands to fall and she did so. "I told him not to let you get involved. Whenever you two show up, chaos follows. And a fair share of bodies in your wake."

"I brought the Kindly Killer to you," she snapped.

"Then who's out there killing in his name?"

Her gaze fell to the desk. Fingers danced lightly along the files. "I was hoping Loren had figured that out."

"Loren…" Ruiz's hand jumped to his brow. "Dammit."

"What?"

Pratchett's frantic call suddenly made more sense. "He did solve it."

"He did?" she asked, excited. "When? Who—"

"He went to Castlemere Institute," Ruiz answered. "Alone."

Soriya moved for the window.

"Stop," Ruiz called.

"I have to go," she said. "I have to—"

"I know," Ruiz said, and quietly cursed to himself. "I wish to God there was another way, but my people are scattered throughout the city. You might be the only one capable of getting to him in time."

She nodded, gratitude clear on her youthful face. She turned for the window and he grabbed her hand.

"Keep him safe," Ruiz said.

"I will. I promise."

"Well?" Ruiz let her go, waving for the window and the storm outside. "Go on already!"

She disappeared in the blink of an eye. The storm swallowed her whole. Ruiz rushed to the window and caught a brief glimpse of her shadow in the night. Then she was gone, as was his only hope of helping Loren in time.

Ruiz ran from the room to his office. He snatched the radio on the corner of his desk and brought it to life. "I need all available units to converge on Castlemere Institute."

CHAPTER FIFTY-THREE

The car halted just inside the gates to the complex. Loren lingered in the driver's seat, staring at the looming building completely wrapped in shadow. The storm whipped through the air in a frenzy and torrents of rain pounded the ground without an end in sight.

He didn't want to be back at Castlemere. Loren had left this world behind him. He had been free. That fleeting moment, unshackled from the never-ending murder and mayhem that seemed to fuel this city, had been wonderful. He'd felt almost human again.

That freedom wasn't for him, though. No matter the joy of the last week, the lack of burden and responsibility, none of it was truly what he needed. He had refused to admit it to himself, though. It took two strangers to knock him back on track: Soriya, who he had pushed away rather than hear her theories, and Gates, who he was a complete ass to from start to finish.

They had been there for him, poking and prodding the sleeping bear within for some spark of life. He should have appreciated the gesture more, instead of lashing out the way he always did. Why did he have to tackle everything alone?

This time, though, the responsibility fell on him.

Loren left the confines of the car. He tucked his jacket tight around him. Keeping his head down, he ran through the rain for the front steps of the institute.

Gates' car was parked outside the loop. Worry filled his eyes. She had figured it out as well. Of course she had. If anyone had the drive to find out the truth, it was the officer hoping to bring some good back to her hometown.

Loren took the stairs two at a time. He didn't bother to knock on the great double doors to the institute. Pushing them open,

Loren stepped out of the storm and into the darkness.

The reception area was devoid of personnel. There wasn't a sign of life throughout the entire room. A small flicker of light came from the security monitors facing the back wall of the space. It offered him enough to navigate deeper into the facility.

Loren pulled out his Glock and took his first step. He stopped with his third, as a voice echoed through the intercom speaker in the corner of the room.

"You should have let this one go, Detective," the voice called. Garbled from the age of the system, Loren could still hear the anger behind the words. He closed his eyes and heard Shriff saying them, though he knew this went beyond Shriff now. The voice sounded like pure evil. "You still can. Turn around. Go home."

"Can't do that," Loren said. "Not after everything you've done."

Laughter filled the speaker. "You don't have the first clue what *I* have done. A blind man has better perception than you."

Loren ignored the taunting laughter of the killer. He moved for the security station, rounding the counter for a better look at the monitors. He hoped for some sign of life in the institute. "I'm here to end this. Tonight."

"There is nothing but death if you walk this path." The monitors shifted from empty corridor to empty corridor. A sudden break in the picture diverted the screens to a single room and a lone figure. Gates sat strapped to a chair, her hands and feet bound and her mouth gagged. "Starting with hers."

She screamed at the camera, but her words were cut short. A shadow passed behind her. A knife, the only clear element on the screen, glinted in the dark.

"Damn you," Loren said.

"We're all damned, Detective," the killer replied. "Last chance."

Loren lifted his gun. He shot out the speaker. Twisting from corner to corner, he took out each camera until none were left operating. The clip slid from the gun and he quickly found another to jam into place.

He started for the stairs to the administration wing. Before he could reach the doors to gain access, a lock clicked. He slammed his hands against the metal slabs, to no avail. The doors refused to budge. Loren was cut off.

Behind him, the security door to the patient wings opened.

Deep shadows stood within, waiting for him. It was an invitation Loren couldn't refuse. He hurried to the open door and entered the institute.

"I'm coming, Gates," he said as the darkness enveloped him. "I'm coming."

CHAPTER FIFTY-FOUR

The restrained officer continued to cry out toward the camera. Eyes burned with a mix of fury and panic, the words completely lost on the cloth jammed between her lips.

The shadow watched it for a moment, letting her fear win out. Once the monitors died in the reception area, the shadow moved for his victim. The knife was still in his right hand and he kept it at his side. His left hand, though, swept the air and collided with her cheek.

She took the blow in stride. Angry words filled the air again, suppressed by the gag. He pulled his hand back, then snapped it across her face once more. This time, no words were spoken. Only the glaring eyes of the restrained and powerless met him. He had certainly seen the look enough in his life to recognize it.

"This isn't what I wanted," the shadow said. "All I've ever wanted was to help people. Why can't any of you see that?"

No answer was desired and none came. The officer's cheek reddened, her right eye watering from the strikes.

The shadow paced the length of the room, conscious of the knife at this side. He paused over the corpse along the carpet and seethed with mounting rage. "You constantly stand in my way. Pushing me. With your criticisms and complaints. With your lawsuits and your damned condescension."

Thin eyes peered at the office door. Loren was coming. The shadow knew it would be him in the end. They were connected and had been since the beginning. Loren had always dogged his trail, mindful of each move made against the city. Even now, even with the young woman as bait, Loren's priority was no doubt the killer behind the curtain. He wanted the truth to set him free. The shadow was more than willing to oblige.

The truth, however, came at a cost.

"The detective is different, though he might not see it yet." The shadow returned to the captive Gates. "He needs to be made to understand the way of things."

He slammed his right hand to the desk behind his captive. She jumped against the chair, but her hands and feet kept her pinned. Her terror widened the satisfied grin on the shadow's face.

"He'll try to stop me," he said in a calm voice. "He's always tried to stop me, though he might not realize it." The emergency controls filled the computer screen. Every system fell under its purview and only the head of the facility, the chief security officer, and a select few others maintained access. Lights, the HVAC system, security cameras, and more were contained in the system and he thumbed through the many options available to him.

It had been set up as a fail-safe in case of a total calamity at Castlemere. Instead, it would serve as the ultimate test of Greg Loren's resolve.

"He didn't leave me a choice in this, I'm afraid."

The shadow paused. Loren had been a worthy opponent, always only one step behind each victim taken by the Kindly Killer. It was a shame to lose such a valued foe, especially when the shadow felt so connected to the man. Still, there was more work to be done and only those willing to sacrifice were allowed to continue in this sacred task.

Hesitation overcome, the shadow found the system required to halt Loren's progress through the institute. The master override key to the cells of the violent wing shined in bright red on the screen. The shadow smiled as he activated the override.

"I warned the detective," the shadow said. "The repercussions fall on him and him alone."

CHAPTER FIFTY-FIVE

Feet pounded against the concrete. Loren ran with reckless abandon through the institute wings toward the back of the facility, the only clear path left to him. He had to reach the administrative wing and quickly. Who knew how long the Kindly Killer would leave Gates alive?

"Come on, come on," he muttered under his breath. His lungs burned, and he cursed his desire for another cigarette.

With the first hall under his belt, Loren entered the violent offenders' ward. He turned right for the connecting wing. Halfway down the corridor, a sharp click echoed all around him—a terrifying symphony in his ears.

Every cell door opened. The technological wonder that was the state-of-the-art ward failed at the precise moment Loren happened to be in reach. There was no chance it had been a coincidence. This was the killer's play.

Loren scrambled for the end of the ward. As he approached it, two inmates left the confines of their cells and barred his path. He didn't know them by name, but the tattooed mess on their clenched fists and the murderous look in their eyes made it quite clear why they belonged in the ward.

Turning around, Loren noted the arrival of a dazed Saprowski, still waking with the clicking sound of the door. A dozen more convicts joined the festivities. Some cheered their freedom, while others peered quizzically at Loren for some clue about what the hell was going on. Behind them all, waiting patiently, stood Tragedy. He didn't question anything. He seemed to understand exactly what was happening.

When the inmates noticed Loren's weapon, they encircled him. "Guys," he said, his left hand before him in a peaceful gesture.

"Let's not turn this into a thing, all right? Go back to your rooms, and—"

"Their cells." The screech of the intercom came to life above them. The voice carried a bottomless rage. "You mean to say their cells. Is that what you want, gentlemen?"

They didn't need to answer. The sudden spark in their eyes made their intentions clear. They tasted freedom. Nothing would keep that from them now.

"Listen to me," Loren said. "He's using you. Just like he did with Saprowski. Remember that, big guy?"

The giant scratched at his head, confused by everything happening around them. He barely knew where he was, let alone why he was there. The medications were too strong, addling his mind yet not enough to keep him under for the duration.

Lucky me.

"You can't let him do it to you again."

Saprowski stared at Loren, aimless. The cheers and jostling of those around him, though, snapped him to the room. One pointed to the end of the hall, which met up with reception and the exit beyond. Saprowski nodded, and excitement grew in his heavy frame.

Looking back at Loren, he cracked his knuckles loudly with anticipation. Loren's shoulders slumped. Saprowski had never been the smartest in the room. Now he was being deliberately ignorant.

The voice on the intercom returned to inspire them more. "He's the only one standing in your way, gentlemen. Freedom is on the other side. Wouldn't you like to be free?"

They required no more prodding. Each inmate took a step closer to Loren. His Glock offered no caution on their part. It did little to fill the detective with confidence, either. The killer had offered the one thing Loren never could, not after the crimes they must have committed to end up in Castlemere.

"Crap," Loren whispered.

The first punch followed immediately. Loren ducked under the blow. The second, though, landed along Loren's left side. He slammed into the nearby wall. Before he could bring his gun to bear on his attackers, Saprowski grabbed him and lifted him from the ground.

"Come on, Saprowski," Loren pleaded. He felt his ribs cracking under the behemoth's squeezing. Then there was nothing but air as

Saprowski sent him flying across the ward. He crashed amid the other inmates. His gun skittered out of reach toward Tragedy.

The masked ghoul stood in silence. He made no move for Loren. Instead, he used his foot to trap the loose weapon, while he continued to watch the other inmates close in on their prey.

"You see, Detective," the voice screeched through the intercom. "The darkness is always in all of us. Why struggle to bury it beneath a life of wasted potential? Why hide what we are when we can show it to the world? You'll need that darkness before the end. I'm sure your wife would have understood."

A kick jutted for Loren's skull. He batted the foot away and rolled for the other side of the crowding mob. Another kick hit him on the right side, followed by another. Someone moved to stomp on his chest, and Loren grabbed the shoe. He threw the attacker back, who barreled into his neighbors and three more behind him.

With some breathing room available, Loren jumped to his feet. His fists clenched tight before him, ready for the fight. "You don't get to talk to me about my wife. You don't know anything ab—"

Loren didn't even see where the punch came from. It slammed into his cheek and he fell to his knees. Another shot from the other side sent him crashing back to the floor, and the kicks returned on all sides. Loren struggled for his next breath. He struggled to go on.

"Stay down, Detective," the voice called softly. "Let them win. Your fight is over."

Blood spurting between his lips, Loren gritted his teeth. "Never. You hear me? Never!"

Glass shattered from the connecting wing. A shadow fell in the corridor. The inmates backpedaled, confused by the newcomer. Twin strands of pink shot out of the darkness and ensnared two of the attackers. It pulled them from the ground, then slammed them into the walls, where they collapsed into unconsciousness.

Loren fought to open his eyes as he worked his way to his knees. He tried to find his feet, but his body defied every attempt. Blood spat to the ground. "I won't give up. I'll never give up. Not to the likes of you."

A figure loomed over him. A hand dropped to help him to his feet. "Good to hear, Loren."

"Soriya?"

She lifted him up, a smirk on her face. They peered around at

the foes still standing, which only caused her grin to widen.
"How about we try this together?"

CHAPTER FIFTY-SIX

Shock overtook Loren. Soriya was next to him, ready to fight with him. After everything he had said to her, his absolute refusal to listen to her story and see the world from her point of view, she still came to his rescue.

Loren didn't know where to begin with her. That had been the problem from the start. Soriya saw the world from a completely different perspective. Her eyes had been opened to possibilities he had never come close to fathoming, maybe out of fear or simply because he'd never had the opportunity.

The chance should have been given. Loren knew that now. Soriya deserved that much, at least for all she had done.

So lost in thought, Loren barely felt the soft smack of Soriya's hand against his arm. One brute from the violent offender's ward charged at him. Screams of misplaced anger rose in the air, much like his fists, as he careened for Loren's position in the hopes of freedom.

Soriya pulled him out of the way at the last second. As soon as he was clear, she laid into the brute with a kick to the jaw. He fell and his momentum carried him into the nearby cell. The ribbon along her left arm shot out, grabbed hold of the door to the cell and slammed it shut.

Loren stared in utter amazement. Standing at her side, he glimpsed a large truncheon strapped to her jacket.

"What's that on your back?"

Soriya held back a laugh. "That's your first comment? Not 'thank you for saving my life?'"

They shifted back to back and faced their attackers. Angry eyes shot their way. The inmates closed in on all sides.

"I was doing fine," Loren said with a shrug.

"Oh yeah," Soriya replied. "It looked that way."

Loren sighed. "Thank you."

"Better."

With that, the first blows rained down on them. They dodged as one, working together almost intuitively. Loren perceived each movement at his back and followed through against his own assailant.

Working through the pain in his side, and the blood pooled in his mouth, Loren beat back one, then two, of the inmates with a pair of blistering punches. Bodies fell behind him as well.

The next wave hesitated for a second. The momentum had shifted against them, and even through their medicated haze, they recognized the threat.

Still, something continued to bother Loren. "And the back thing?"

"A present for Mr. Kindly."

Loren grimaced. The reminder brought back the ticking clock against him. "He has Gates."

"Gates?"

"A colleague," Loren said. "She figured everything out. I should have listened. To both of you."

Soriya blocked a punch from her left before delivering a reply that sent a man barreling into the cell behind him. The blow left her vulnerable, but Loren shifted to defend her from the advancing wave of assailants. He tackled them to the ground, a scream on his lips. Once down, Loren grabbed them by the hair and slammed their heads against the concrete.

When he glanced up, Tragedy was there. He stared down at Loren, twin black voids of nothingness locked on Loren's very soul. Loren's gun was in Tragedy's hand, aimed for the detective's forehead.

"A tragedy, for sure," the masked fiend remarked. "So sad."

A driving kick slapped Tragedy's arm up. The bullet snapped the air before connecting with the emergency lighting above. The section dropped to complete darkness. Even so, Loren watched Soriya knock Tragedy back. The gun fell from his hand to the ground before Loren.

"Go," Soriya said.

Loren grabbed his fallen weapon and tucked it at his side. "What?"

Saprowski jumped between them. He charged at Soriya like a rampaging rhino and slammed her into the wall. Loren leaped on the behemoth's back, pummeling his head to no avail. Saprowski lurched to the opposite wall, and all breath left Loren as he connected hard.

Loren fell, his feet hardly able to carry him any longer. Saprowski whirled around to strike. His fist hung heavy in the air. Before the blow fell on Loren, a hand jutted out and caught Saprowski's fist.

Soriya was in front of him. She diverted the blow to her right, then led with a powerful left to the giant's side. Saprowski cried out and fell away from the pair.

"Well, what are you waiting for?" Soriya asked, her eyes keen on the inmates.

"What do you mean?"

"Save Gates," Soriya said. "I've got this."

"There are eight of them."

She whipped the hair from her eyes, the glint of her teeth shining in the darkness. "Exactly." She leaped back into the fray, her fists flying. "Go, Loren. Save her."

Loren lifted his sidearm and raced for the connecting wing. The second he was clear of the ward, the door slammed shut behind him. The locking mechanism clicked loudly into place.

"Soriya!"

It was too late. The Kindly Killer had set his path. Loren took off down the wing for the stairs to the second floor. He only hoped he wasn't too late.

CHAPTER FIFTY-SEVEN

"Kill her already!" The voice bellowed through the intercom.

Soriya made the task as difficult as possible. She leaped between assailants, danced around blows, and delivered her own bone-crunching justice with every move. There was no opportunity to lock her down, even in the tight quarters of the ward. She constantly moved, shifted, and dodged—a blur of color in the darkness.

Four inmates fell in seconds. Despite her confidence, though, Soriya knew it was more luck than anything else. These men did not know who she was or her capabilities. Those that remained standing, however, learned quickly. They tempered their rage and encircled her, waiting for an opening rather than jumping at the first chance.

"Let's even the odds, shall we?" the voice called.

The doors to the ward opened. From a distance, the sound of unlocking cells echoed through the building. Inmates staggered to their freedom in the corridors, and a fresh wave of attackers arrived, ready for a fight.

"Freedom is yours when she is dead," the voice announced.

That was all the incentive they needed. Dozens rushed for her. Backing away from them, Soriya ran headlong into another pair. A blow connected with her cheek, which drove her to one knee. She rebounded and delivered a jaw-shattering uppercut to the closest inmate. He crashed along the growing crowd.

Soriya spun and met his neighbor with a spin kick that sent him whirling in the air. His head cracked against the glass of the nearby cell and he collapsed in a heap.

There were still too many. She needed room to maneuver. Reaching for the pouch at her hip, Soriya released the Greystone. She held it before her and channeled her will into the stone.

R

Bodies flew to the walls and out of the ward. The wind swirled from every crack and through the broken window in the neighboring hall. The bizarre assault of the elements brought out terror in some prisoners. They fled rather than face the Greystone again. Others struck the walls hard enough to knock them out for the duration.

Few remained in the ward. Those that did struck Soriya while her back was turned. The rune upon the Greystone dimmed as she fell forward. A quick flip along her heels brought her face-to-face with those still standing. Four men, including the one Loren had called Saprowski, looked upon her like a prize meal. They lashed out with reckless abandon.

They were sloppy, too impatient at her seeming weakness after using the stone. Soriya let them in close, then took the first one out at the knee. His leg snapped from the blow, and his cries followed him face-first to the floor. The second caught her on her side, driving her to the wall. Soriya kicked out for the glass of the open cell. She climbed over the attacker, flipped behind him, then knocked him into the cell. The door slammed shut behind him and locked with the press of a button.

A punch landed to the left of her head. Soriya barely shifted to the side in time, as Saprowski made his presence known. He wailed in the dark, striking at nothing but shadows. Soriya stepped back with each blow, out of reach of the massive mitts of the inmate.

The second he overstepped during one of his punches, Soriya launched into the air. She kicked him in the jaw, then somersaulted over his head. Her hands reached behind her, looping under his double-chin. With all her strength, Soriya pulled at Saprowski. His feet left the ground, lost to her momentum, and she threw him across the ward to the far end.

He slammed into the wall. As he slid to the floor, dazed but not out, he grabbed at the conduits running from the terminal box. One ripped loose and angled dangerously in the air. The sharp metal hanger from the wall twisted along the end, pointing like the blade of a spear.

Only a single inmate remained. He had waited patiently, watching through black holes for eyes. Tragedy, head crooked, appeared to have enjoyed every second of the show.

"Look at how you struggle." His arms were outstretched to showcase the fury unleashed on the ward. "This is your life now, isn't it? Forever fighting. Forever suffering. How tragic."

Soriya cringed at the word. She wanted nothing more than to pummel the masked cretin. Her body, though, struggled against her. The effects of the last few minutes had taken their toll. Her hands were numb from taking out Saprowski, her side a welt of a bruise from too many blows. Still, she fought through every ounce of pain and took a step toward her foe. "Better to stand up for a cause than simply create chaos for no reason at all."

"Is that what I've done?" Tragedy asked, laughing at her.

"Enlighten me."

He circled her slowly. "You believe the timing of my arrival to be a mere coincidence?"

She had never considered it, in fact. Tragedy, as well as his deceased partner, had plagued the city for months. Random acts, with no apparent purpose, had offered the police no clues. She thought chaos had been the point, but looking back, she suddenly realized the truth. Every act had occurred for a reason.

"You pulled resources from the investigation. You're in league with…"

"I hate the name," Tragedy interrupted. "Don't say it."

Soriya huffed. "Well, I wouldn't want to upset you. What should I call him?"

"The start of something new."

Soriya tired of the discussion. With a leap, she closed the gap between them, her leg jutting out to strike at the waiting Tragedy with a blistering kick. Instead of battering him back, Tragedy caught her by the left ankle and twisted hard. Soriya fell to the ground, her ankle pulsing with pain.

"He opened a door. One you will never close. A change is coming to Portents, Greystone." Tragedy loomed over her. "You have no place in the new order."

"Ambitious," Soriya said. She fought to stand, her left side nearly useless. "Doesn't sound like you at all."

"We all have our roles to play. But after you took my love from me?" Tragedy cracked his knuckles and cocked his fist back. "I'm going to enjoy this."

"Finally, something we can agree on."

His fist crashed toward her. Soriya rolled to the right. His punch connected with the concrete, and the ground quaked from the impact. His strength was overwhelming, sending cracks out from the epicenter.

Soriya grabbed hold of the wall and forced herself to stand. She wouldn't die on her knees or on her back. If this was the end, she would stand.

When Tragedy moved to oblige, he carried the device from her back. He held it before him, confused. Then he tossed it aside where it rolled to the corner. "A weapon? You surprise me."

"It isn't for you," Soriya said. "This is."

ᚱ

The Greystone lit up with enough force to drive Tragedy from his feet. He sailed to the end of the ward. His laughter followed him, unafraid of her strike. What he failed to see, however, was the conduit still hanging loose off the wall. The angled metal sliced through his mid-section, impaling him to the spot.

Soriya let the wind die down. She could barely stand; her body wanted nothing more than to give out. "It's over."

"No, Greystone." Tragedy's hands gripped the end of the conduit. He fought in vain to free himself. "It will never be over for you."

"What are you—"

Tragedy let go of the conduit and grabbed his mask. His body crumbled as he slipped the obol from his face. Before the devastation could reach his hands, Tragedy dropped the mask into the lap of Saprowski beneath him. His carcass collapsed, spilling loose from the conduit and showering the dazed Saprowski with a bath of diseased flesh and maggots.

The behemoth gawked at the mask before him. Soriya crept closer, a hand out to stop him. "Listen to me. Don't—"

He didn't bother to hear the rest of her warning. Saprowski slipped the mask on. The brand instantly appeared along his neck; the image of the masks was clear even in the dim emergency lighting of the ward.

Standing, he cracked his neck and clenched his fists before him.

The mask had replaced Saprowski, body and soul. "Much better."

Soriya seethed. "That's the last life you claim."

"Doubtful," Tragedy replied. "There's so much left to do."

"Not for you."

"You think you stand a chance at what is coming?" Tragedy boomed, rushing toward her. "You're nothing. There's only one way this can end!"

"I agree." The Greystone pulsed in her hand. She felt every last ounce of strength rush through her body and into the stone for one final attack.

Strength coursed through her. She released every erg built up in her lithe frame in a single punch.

Tragedy never saw it coming. Running toward his supposed destiny, he had no time to dodge or block the blow.

Her fist connected with Tragedy's mask. It fractured from the impact, splintering in a dozen directions across the ancient obol. The mask shattered like glass and Saprowski fell before her. The brand dissipated, unable to maintain its hold after so short a period. He was still breathing, free from Tragedy's grasp.

Soriya wiped the sweat from her brow and collapsed along the wall next to her.

CHAPTER FIFTY-EIGHT

Loren raced up the steps to the administration wing. All thought to the pain in his body vanished. There was only Gates to consider. He listened to the hysteria below. Inmates ran through the wings with reckless abandon. They searched for freedom, frantic in their need to escape.

He pushed it all aside. Loren could do nothing against so many. At least Soriya was safely locked in the violent offender's ward, or as safe as one could be, surrounded by raging homicidal maniacs. She certainly seemed capable of handling herself, at least.

If only Loren felt the same. His hands filled with nervous sweat, afraid to face the truth. He turned left at the landing down Deckart's private hall. At the precipice, Loren stopped and headed right instead. He reached Finney's office door. It was open a crack, and he stepped inside.

"Gates?" Loren called, inching his way through the office.

She sat at the desk, bound and gagged. The killer held a knife to her throat. On the carpet in the center of the room was the body of Clyde Deckart. He had been Loren's last hope, but then, Loren always knew who the killer was going to be.

It was in the connection between the last three victims. They had all served on the same medical review board, where they granted and revoked licenses to medical professionals, including the man with an upcoming review to gain his practice back. The same board had taken it away from him years earlier.

The killer had to be Arnold Finney.

"She's fine, Detective," Finney answered. None of the empathy he had displayed during their previous conversations was present, or the heart for his work and for humanity he'd shown Loren. Only the deep malice he had masterfully hidden from view remained.

"She'll stay fine as long as you keep your distance."

"It's over, Finney," Loren said. "I wanted to believe I was wrong, that there was no way it could be you. Why? How could you do this?"

"They brought it on themselves!" His eyes bulged as he yelled. The knife remained in place, secure to Gates' throat. "They ripped my practice from me over a mistake. They took my livelihood and left me with a paltry position dealing with the worst of the worst."

"That's not…" Loren stared at the stranger before him. How had he not seen the truth sooner? "Did I ever really know you?"

"We all hide our darkness, Detective," Finney said. The way he said his title sent chills up Loren's spine. Finney knew the effect Shriff had had on him and played into it well. "I grew tired of holding mine back."

"I've heard that before." Loren took another step closer, gun at the ready.

Finney shook his head. "That's far enough."

"What are you going to do, Finney?" In the distance, flashing red and blue lights filled the air. The sound of sirens carried on the wind. "There's nowhere for you to go. This place will be crawling with uniforms in a matter of minutes. Let Gates go."

Finney's eyes flitted to the windows and back again, twice, then three times, in the passing of a few seconds. "No," he said, sweat along his brow. "I've been walked on my whole life, snubbed by inferior minds. I won't let it end this way. I'll see her dead first."

"I won't let that happen," Loren said. He wasn't looking at Finney. Gates had drawn his attention. Wide eyes communicated all he needed to know. So did her hands, which were no longer bound to the arms of the chair. "And neither will she."

He raised his Glock and shifted to the left suddenly. The quick movement drew Finney's attention away from his hostage. In that instant, Gates grabbed Finney by the arm and shoved the knife away.

"Don't you—" Finney cried out, rage unbound. His free hand connected with her cheek and pushed Gates aside. She fell, chair and all, with a crash. The legs snapped loose from the seat and Gates slipped free from her bindings.

Finney continued to stand over the fallen Gates. The knife arced downward toward his victim. Loren seized his opportunity and pulled the trigger. The bullet caught Finney in the right shoulder.

He staggered back toward the window. The knife remained firmly in his grasp, his free hand over his bleeding wound. His eyes flashed with anger, wild and frenzied, then changed in a blink. He looked at Loren with sadness and remorse.

"Greg…" he pleaded. "Wait, I… Listen to…"

The knife was in the air, the threat still apparent.

"I've heard enough from you!" Gates shouted.

A powerful kick collided with Finney's chest. He toppled back, too far from Loren to be saved, and crashed through the window. Finney's cry echoed in the night as he fell.

Loren raced to the window. Finney lay on the ground in the pouring rain. Ruiz and a dozen armed officers surrounded him. They kept their weapons trained on him while the captain checked the fallen doctor's vitals. When Ruiz glanced up at the shattered window, Loren waved.

A rustle of movement behind him brought Loren away from the storm outside. Gates struggled to grab the side of the desk for leverage. Tears ran down her cheeks, her body visibly shaking from the ordeal. Loren was immediately at her side. With a helping hand, he pulled her close and held her tight.

"It's over," he whispered. "It's finally over."

CHAPTER FIFTY-NINE

Loren held Gates close to his side. They traveled down the steps from administration and directly to reception for the exit. Officers rushed through in all directions. They dragged patients back to their cells and restrained those still resisting. The fight had been knocked out of most from the looks of things, not that Loren cared in the least.

His thoughts were stuck on Finney. For as short a time as they had known each other, Loren had honestly cared for the man's future as a doctor. He had even contemplated offering a personal recommendation for the review board hearing. Finney had exuded nothing but kindness and empathy, yet the truth had been hidden deep, waiting to be unleashed. Shriff had offered the perfect opportunity to do so and Finney had jumped at it.

Loren felt like a fool. So did the rest of the staffers and security personnel of Castlemere, who had been found in a conference room behind the security station.

"He asked us to meet him for an update," Olson said. "We were all there and then… the door locked and every system shut down. We were trapped."

The same bewilderment followed Loren and Gates as they left Castlemere for the storm outside. The rains attempted to wash away the stain of the night, though Loren wondered if he would ever feel clean again in Portents. Chaos seemed to trail him like a shadow, waiting to swallow him whole.

At the base of the stairs, EMTs strapped Finney to a medical bed. The fall had left him bruised and battered, but still breathing. His eyes were shut tight, lost to the nightmare that would be the rest of his life. The emergency technicians carted him away toward the ambulance at the far end of the loop.

Ruiz nodded to them as he passed. When he spotted Loren and Gates walking down the steps, Ruiz rushed over. "Greg!"

Loren grinned. "About time you showed up."

"Cut the crap," the captain spouted. "Gates, are you—"

"I'm fine, sir," Gates said weakly. Her head stuck close to Loren's side, her body still shaking from the experience. "He didn't hurt me."

Ruiz peered at Loren for confirmation, then back at the officer. "Yeah, well, the medic will determine that."

He waved them over. Two medics helped Gates over to a secondary ambulance. Loren called after her. "Looks like a couple days of rest. Hope you can stomach the time off."

Gates glanced back, her eyes lost to the shadows. "Oh, I'm sure I'll find something to do. Thanks, Detective."

The medics continued toward the back of the ambulance to treat her. Loren paused for a moment, the sound of his title chilling him to the bone.

He took a step to follow Gates when Ruiz cut him off. "You want to tell me what the hell you were thinking?"

Loren stared at him, bewildered. "Hold up. Why isn't Gates getting this treatment as well?"

"I like her better."

Loren laughed. "You're all heart, Ruiz."

"And you look like a massive bruise," the captain replied. "You should join Gates to—"

"I'm fine," Loren said. His body ached in places he never knew existed, but he pushed the pain away. Rest would come soon enough.

"Greg…"

"I'm fine."

Ruiz nodded a silent surrender to the argument. The pair started back up the steps for the institute. Chaos continued through reception. Staffers were sent home for some much-needed rest. Olson debriefed his security guards, as well as Quinn and Messick. All others weaved their way through the complex to lock everything down.

Loren led Ruiz into the violent offender's ward. Everyone had been secured in their cells, the power back up and running in the fight's aftermath.

"Why did you do it, Greg?" Ruiz asked again in a softer tone.

"What made you come here?"

"I didn't want to," Loren answered. "I wanted to walk away, but that felt like giving up instead of helping my situation."

"What changed your mind?"

"Gates did," Loren said. He peered down to see a shattered shard of Tragedy's mask on the blood-soaked concrete. "And someone else."

"Yeah..." Ruiz ran his hand through his salt-and-pepper hair. "We're going to have to talk about your someone else at some point."

"You know about—"

Ruiz stopped him with a look. He patted the detective's shoulder. "We'll talk."

Ruiz started toward Quinn and Messick. Hours of work awaited them. Loren called to him before he was out of view. "It's going to be a long talk, isn't it?"

"Oh, yeah."

"Figures," Loren muttered to himself. He circled the facility, winding down the paths he had run through to save Gates from Finney. At the steps to the offices on the second floor, Loren caught a brief glimpse of a pink ribbon.

He climbed after it, but by the time he reached the second floor, the ribbon was gone, along with its owner. Loren turned right, a step back to Finney's office. Forensics crowded around the door. Hady's people were already inside to deal with Deckart's body.

Loren went left instead to the quiet of the administrator's private wing. The door to the office was open, and Loren stepped inside and closed the slab behind him.

Soriya stood by the window, looking out over the parking lot. Flashing lights from the multiple squad cars below illuminated her beaten and bloodied frame. Her smile refused to diminish.

"I suppose I should thank you properly," Loren said. He leaned along the bookcase on the opposite side of the window frame.

Soriya continued to stare into the darkness. "Let me know when the shower of gratitude arrives."

He chuckled, then sighed. The doors to Finney's ambulance closed and headed off into the night. So much pain, so much death, and all caused by one man.

"You were wrong, though," he said as he stared into the storm.

"There was no possession. Finney took advantage of the information at hand to create a boogeyman in the city. He used the details of the previous victims to take out the people who hurt him the most. Just another murderer. And I thought so much of him."

Soriya said nothing. Her fingers stretched around her back for the item secured to her jacket. Her gaze, though, remained locked outside. When Loren trailed her, he realized she was watching the other ambulance closely.

"Hey," he called, drawing her back to the room. "Did you hear me? It's over."

"Hmmm? Oh. Sure. Of course."

"What was the deal with the weapon?"

Soriya kicked off the window ledge and shifted back through the office. "Just a precaution, Loren. Unnecessary, I guess."

They headed for the door. Soriya led him down the private wing. A large window overlooked the forest that extended north across the massive estate. Her fingers unlatched the casement and opened the window. The wind blew in, sharp and cold.

Soriya smiled at him through the darkness. "I'm glad you were here, Loren."

"Yeah," he replied. With his hand raised to the back of his neck, Loren glanced back down the twisting halls of the institute. "You know what? I'm glad I was too."

Wind whipped along the corridor. Loren turned to his companion, but Soriya was gone.

Loren rushed for the window, but all sign of the mysterious woman had vanished. He didn't think he would ever get used to it.

He wasn't lying, though. Putting an end to the case, standing up to the killer, it felt like Loren was right where he belonged in the world.

Loren tucked his hands in his pockets and started for home.

CHAPTER SIXTY

Loren closed the lid on the box. Every scrap of data, every piece of evidence cataloged over the course of the last year, sat within. The case was over. The Kindly Killer was truly gone this time. Arnold Finney had been the last chapter of the story.

Sitting back along the couch, the weary detective reached for his stale ginger ale. A beer would have been nice to celebrate the occasion, but he was proud he'd been able to resist the urge. The painkillers for his injuries certainly helped deter his poor judgment. Still, the days of his downward spirals had to remain in the past, for as long as he was able, at any rate.

Something glinted from underneath the table. Loren set the glass down next to the box, then reached down to retrieve the small shiny item: his badge. A grin widened on Loren's face. He stood, holding tight to the gold shield, and headed for the window.

There had been days he wondered if it would ever mean the same to him again. The job had become nothing but a burden, one threatening to drag him under with every case, with every lead, and with every crime. No light remained in his world. His wife had provided that glimmer for so long, but with her death darkness enveloped his every waking thought.

He had Gates to thank for bringing him back—her and Soriya. Two strangers had shown him the power of his badge, and the responsibility he bore in helping bring the light to the rest of the city. Loren now understood why, and definitely where, he was needed.

The sun set in the distance. Another night was on the horizon, with deep waves of purple running to pinks and oranges across the sky. The storm had finally ended. The rains had petered out, and the winds had fallen to a warm breeze from the south. Clear nights were in the forecast, no extra shadows needed.

A knock at the door pulled him from the calm outside. Loren's first thought was of Pratchett. He had left the officer in the lurch the previous night by taking his car to Castlemere. He owed the man for trusting him so much. Pratchett was a good friend and there were few left in Loren's corner.

A second knock brought with it a sense of urgency. Loren wondered when he'd become so popular. He opened the door, surprised at the woman waiting outside.

"Gates? What are you doing here?"

The young woman wore a t-shirt and jeans. Her hands were tucked behind her back and her gaze lowered to the floor. Bruises were clear on her face from Finney's assault on her the night before, but her eyes were bright and vibrant. "I…"

"Should you even be out of the hospital after everything you went through?" he asked, cutting her off. "Ruiz will have your hide if he learns you checked yourself out without a clean bill of health."

She said nothing, unable to come up with a defense. Loren rolled his eyes at his behavior. Why he had yet to master some common courtesy, especially with the amount of visitors to his apartment of late, was something he needed to address. "Sorry, Gates," he said. "I'm the last person who should lecture anyone about personal choices. It's been a strange few days.

"Come in." He waved for her to follow as he crossed the living room. Upon her entry, Loren turned for the kitchen. "Would you like a drink? I can't offer much, but the flat ginger ale has a decent aftertaste. Better than the water, anyway."

The door shut, and the lock engaged with a solid click. "I only need one thing, Detective."

Loren stopped short of the kitchen. His eyes thinned at his company. "Gates?"

She raised a pistol at him. "To tie off a loose end."

CHAPTER SIXTY-ONE

"Put the gun down, Gates."

Loren raised his hands slowly. He approached the wide-eyed visitor at his door with slow steps.

At the third, she shook her head to stop him. "I'd rather not, Detective."

"This isn't you," Loren said. She kept calling him by his title, just as she had the previous night. At the time, he'd thought it odd considering his request to call him Greg. The way she now said it mirrored the way others had over the last few weeks too closely to be a coincidence. Suddenly, Soriya's theory made much more sense. "Oh. Oh, Gates. This *isn't* you, is it?"

"Ding, ding, ding," she said, a finger to her nose like a buzzer. "Give the man a prize."

Her deadpan laughter filled the room. There was no life behind it, only misery and pain.

He couldn't believe it. Possession. How was such a thing possible? And if it was, that meant Soriya had been right from the start about Shriff. Somehow he had passed on his instability—the Kindly Killer persona—to Finney. How had Finney made the transfer?

Loren's eyes alighted, recalling when Finney had pushed Gates away from him. He had touched her cheek for only a second, but the contact was enough to solidify his hold on the woman. Loren had no opportunity to discover the truth because Gates had kicked Finney out of the damn window to cover the change.

"Dear me, Detective," Gates said. "I waited and waited for you to see the light, but you never got there. I pushed it with Shriff."

Loren's brow furrowed.

Gates rolled her eyes, exasperated. "Come on. How would an idiot like Shriff know anything about your wife? He was a self-obsessed twit who deserved to be stepped on, truth be told. He still had his uses, though. Gave me plenty of fun. Until you and your pal got involved."

Loren's fist clenched at his side. "And Finney?"

"Even sicker, if you can believe that!" Gates said with a laugh. "His *tiny* mistake? He was diddling his patients. Like a lot of them. He would put them under to explore their dreams, then have his way. All in service to their treatment. He was so convinced he was right, it barely took a nudge to throw him over the edge."

Gates took a deep, cleansing breath. The gun wavered in her hand, but Loren made no move against her. Confession was much too good for her soul, and he wanted to hear the rest.

"They were pleasant diversions, but it's time for me to get to work," she said. "I can't have you dogging my trail any longer, fun as it may be. Time to tackle my real reason for being here."

"Which is?"

"I like you, Loren." Gates exclaimed. "So many questions. All the time!"

Loren shrugged. "How else am I supposed to appreciate your motivation for killing me?"

"Cute," Gates shot back. "But I'll grant you that. A little appreciation goes a long way."

"Why are you here? Why do you need Gates?"

"I'm the Alpha," Gates proclaimed with pride. "No form. All power. I'm here to bring about the end."

"How?"

"The Omega, Detective. I am the beginning to their end." She stared at Loren, reading his obvious confusion over everything. There wasn't a damn word he understood, and she knew it. "You're so lost. Oh, not just you, but the look on your face doesn't help humanity's argument for survival. Do you know what lies at the heart of this place? At the heart of Portents?"

"What?"

"Forever, Detective," Gates said. "I'm talking about for-ev-er. An eternity the Omega will rain down on this world once it's free. It's going to be glorious. Too bad you won't live to see it."

Her grip tightened on the pistol. Panic filled Loren's eyes, his hands before him. "Gates!" he cried. "Gates, listen to me. You can fight this. Fight against whatever this thing is inside you."

The gun went off. The bullet pierced the floor scant centimeters from his right foot. Gates raised the weapon level with his chest once more. "Nope," she said. "She can't hear you. Gates is gone. Lost in the darkest part of herself."

"She doesn't have one, you piece of shit," Loren snapped. Spit flew from his lips. "She's the light this city needs. And I believe in her."

"Not enough to make a difference." She started to depress the trigger. There was no more debating, no more delaying. Gates had no control over her body. Loren had to make a move, but he couldn't—not against her. Not after everything she'd done for him, all her efforts to save him.

A knock at the door interrupted them.

Gates turned for the door. As she did, a foot crashed through the lock and the wood fell loose from the frame. "What the hell?"

Soriya leaped into the room. She dove for the extended weapon, but Gates was too quick for her. She tucked close, backpedaling away from Soriya.

With her chance stymied, Soriya circled the perimeter, then stopped between Gates and Loren. She spread her arms, a human barrier.

"Hey," she said to Loren.

"Uh, hey. You—"

"I was about to knock when I heard her monologuing," Soriya said. "Who does that, anyway?"

"What are you doing here?"

Soriya ripped the weapon from her jacket. "Putting an end to this once and for all." She removed the Greystone from her hip, settled it against the base of the weapon, then held the pair out for Gates to get a better view. "Recognize this?"

Fear sparked in Gates' eyes. "You wouldn't."

Loren shifted to Soriya's side. "Wouldn't what?"

"The spirit inside your friend can body hop," Soriya explained. "Through touch, most likely. It needs that freedom. See, there's no obol like the masks to offer to new hosts. This, however, will trap the spirit in place."

He recognized the truncheon now. It wasn't some blunt force object. It was a brand, the mark on it now clear to him, though he failed to understand its meaning.

"You trap me in this body, and my presence will destroy her mind," the frightened woman said. "I'll corrupt everything within her."

Loren's hope rekindled with her words. "So she is still in there. That's all I needed to hear."

He drew his sidearm from the holster off the side of the couch. At the sight of his weapon, Gates tightened the grip on her gun. Soriya smirked, edging closer to the possessed woman. Before she could get within reach, Loren cut between them and leveled his gun at Soriya.

"Loren?" Soriya asked, confused by the sudden turn of events.

He wasn't looking at Soriya, though. Loren caught Gates' excited glance and held it in his own. His bare arm extended toward her. "Take me."

"What?" Gates exclaimed.

"She doesn't deserve this," Loren said. "Gates is innocent. Possess me." Both Gates and Soriya said nothing, hardly able to comprehend the offer. "We're connected. You've felt it the same way I have. Through Shriff. Through Finney. I was always there. Always waiting for you. Come on. I have to be more appetizing than Gates. I'm probably the buffet of darkness you've been looking for this whole time."

"You..." Gates hesitated. Her gun lowered slightly, and she staggered backward, fumbling for balance. When she looked up again, her entire posture changed. A soft voice called out, "Greg."

Loren grinned. "Gates! I knew you could—"

She stopped his approach with a raised hand. Her other hand cradled her gut like something churned inside. "I can't fight it." Gates turned to Soriya with piercing eyes. "But I can hold it back."

"That's not going to happen." Loren cut between them. "I—"

"I can do this, Greg," Gates pleaded. The strain on her body was clear. "The good in me can beat this back. Trust me."

"I can't," Loren said. "It should be me. I have nothing worth—"

"You're wrong." Gates fought back the growing pain rampaging through her body and stood tall. "Here's your chance to prove it.”

Gates leaped at Soriya. In mid-air, her entire demeanor changed. All the pent-up anger, the malicious intent of the Alpha, exploded from her in a guttural roar of fury.

Soriya squeezed the Greystone. A light beamed along the surface.

Heat channeled through the branding iron in her grasp, and the surface burned a deep red.

“No! Wait!” Loren reached out to no avail. It was too late.

Soriya jammed the iron up at Gates and caught her in the neck. The brand burned into her skin, sizzling on impact. Soriya held it in place, trailing Gates’ falling body from her failed leap. Soriya pulled back and Gates slammed to the ground on her knees. Her hand shot up to the searing wound embedded in her flesh, then flinched away at the heat still rising from the brand. Gates’ scream boomed through the apartment in a voice not her own. It was the pain of the Alpha.

“No, no, no,” Loren begged. “Why did you—”

“Because she was a fool,” the Alpha seethed. “You all are. Nothing will stop what is coming. Nothing!”

Soriya kicked Gates across the cheek. “I will. I will always be here to stop you.”

The possessed figure fell to the ground. Her eyes closed to the world.

Loren could do nothing but watch it happen. Horror filled him, incomprehension at what had occurred. He swung toward Soriya, hands tight to his temples.

“What have you done?”

CHAPTER SIXTY-TWO

It should have been him. Of all the people who deserved to live in a hellish limbo for the rest of their days, it was surely Loren. He had already lost everything that ever mattered to him. His mistakes far outweighed any contribution he'd brought to the world. Gates was too young, too hopeful, to have lost her entire future in a single act.

He stood over her fallen frame, tears in his eyes. He didn't bother to hide them, thinking of all the bright days ripped from the young officer who cared too much to see anyone else suffer. She was selfless. What the hell was he?

"Gates…"

A hand fell on his back. "You have to call this in, Loren."

He knocked the hand away, then stepped across the room. "I have to help her!"

"You can't," Soriya said in a soft voice. "You heard her, Loren. She made her decision."

"You forced it on her!" he shouted. "She's gone, trapped behind that monster—that Alpha—because of you."

"I didn't have a choice."

"Bullshit!" he railed. He threw his hands in the air, wringing them out before him. "I gave you an out."

"Losing you wasn't an option."

Her words barely penetrated. His life meant so little to him. How could it mean a damn thing to anyone else?

"W—We…" Loren stammered as he paced the room. "We could have forced the damn thing out. Put it in Finney or some lifer with no chance of seeing daylight again. It took me ten seconds to find alternatives. You had a full day." His eyes widened, and he spun to face Soriya again. "That's when you knew, wasn't it?

At Castlemere?"

Soriya's gaze fell at the accusation. "I wasn't sure."

"You didn't say a thing!" He rushed her. Grabbing her by the collar, he slammed her against the wall. "Who do you think you are? You and that stone of yours? You get to do whatever you want? Take any life that gets in your way and claim the moral high ground?"

"Sometimes." Her look hardened and she stood taller under his grasp. "And sometimes a brave woman makes the necessary sacrifice when I wish there was another way. I wasn't sure, Loren. Not until she showed up here. Not until she was about to kill you."

Loren let Soriya go. Backing away from her, he almost collapsed against the side of the couch. Shaking fingers gripped the fabric for balance, to keep him from falling completely. He wasn't sure if he would ever get up again.

"She should have," he muttered.

"Loren—"

"You took away her future, Greystone. And I didn't do a thing to stop you." Hate filled his eyes. It carried him back to his feet. "I never should have let you in my life."

Soriya's head bowed, crestfallen. All her efforts had been to bring them together. For what reason, Loren had yet to learn. Now he couldn't care less.

"That doesn't make the truth go away, Loren," Soriya said. "You've seen the true face of Portents. You're going to need my help to deal with it."

Loren refused to meet her gaze. He moved for Gates, still unconscious on the floor. "What I need is for you to leave."

"Loren, don't push me away," Soriya said. She reached for him. "Don't—"

He slapped her hand away. "Now!"

She nodded, retreating to the broken doorway. "I will. I'll go. But not forever. I have a feeling this fight is only beginning."

When he looked up, she was gone.

His entire world had been turned upside down. He had tried to escape it, but found the pull irresistible. It demanded a sacrifice, and he begged for it to be him, only him. Instead, he'd lost the light that had saved him.

He wanted to surrender again, to retreat into the darkness he had tried to resist for so long. That was no longer an option, not after Gates' sacrifice. She had given him a second chance at life, though Loren worried what kind of life was left to him.

Soriya's whispered warning caught on the breeze and echoed through his weary thoughts. *I have a feeling this fight is only beginning.*

"That's what I'm afraid of." He reached for his phone. His eyes remained locked on Gates as he dialed the precinct, a silent good-bye on his lips. "Will there be any light left by the time it ends?"

CHAPTER SIXTY-THREE

Soriya didn't go far. After Loren had demanded her departure, she headed around the apartment building and back up the fire escape. Tucked out of sight, Soriya waited until backup arrived to help secure Gates—and whatever was now locked within her.

Loren offered explanations. He played the truth angle, which surprised Soriya. It wasn't believed in the slightest and all weighed in that Gates had snapped from her experience with Finney the night before. As if one could catch homicidal tendencies like the common cold.

Loren didn't bother to fight for his version of events. He was too broken, too overwhelmed by everything.

The fault lay with Soriya. She should have trusted him with the full story. She should have told him her suspicions at Castlemere. They might have saved Gates. They might have been killed in the process as well. Playing their hand early held as much risk as holding back information. Mentor's lessons rang out through her mind and she cursed his every word, the same way Loren cursed hers.

He wanted nothing to do with her now. His fears had been justified through the loss of Gates. But Soriya couldn't leave him behind—not now. It was more than guilt over Beth's death. She had failed him just as much, in some regards.

No, she couldn't leave him. She would watch from afar, as she had for months prior to their introduction.

Loren now knew the truth, at least. He was aware of the city in a whole new way. His anger kept him from hearing all of it, but the knowledge remained, waiting for him to unlock it. She would be by his side when he did.

When Gates was escorted in cuffs from the apartment, Soriya left the comfort of the fire escape. She traveled back up the road for a clear view of the police cruisers parked on King's Lane.

Gates kept her gaze on the ground. Her shuffling feet were prodded along by the pair of officers on either side. Outside the car, Gates looked up and scanned the block. She caught sight of Soriya at the corner. No anger sat in her wide green eyes. None of the rage of the Kindly Killer presented in that brief glance.

Instead of screaming rage, Gates offered only a steadfast nod of acceptance to the woman who had branded her neck. The killer was locked inside, where it would remain for all time now. With that, the police ushered Gates into the cruiser. The door closed behind her and she was off into the deepening dark of Portents, her last trip through the city.

Soriya fought back tears. Regret had its place, but not here. She had done the right thing. Gates knew it. Someday, Loren might as well.

She needed him to understand. More than that, she simply needed him, as he needed her, though he failed to see things in that manner at the moment. They were light to each other's dark. Loren was the balance she had sought since she undertook the responsibility and the weight of the Greystone.

He might not want Soriya in his life, but she would always be there for him. Their relationship was only beginning.

Soriya started down the Knoll, the pink ribbons at her side and the stone in her hand. The night was young and there was work to do.

CHAPTER SIXTY-FOUR
Three Weeks Later

Loren returned to Castlemere out of necessity, not some inane desire to torture himself. He had avoided the trip following the arrest of Gates to cope with everything that had happened and why.

He was back at work full time again. Ruiz had even cleared him for active duty, and his caseload was picking up. The leash remained tight, with plenty of oversight thanks to his previous mistakes, but he had kept his nose clean and his work pristine... mostly. There was always the occasional head butt with superiors, with other departments, and with obstinate witnesses, but he dealt with them in stride.

The work was exactly what Loren needed. Keeping busy, keeping his mind distracted with the murder and mayhem of Portents, allowed him to focus on something other than himself. Closure, though, continued to elude him from his experiences. His return to the institute attempted to rectify that error.

"Thank you for taking the time for me, Dr. Nevins." Loren walked with the stout psychiatrist down the steps from the administration wing. Her heels sank into the carpet with each stride, causing Loren to tower over her. She was of a different breed than her predecessor. Where Deckart berated and bellowed for results, Nevins appeared to care for those around her as much as she did her patients.

"Stephanie, please."

They started through the wards. Painters worked to hide the mistakes of the past with bright colors that brought positivity throughout the well-worn facility. Loren wondered how long the makeover would last.

"I hope you won't take offense if I keep it to Dr. Nevins," Loren said. His eyes were always on the closed cells of the inmates of the wards—the few present during the mid-afternoon hour.

Nevins nodded in understanding. "You were close to Dr. Finney, weren't you?"

"He was a friend when I needed one," Loren replied in a sad tone. "Or so I thought. Is he—"

"Through here."

Nevins pointed ahead toward the violent offender's ward. She had restructured it as the solitary wing, with more guard details posted throughout. Work crews continued to repair the damage wrought from the night of the breakout, including the shattered window just outside the ward.

"The cleanup is almost complete," Nevins continued. "Most prisoners have been transferred to other facilities for the duration, but we've kept the wing locked down for a few special cases."

Loren noted the presence of Saprowski to his right. He sat hunched in his bed, docile. On the floor, he worked on a detailed drawing depicting the masks of Tragedy and Comedy. Their memory was clearly locked in his brain from his experience.

"Is that what Finney is now?" Loren asked, surprised. "A special case?"

Nevins sighed. "I read the man's work. He was brilliant. His sudden descent is nothing more than a tragedy. One of his own making, however."

They stopped outside the glass of Finney's cell. He sat on the ground with his back to them.

"Then why is he here?" Loren failed to understand. "Why isn't he in the maximum security ward at Caldwell Correctional?"

Nevins shifted for the controls next to the cell. Beneath a small speaker, she inputted a code. "We've had to take away his control to give ourselves a reprieve every once in a while. Take a listen."

The sound kicked on. Finney's voice filled the speaker, his words sharp and bitter. "It was the voice! He told me to do those things. Those awful, terrible things."

His body rocked back and forth, his gaze locked on the ground before him. "They deserved it," he said in a completely different voice.

Another twitch and Finney returned. "I would never, no matter the anger. I…"

He trailed off as he spun toward the glass. His eyes alighted at Loren and he shot to his knees. "Greg! You believe me, don't you?"

Loren didn't know what to say. Unfortunately, Finney filled the silence. Another twitch and his voice altered, his very mannerisms shifted. "Don't you believe me, Detective? You know the truth. Murder was too good for them."

His mind was gone, snapped in two by the Alpha's presence in his body. The possession warped Finney's sense of reality. Loren wondered if there was ever any chance to save the man who had been his friend, or if this was always the path he would travel—with or without the Alpha.

The sight saddened him. Nevins read the look on his face and turned off the speaker. "He's been that way since he woke in the hospital after his fall."

"He never displayed a split personality before. Could the fall have—"

"No," Nevins answered quickly. "This was a deep schism, most likely triggered the moment he took his first life. The one voice is a justification to the deeds. The other, Finney's own words of regret at committing them."

She ushered him away from the cell. Loren followed, though part of him held on for a moment for some sign of the real Finney, hoping the man he'd met during his first visit to Castlemere was still in there somewhere.

They continued through the ward, toward the far end of the corridor. "We'll do what we can to help him," Nevins said. "The same with your friend."

"May I?" Loren asked, cocking his thumb ahead.

"Please," Nevins said with a nod. "She has company, but take all the time you need."

"Thanks."

Loren proceeded without his escort. An older woman stood before the cell. She held her fist against the glass, her eyes thin with anger at the sight of the woman inside.

Gates sat against the wall near the glass. Restraints locked her arms to her chest to keep her from hurting herself. A dazed look from the medication kept her attention aimless.

Loren moved beside the woman outside the cell. "Mrs. Gates?"

She didn't acknowledge his arrival. The sight of her daughter continued to draw her in. "That isn't her. Where did my Melanie go?"

"I'm sorry," was all he could think to say.

"It's this city. I've always said so. It takes and takes until there's nothing left. I tried to warn her." She glanced at him with tears in her eyes. "I begged her to escape. To go abroad. Meet a boy. Live a life in the sunshine."

She reached into her purse and pulled out a pack of cigarettes and a lighter. She took one out, then offered the pack to Loren, who considered the proposition for a long moment before passing. He grabbed at the pack of gum in his pocket, removed a stick of the fruity monstrosity, and slipped it between his lips. *Filthy habit.*

The woman lit the end and puffed hard on the cigarette. "I hate Portents."

"Yeah," Loren agreed. He shifted a little closer to the rising smoke around her. "I can't really argue with that sentiment."

"Ma'am?" A guard rushed toward them. "You can't—"

"I will do whatever I damn well please!" Gates' mother yelled. "You hear me?"

"But you can't—"

"Did you hear me?" she repeated in a shrill tone.

The guard shrank back. "Y—yes."

Mrs. Gates huffed, then stalked past Loren and down the corridor. A sad gaze flitted back to her daughter before she departed for the day. Her shoulders were slumped, and a cloud trailed her until she was gone.

"That poor woman," Loren muttered.

"She'll be all right. She's strong." Gates stood at the glass. Alert eyes trailed her mother's exit from the ward. Then she smiled at him. "Hello, Greg. Thanks for visiting."

CHAPTER SIXTY-FIVE

"Gates?" Loren put his hand to the glass. "Is it really you?"

"It's me, Greg."

She was still in there. He could tell from her wide green eyes and the hopeful tone of her voice. They had barely known each other a month, yet Greg felt completely connected to her after all they'd endured. They were like old friends who had been through a singular experience no one else could possibly comprehend.

Even he had trouble with it, especially with how it ended. "Gates, I…"

"You're tearing yourself up over this," Gates said with a nod. "John said you would. That's how you were built."

"It's my fault."

"No," Gates said, her voice soft and self-assured. "I made a choice and your friend was right to act when she did. No more Kindly Killer. No more death."

"I don't know." He had debated the event every second since it had happened. Soriya had acted as judge, jury, and executioner. How was he supposed to handle something like that? How was he supposed to work with someone like that? It all boiled down to the same thing in the end. "I don't think I could ever trust someone like her."

"You'll have to trust someone," Gates said. "She cares about you and about this city. Don't give up on either. They'll both need you… before the end."

The brief pause in her speech caused a complete shift in her. Her voice, so hopeful throughout, finished with bitterness and rage. Malicious intent spewed from her lips, and Loren immediately noticed the change. It was in her eyes, the way her head tilted to the left at an angle. The smile, most of all, sold him on the change.

Once serene, now nothing but pure evil remained behind her toothy grin.

"Gates?" Loren called, hopelessly. "Melanie?"

"She thinks this city is worth saving," the voice spat at the glass. Saliva ran in a thin stream between them. "She's wrong."

"Alpha."

"The mother has it right," Alpha continued with a sneer. "What a cesspool. Portents deserves to be ground zero for what is coming." She danced away from the glass, jubilant at her own fantasies. "Do you remember, Detective? What lies at the heart of Portents?"

He would always remember. No matter where his life took him, no matter what he did, Loren would never forget the answer to Alpha's question.

"Forever."

She giggled with glee, then sidled up to the glass once more. "There is a darkness in there, Detective. It's locked in the heart, chained and angry as hell. When it breaks free—and it will—it is coming for you and everyone you love."

More laughter filled the cell. It rang out through the speaker and echoed down the corridor. Looks shot their way as guards walked their beat. None intervened.

For Loren, the sound was chilling. It rattled his bones, but he didn't blink or flinch at the mad cackle. He refused to back down to the menace buried deep within his friend.

"There will be no more light, except what it chooses to provide," the Alpha said, relishing the notion. "The Omega is coming, Detective."

"Not if I have anything to say about it."

She laughed at his false bravado.

Loren slammed his hand against the glass. "I won't let it happen. I will stand in the way. No matter the monster, no matter the threat, I will be here and I will stop it."

He meant every word. As much as Portents had taken from him, despite all the pain and misery it had caused him to endure during his tenure at the Central Precinct, Loren held tight to his role and his responsibility.

Nothing would stop him from the work. He knew he might falter and fade over time, that the darkness would find him on weaker days and he would lose his way. He also knew others would always bring him back—like Soriya had and, like Gates continued to do, locked away behind the eyes of a monster.

Loren would always fight his way out of the darkness for the light. He would be there when needed.

Always.

CHAPTER SIXTY-SIX

Loren left her in silence, sadness in his stare and in his steps. The guards followed suit soon after, and the emptiness struck her.

Alpha fell quiet once more. The evil presence never left her completely free. She felt it worming deeper through her body and through her mind. Thoughts shifted under its influence, and the sunlight appeared duller thanks to the presence.

She couldn't tell Loren everything. He would have broken, just as she almost did. The Alpha had shown her the world to come. Portents burned in the vision. Buildings fell, bodies lined the streets like refuse, and a blood rain poured down from the heavens. No one would be safe. No one would survive.

The Omega was coming.

"You can't stop it," she muttered, her words weak and lost. Her body gave way beneath her and Gates fell to her knees before the glass. Head against the cool surface, she gazed in all directions for someone to hear her, for someone to stop her from seeing it happen over and over again.

The Alpha might have been trapped, its mission a failure, but someone or something else would pick up the search. The heart was out there somewhere, hidden away in Portents, waiting to be found.

"You have to destroy it," she said. "You have to destroy the Heart of Forever!"

If they didn't, Portents was doomed. From the docks of Riverside, down the RDJ, and out to the Grove, every inch of the city would be lost. The screams of the dying would overwrite every story that had created her wealth of imagination. Portents was in her blood, and its end was being written in the shadows by a darkness greater than any ever known.

A chuckle escaped her. It grew from the depths of her mind, then sprayed out in a massive wave of laughter that rocked her body to the floor. Manic and screaming, tears flooded from her eyes in a laughing fit that resounded through Castlemere to the grounds beyond.

All at the thought of Portents burning. All at an ending no one could stop.

Not even Greg Loren.

ACKNOWLEDGEMENTS

This book would not be possible without the support of my incredible patrons:

Matt Patrick
Sally Hall
Sara Frandina
Paul Sardella
Vicki Wilkinson

Returning to the beginning of Greystone was quite the challenge. I wanted to make sure everything lined up, while also serving as a bridge for what is to come. Thankfully, these wonderful individuals were available to help me work through every issue that cropped up along the way.

I am eternally grateful for your patience and understanding.

ABOUT THE AUTHOR

Lou Paduano is the author of the Greystone series of urban fantasy adventures, which follow Detective Greg Loren and Soriya Greystone as they hunt myths, monsters, and legends in the city of Portents.

He is also the author of the conspiracy thriller series, The DSA, a serialized tale about a clandestine government agency trying to discover the true power behind humanity's future.

Lou lives with his wife and three daughters in Grand Island, NY. You can learn more about his books, including upcoming releases and free content by visiting his website at loupaduano.com.

THE GREYSTONE SAGA
AVAILABLE NOW

Follow the adventures of Soriya Greystone and Detective Greg Loren as they hunt dangerous myths and legends in the city of Portents.

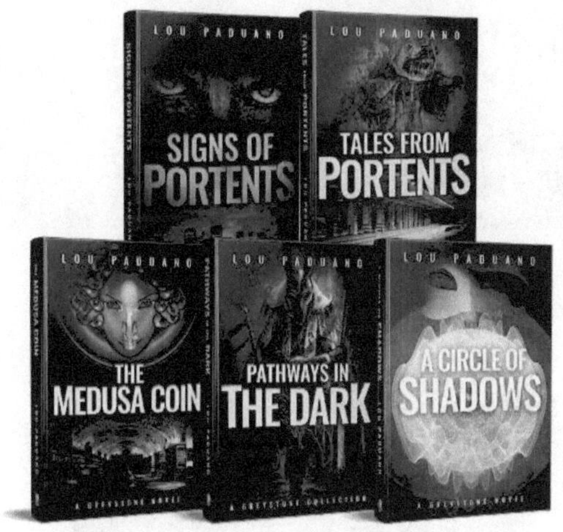

BOOK ONE - SIGNS OF PORTENTS
BOOK TWO - TALES FROM PORTENTS
BOOK THREE - THE MEDUSA COIN
BOOK FOUR - PATHWAYS IN THE DARK
BOOK FIVE - A CIRCLE OF SHADOWS

GREYSTONE-IN-TRAINING

For years, Soriya trained to become the Greystone.
Follow the trials that made her the protector
Portents needed to fend off the darkest of threats.

BOOK ONE - HAMMER AND ANVIL
BOOK TWO - THE GIFTS OF KALI
BOOK THREE - THE FINAL GAUNTLET

GREYSTONE LOST TALES

ARMY IN THE OBELISK
THE LAST KING

GREYSTONE CONTINUES IN…

A knight's destiny spells the end for Portents.

In the final days of Camelot, Merlin foresaw a great darkness rising. He dispatched five knights to combat this evil—and safeguard the world from its insidious threat. The knights built a fail-safe device, should all hope fade, and awaited the day it became necessary.

The clock starts ticking when a prominent philanthropist is found murdered. Detective Samantha Myers, with the aid of a centuries-old siren Thel, is pulled into the case. Stymied by the secrets uncovered, Myers turns to the only man capable of solving the mystery: Greg Loren.

Can Loren protect the last knight and the key he bears or will Portents fall in the wake of his failure?

The restoration of Portents may be over before it has even begun in this epic installment to the Greystone Saga.